The Coal Elf

By Maria DeVivo

Twilight Times Books
Kingsport Tennessee

The Coal Elf

This is a work of fiction. All concepts, characters and events portrayed in this book are used fictitiously and any resemblance to real people or events is purely coincidental.

Copyright © 2012 Maria DeVivo

Paladin Timeless Books, an imprint of
Twilight Times Books
P O Box 3340
Kingsport TN 37664
http://twilighttimesbooks.com/

First Edition, November 2012

Library of Congress Control Number: 2012918694

ISBN: 978-1-60619-216-0

Cover art by Ural Akyuz

Printed in the United States of America.

For Bambam – for always supporting me, and telling
me what I needed to hear, rather than what I wanted to hear.

For Juice – for being by my side every step of the way,
pushing me with your excitement and enthusiasm.

For Kookabella – it's always for you, and always will be for you.

Acknowledgments

Thank you to my husband, Joe, for always putting up with me and my weird ways. Your undying love gets me through everything. Thanks to my daughter, Morgan, for being the light of my life; my parents, Joel and Maria, and siblings (Joel, Jen, Jaci, Justin, Martino, Vin) for the bond of family that will never break; my nephews, Logan and Tino- I hope the spirit of the Big Guy stays in your hearts forever; my publisher, Lida Quillen, for enthusiastically taking a chance on this twisted tale; my editors, especially Gerry Mills, for helping to flesh out my labor of love; my agent, Carolyn Jenks, for always having my back; my cousins and extended family, friends, and my Facebook Brigade!

I am so grateful for everyone's help in spreading the word: my students – past and present – for challenging me... always; my second family at Randall Middle School who have rallied for me, been my cheerleaders, and supported me through everything!

I am truly blessed.

Chapter One

EMBER KNEW IF SHE CLOSED HER EYES LONG ENOUGH, SHE COULD FEEL THE warm sun beating down on her face; its heat intermingled with the frosty nip of a breeze that kissed the pointed tips of her ears.

And if she tried very hard, she could smell that scent again—the smell like white and gray—if color had an aroma. A smell that reeked of wetness in the air and ice patches on the ground and sloshing half-frozen dirt between her toes. That smell that indicated the clouds are just heavy enough to burst open their icy insides. Smells of Home.

Once upon a time....

She knew if she squeezed her eyes a little tighter, that the colorful light orbs that flickered behind her closed lids would transform into the hundreds of butterflies flitting about the garden in her courtyard, their iridescent wings catching the thin rays of light from the sun, melting its way off the horizon, moving in and out and back and forth against that gray-and-white smelling wind.

Before she could escape peacefully into another daydream memory, the work siren sounded, rousing her from thoughts of Home, signifying the end of yet another workday in the Mines. She opened her eyes to the surrounding darkness and focused on the line of light coming from the lantern beside her, dropped her pick-axe to her side and wiped the crown of tiny salt droplets from her forehead with the back of her dirty hand. The smell of coal dust from her sleeve was that of burnt dirt and dry rock. Nothing like the smells of Home.

Not so, once upon a time. She tried desperately to inhale deeply and eliminate the ash smell, but it wasn't possible. Breathing down here in the Mines was a conscious effort; it was difficult to breathe in the slightest amount of air and feel satisfied, as most breaths were filled with dirt and dust and particles of ground-up rock, each one covering the back of her throat with grit. Worse yet, she'd been coughing up blood the last few days.

Such was the life of a Coal Elf.

You'd think I'd be used to this by now, she thought. But maybe she'd never get used to it. She wriggled her small body side to side to loosen the work gear from her shoulders. The rough material of her jump-suit scratched the insides of her sweaty thighs and the deep cups of her underarms—a stark contrast to the velvets and cottons she wore growing up.

It itched. Badly.

Her comforting daydreams shattered by the end-of-the-day siren, she now focused on getting back to her cozy den, getting out of her work clothes, and diving into the sea of blankets adorning her bed. Oh, how she longed to close her eyes again, this time for a long, rest-ful sleep, but a second bell told her it wasn't going to happen. Not now. Not tonight.

Not with the Quarterly Meeting to attend. Nor with the deep ache in the center of her chest and that underlying rattle in her lungs. No. No rest for the weary.

No rest for a Coal Elf.

Six elf-years in the Mines had distorted her childhood memories, to the point where she often wondered whether anything she remem-bered was real. Daydreams. Wishes. Memories. Call them what you will, they certainly felt extremely real to her.

There was one particular day, though, that she knew she could never forget: *the day of her ninth elfyear birthday.* She'd been playing in the snow drifts outside the courtyard of her family's sprawling manor in Tir-La Treals. It was a lovely wintry afternoon with a light flurry of snow dusting the rooftop of her home.

Life was good for her then. Charmed.

While she played, Father, Mother, Nanny Carole, and her sister Ginger had gathered in the grand living room of their palatial estate. They anxiously awaited word from the Boss's Council, a letter that would state what Life Job Ember, the youngest Skye child, would assume. Her father had once been a toy maker, but years of superior work moved him up the ranks. Now he was regional manager for the entire parish. Mother, too, was well-respected in the community as a head costume designer; her creativity and keen eye for fashion had made her the most prominent figure in the industry. And Ember's older sister, Ginger, was following Mother's path, apprenticing with the Master Designer Team. Because of this, everyone assumed that Ember would somehow be involved in the toy making guild. This would not have been her first choice for a career (as if any elf had one), but she was comfortable enough with the idea, knowing she'd have much to learn from her father.

Yes, life was indeed good. It was charmed... until the letter was delivered.

Ember remembered Father calling out to her in his "serious" voice, a voice of command. She stopped playing and ran inside. When the family had gathered together, she saw Mother gasp when she silently read the parchment, her eyes growing wide with shock. Mother nearly fainted. While Nanny Carole mouthed the words "Coal Elf" to herself in disbelief, Ginger nearly doubled over with wicked-sister laughter.

Ember sat on the candy cane striped sofa next to the low-flamed fire in the hearth and waited.

Father, his head hung low, treated the official letter from the Boss's Council like a foul and toxic substance oozing between his fingertips, letters on the gold embossed paper spilling out, over, and in between the creases of his chubby hands. When he told her what the letter said, he practically whispered the words, as if in shame and disgust. His dark-brown eyes never once met hers – a clear sign that his heart was breaking.

"This is what the Boss wants for you," he mumbled, lovingly placing his hands on her knees. "Your mother and I never imagined you would end up o'er there in the Mines, but apparently the Boss has got it all figured out."

And that was it.

But Ember didn't understand. What had she just heard? What was going to happen to her?

This didn't make any sense!

Yet she had to put her understandable confusion aside. Elves didn't question much, and elflings, like herself, were supposed to question even less. She'd been brought up, as all elflings were, to believe and obey and never to question.

But Ember *wasn't* a typical elfling. Her curiosity and natural incli-
nation to question had often landed her in trouble. Now, she was
destined to be a Coal Miner?

Even though she didn't understand this at all, she had to accept the
Boss's decision. As Father said, it was the Boss's plan. No one questioned the Boss.

This was just how life was for her people. All throughout the Pole,
elflings her age were being assigned their Life Jobs, handpicked by the
Boss himself. That was their tradition.

It was the way things had always been done. By assigning Life Jobs
at age nine, the elflings were able to enjoy one last year of elflinghood
before their apprenticeship began.

But to become a Coal Elf? That job was for a select few, as Ember
would later find out. In fact, all the people she knew had been
assigned *normal* jobs; for example, pretty little Melody Grubbins,
from across the road, was assigned Chorus Leader of Lollipop Troupe
#5. Cynnamon Stixx of Tir-La Dunes was told by *her* father on
Assignment Day that she'd be apprenticing at the Gumdrop Bakery
as a Cookie Elf. And Hattie Candlewick was patted on the head by
her gleeful mum after the Boss's letter to the family announced that
Hattie would be a Tree Decorator.

Ember Skye would simply be a Coal Miner. She had to accept it.
What else could she do?

No one ever dared to go against Santa Claus.

ℝ℞

Barkuss came bustling up behind her and tapped her on the shoulder. His round face glowed as his broad smile curved around his nose.

"Ready for the meeting, Ember? Last one of the year!" he sang in
his sing-songy voice.

She rolled her dark blue eyes. "You can't be serious," she scoffed.

Barkuss blew a stray lock of ashy red hair from his eye. "Oh, c'mon,
girl!" He clucked his tongue against the roof of his mouth.

She waved her hand back and forth in the air. "No, no, no. It's
not even funny, Barkuss. It's seriously the same meeting every four
months. Doesn't it bother you?"

"It's what we do, E! It's just how it is!"

"Don't you get tired of the same old boring nonsense?"

"Why go against it, right? Ain't no sense in that. Ain't nothing go'n change nothing! Pick up your stuff! I don't wanna be late!" Barkuss gave her one last pat on the shoulder and headed out.

It never failed to amaze her how Barkuss always seemed so eager to do anything related to the Mines. He was eager to work, eager to please, and especially eager to do his job. That's why Barkuss was so happy about the last Quarterly Meeting of the year, because he was happy about everything. He loved his job; he even loved his darkened, ash-filled den, because that was all he knew. That was all he had.

Barkuss had been born and raised in the Mines. He didn't know anything else.

But *Ember* had seen the sun and tasted melted snow on her tongue and danced beneath the pregnant branches of the Nessie Fruit trees. Maybe that's why she didn't enjoy life in the Mines nearly as much as Barkuss.

No, Barkuss was a true Coal Elf. He had *never* been to the surface, and had no interest in going there. He and his brothers were *Ceffles*, or Coal Elves for Life, a fact he delighted in recounting to her. Often.

Regardless, Barkuss was a funny elf with what would have been red hair had it been cleaned properly. At twenty elfyears old, he was always smiling and cheerful. He was a Coal Collector and he took tremendous pride in the work he did. His incessant boasting and flamboyant stories often made him the butt of many of the other elves' jokes. Ember had to admit Barkuss could be a little too much at times, but in the end, he was a good friend.

He can't be right about nothing changing. Not about this.

The Quarterly Meeting was held in the normal spot, a dead end room beyond a small hallway. There, sharp gray rock had been chiseled into semi-circular benches. She found a spot on an empty bench away from the others. Barkuss was already seated next to another crew member, and the two were whispering in hushed tones, or as hushed as possible for Barkuss.

She tried to stifle a sudden cough, but couldn't. Heads turned her way as the horrifying rattle-sound bounced back and forth on the cavern walls.

Barkuss perked up, looked at her and mouthed the words "You okay?" under his scrunched-up nose. She half-rolled her eyes and nodded, receiving a thumbs-up from him before he turned back to his conversation.

She sat with her ankles crossed and gear beside her, deceptively calm. But inwardly, she felt hopeless as she scanned the faces of the elves around her. They looked so tired and worn, disheartened: empty eyes, never to see the full moon hanging in the night sky; gnarled hands wrapped around overworked pick-axes, never to pluck a sweet Nessie fruit from an ice-bitten tree; aching legs beneath burlap jumpsuits, never to kneel before the grandeur of a freshly made snowman.

"The List!" a voice boomed in the entranceway of the meeting hall. Her stomach did nauseated flip-flops at the mere sound of his voice.

Because who could it be, but Sturd?

Sturd was a wretched elf who didn't look like much of an elf at all. His beady eyes were way too small for his face, and they were *red*! His ears were exceptionally pointy—the pointiest elf ears Ember had ever seen. His teeth were gnarled, more animal than elf. He, like Barkuss and most of the other Coal Elves, had been born in the Mines, but instead of eating Nessie Fruit like everyone else, it was rumored behind hushed den walls that he lived off the harmless Graespurs, eating their meat and using their soft furs for blankets.

His demonic visage made her shudder.

Although there was barely an age difference between them, Sturd was her superior in the hierarchy of the Mines. The Mining Guild listed four positions. Miners, like her, harvested the coal and were at the bottom of the hierarchy. Sturd's crews were presently working Onyx Alley, Crystal Cave, and Raker's Cove, three of the prime mining areas. A notch higher than the Miners were the Collectors, like Barkuss. Miners reported their daily stock to the Collectors, who kept the data on what each crew was producing. They also stored and protected the coal.

Above the Collectors were Supervisors, like Barkuss's brother, Banter. Supervisors made sure that the Miners and Collectors were completing their tasks and filling their quotas. They also filled out reports and kept data, reporting directly to their Managers. Managers, like Sturd, were the direct line to the Council, who in their turn, were the conduit to the Boss.

However, her own dealings with Sturd extended beyond the Manager/Worker relationship. She had apprenticed under Sturd's father, Corzakk, her first year in the Mines, and had lived in his den during that time. Now, there were six elf-years of bad blood between Ember and Sturd.

She didn't like Sturd.

Worse, he didn't like her.

"The List," he repeated, quieting the last of the whispered conversations in the crowd, "is our life-force. Our entire operation rests on it. We work in accordance with it. For it. Yes, the Land Elves from Aboveground have their own List, but ours is important as well, for without it…."

Same speech as always. She repeated the words in her mind, along with Sturd, reciting them syllable by syllable, rhythm and all.

Soon the vile elf would be introducing Harold Pennybaker, head elf of List Communications Aboveground. Harold would then come out, compliment everyone on a "job well-done," read the status updates, spout out the facts and figures for final coal quotas, and officially recognize the "fastest elf" and "most productive elf." All would smile and clap. Barkuss would eat it up.

Her musings stopped and her ears pricked forward when an unfamiliar word "but" crept into the script. Sturd had never said that word before.

"But," he repeated for emphasis, "Harold has a very interesting piece of information that I think you will much rather enjoy. So, without further ado, brothers… and sister." Here he paused, glaring hard at Ember. "I give you Harold Pennybaker."

Chapter Two

EMBER HAD TO ADMIT TO HERSELF THAT STURD'S CHANGE IN THE SCRIPT piqued her interest. She rubbed her hands together with antici-pation when she heard the echoing footsteps bounce off the cavern walls.

Harold Pennybaker half-ran from the hallway to meet Sturd in the center of the seated elves. Despite the smile plastered on his face, she knew that Harold wasn't happy to be back in the Mines; he never was. His smile drooped a little at the edges after Sturd put forth his ferret paw to be shaken.

The welcoming applause from her fellow Miners was half-hearted. Just as it always was.

So far, she didn't see one thing that warranted Sturd's "but." Not one thing.

Then why did Sturd say it?

Ember wrenched her mind back to the present. She could say one admirable thing about Harold: he had plump, rosy cheeks. He looked healthy and glowing—so alive!

Coal Elves were much different from the Land Elves she'd grown up with. Coal Elves were thinner; their muscles taut against their skin. Layers of coal dust caked onto their hands and faces, creating thick gloves and masks that hid many scars, sores, and wrinkles. Their once-blond and sandy brown hair permanently transformed to black and gray.

Instinctively, she felt her own emaciated cheeks with the back of her hand, huffing at the hollowness there. *Not healthy. Not glowing. Barely alive.*

Harold quickly wiped his hand on his black pants' leg after Sturd's firm handshake. Everyone except Sturd noticed.

She tried to muffle a chuckle, but a fresh coughing spell took its place in her throat. Eyes turned her way as if to say, "keep quiet." Barkuss bit his bottom lip, Harold Pennybaker's mouth formed an "Oh, dear" shape and Sturd glared—again. When the coughing finally ceased, she raised her hand so the meeting could proceed.

Harold smiled cheerily. "Good evening, everyone," he began, phoniness dripping from every syllable. "So, this is the last Quarterly Meeting of the year, and I'm sure you're all anxious to hear the final numbers." He paused, waiting, but there was only silence. "Well, then," he huffed, straightening his tie and motioning to Sturd, "Mr. Ruprecht here has stated that I have some interesting news."

Sturd nodded.

"And, yes, I actually do," Harold continued. "Everyone has done a fabulous job this entire year. We have one last four-elfmonth stretch until the Big Night, and the Council is extremely impressed with your progress. Goals have been met, quotas filled. There's enough coal stored away for many elfyears to come. Your efforts have not gone unnoticed, and I applaud you for your work and dedication." He started clapping and a few of the workers followed suit, but when he stopped, they stopped.

"Things in the human world are also at an all-time high. After much review, deliberation, and calculation, the Council and I have decided that this year we will have…" He paused dramatically, slowly raising his fist in triumph. "…a Light List!"

The Coal Elves just looked at one another in confusion.

Sturd interrupted. "A Light List means we can all ease up a little in the Mines. Breaks will be extended to an hour, and days will end an hour earlier."

Like light bulbs going off in a collective brain, everyone around her started to hoot and holler and cheer. *Light List? Was that what Sturd and Harold were saying? Was it possible?* she thought. The Light List rumor *always* started right around this time, the end of August, with only four months left to go before the Big Night. Coal Elves were always saying things like, "Oh boy! If we work real hard we might get a Light List!" or "Man, oh man! Let's pound out this here cavern so the Council will reward us with a Light List!"

She remembered how she'd gotten excited and giddy the first time she'd heard the term. Come to think of it, she'd worked *harder and faster* after the insinuation of "lighter work" was injected.

And now, it was actually happening!

Ember was skeptical. She couldn't believe this was an actual elf-year with a Light List. On the other hand, she could easily believe the so-called Light List was all a lie—a lie to drive the Miners to work harder, faster, and more diligently.

Lies were a mainstay in her life. Even conversations between her mother and father had always amounted to *some* sort of fabrication in the long run.

Ember remembered her mother and father arguing heatedly in their bedroom not long after she'd been assigned her Life Job, unaware that she could hear them. Their voices, muffled as if underwater, came through clearly enough to Ember as she pressed her pointy ears to her bedroom wall.

Her mother sounded distressed. "Being a Coal Miner is strictly reserved for male elves. Plain and simple!"

"I know, I know, but there are plenty of girls who—"

"There are plenty of girls who reside in the Mines," Mother interrupted, "but they are there for very specific purposes, mining *not* being one of them! A Coal Miner? This is unheard of! Outrageous! Girl elves do *not* work the Mines!"

"So, what should I tell her?" Father sounded weary, defeated.

"I don't know!" Mother huffed. "And I honestly don't care! You'll think of something. You're better with her than I am."

Later, Father had tried so hard to sugar-coat the debacle. "You *must* be a very special little elf, Ember," he'd cooed. "The Boss doesn't very often choose girl elves for the Mines. He must have some big plans for you." He'd smiled and patted her blonde hair.

"But, I don't understand!" she'd cried. "Why is this happening to *me*? Did I do something wrong? Am I a bad elfling? Will I ever see you and Carole, and Ginger, and Momma again?"

She'd thrown herself onto the floor at her father's feet, curled her knees to her chest and sobbed uncontrollably, but he gripped her shoulders and brought her back to her feet.

"Ember, listen to me. Of all the elflings, the Boss chose you… *you*!" He nervously wiped his hands down his sleeves. "So stop your crying right now. You have to be strong," he continued. "Do you really think the Boss is going to make a girl elf work in the Mines? He'll probably set you up in a really nice cave where you'll have to take care of all the workers' needs. It'll be a piece of cake... trust me... you'll be cooking and sewing and singing all day long like a Nanny Elf, except you'll have to take care of all the worker elves, not just one elfling. You'll probably get to come back to the manor on weekends and for holidays. For all I know, when you get there, they'll honor you with a big party. A big induction. That's what happened when Ginger took her Life Job. The Big Man was there, and everything! Now wipe your eyes. There, there. See, everything is going to turn out candy canes and lollipops."

That had been long ago. None of what her father said had come true—not the slightest bit.

Now the meeting was breaking up. Coal Elves were dispersing and she swore she heard the others humming some old familiar Christmas songs. At least *they* were happy; at least *they* were buying the lie.

Harold Pennybaker was gone, escaped to the Catta-car to make his way as quickly as possible to the Mouth. That was typical.

Sturd was gone, too.

But not Barkuss. He bopped up from behind her and tugged on her shoulders, showing a toothy grin. "Isn't this great?"

She lifted her shoulders. "Yeah, I guess so."

His eyes narrowed. "Oh, c'mon, girl, why the shrug? This is *exciting*. We've always talked about a Light List, but now, it really happened!" He jokingly punched her on the shoulder and winked. "Wanna come back my way and have a bite to eat? We could celebrate the good news."

"No, thanks," she replied softly. "I'm going to bed. I'm exhausted." With that, she stood, flung her pack over one shoulder and ignored his raised eyebrows.

"Whatever," Barkuss said. "Catch ya later, girl." And he flounced down the hallway.

She bent down for her lantern, but as she straightened up, her head felt fuzzy. A tickle within her chest warned her of an impending coughing fit. She sensed the familiar metallic taste rising in her throat and with one forceful cough she spewed out a half-cup's worth of blood. It splattered on the floor, a deep, dark red pool, from which slithered a thin white worm.

Her worst fears had been confirmed: Coppleysites. Again!

Great, just what I damn well needed! With that, she headed back to her den.

Chapter Three

Her rocky "cottage" had been chiseled out for her the day after she was assigned her Life Job. Not knowing what to expect or even how to deal with a female worker elf, the Builder Elves took extra care in creating a suitable dwelling. They overdid their efforts by trying very hard to make elaborate accommodations for her: a living area, fully-stocked kitchen, lavish bathroom, and a bedroom suite that could sleep three elves at the same time. Niches carved into the stone walls were draped with thick velvet curtains to give the appearance of windows. The elves also planted a garden next to the small rocky front porch with night-blooming flowers. The Alcanthia flower grew lavishly in her garden, its purple petals adding a rich, deep color among the white petals of the Moon Glow plant.

But even the garden brought minimal joy to Ember's life. *You could cover reindeer droppings in chocolate, but in the end, you still have reindeer droppings.*

She flung open the wooden cottage door and coughed a few more times. It had been a long walk back from Onyx Alley. Barkuss had often told her to take advantage of the trolley, especially after working a long shift, but she had her reasons for not doing so even though her feet hurt from standing all day, and her belly ached with a ferocious growling hunger. She ignored these pressing issues of wants and desires, and concentrated on the need at hand.

"Coppleysites!" she huffed. She lowered her aching body onto the dust-caked couch and pressed her hands to her throbbing forehead. This was her third bout of Coppleysites in recent months.

Coppleysites only afflicted Coal Elves. The nasty parasites found their way into an elf's lungs and settled down to stay, slowly growing and increasing every time coal dust and ash were inhaled. An early warning sign of this parasite was frequent coughing (but which Coal Elf *didn't* cough on a daily basis?) that produced dark red splatters of blood.

If she didn't take care of the Coppleysites soon, she'd be in even more pain—constant pain. She could even die. An elf's lifespan was usually around one hundred and fifty elfyears, so her own life was all ahead of her.

I really don't see myself doing this for another hundred- some-years, she thought. Would death be such a bad thing?

A muffled voice outside her den interrupted her morbid thoughts. "Did I hear someone say Coppleysites?"

Barkuss? she thought. *What was he doing here?* "Come in," she called.

"Did I hear that nasty word?"

"Yeah," she nodded, muttering her response. "I saw blood today as I was walking back from the meeting. Blood, and the worm. What are you doing here, anyway? I thought you were going back to your den to eat?"

He gasped, putting chubby hands to his mouth. "Oh, E! I just *knew* something was off with you. All that coughing, I suspected as much. This is the second time in three months, isn't it?"

"Third," she corrected.

He gasped again. "Oh no, oh no, this is not right, girl! You need to get rest and get better. Those little buggers will kill you!"

"I know."

"I'm going to talk to my brother, Banter, and I'm going to tell him straight up, 'Banter, this girl needs to rest and she needs to rest *now!*' Besides, the Big Night isn't but four months away and now we got a Light List and—"

"Don't!" she interrupted. *"Don't* talk to him. I'll be fine. I'll drink some grulish. That should take care of it."

"Absolutely *not!*" he exclaimed in horror. "You'll drink the grulish *and* get rest *and* take some time off."

"No, Barkuss, really, you're making too much of this. I—"

She couldn't finish. A coughing spell rocked her body something awful, bringing up blood that landed right at Barkuss's feet. Another white worm slithered past his shoe and under a rock tile.

He winced and let out one of his trademark girlish squeals. "Set yourself down right now, girl! I'm making that grulish and talking to

Banter as soon as I leave! He shouldn't have a problem with his best worker needing some healing time."

"Please don't fuss over—"

"Shush!" he practically screamed. "I'm taking care of you right now!"

It was no use arguing. Once Barkuss had his mind set on something, it was going to happen—like it or not.

Ember knew that Barkuss had nothing but noble and genuine intentions, but what she needed right now was to be left alone. No, that wasn't quite it. What she *wanted* right now was Nanny Carole, who'd been in her life since forever. Ember missed the way Nanny Carole sang to her, bathed her, and played with her. Those were times when life was carefree and without worry. Right now, Carole was probably taking care of some other elfling, brushing *her* hair, singing *her* the same songs. How could Carole know that her previous charge, Ember Skye, was suffering, unable to breathe, and worse, unable to escape? Who would tell her?

Barkuss prepared the sweet grulish drink and brought a blanket from her bed. She spread her little legs out on the couch as he gently covered her, gave her the drink, and lovingly patted her head. His affectionate mannerisms made her smile with temporary comfort. Eyes closed, she clutched the warm, ceramic cup in both hands and let the rising steam fill her nostrils. Knowing that this strange and overly sweet concoction would bring immediate (albeit temporary) relief from the heavy feeling in her chest, she drank deep and smiled again, surprised at the brew's glorious flavorings.

Barkuss wore a satisfied grin. "Good, eh?"

"Hmmm...yes, I do say!" She quickly swallowed another draft. "Why didn't you make this for me the last two times I suffered through this?"

Barkuss blushed. He loved attention and adoration and affirmation, even if it was all over a silly cup of grulish.

His grin turned impish. "You like... a lot?"

"*Like* isn't the word, Barkuss," she gushed. "This is the best grulish I've ever tasted. It's like drinking a strawberry fizzy drink without the fizz, and not too sweet at all. Thank you so much. Where did you learn how to make it like this?"

His round face reddened under the coal dust as he made his way to the lounge chair next to the couch.

"It was my mother's secret recipe." He waved a hand that reminded her of fat gossiping Nanny Elves who ate peppermint sticks all day while their elflings flounced around the playground.

Mother: it was a forbidden word in her vocabulary. Even when she did live Aboveground, *mother* was just that... a word with no real meaning.

"You loved yours so much, didn't you?" She'd asked the question as he hung his head low. He slowly lifted it, eyes closed, nodding.

"She was a great mother. Always took care of me, my father, and my brothers. Incredible lady! Soft ashy hair that she kept tight in a bun, and for all the dirt down here, her cheeks were always rosy. I think that's 'cause she was always working over a blazing fire. Best cook. Knew how to make a killer grulish!"

She was about to tip her mug forward in a toast-like fashion, but was suddenly overcome with the sense of the room shifting. The grulish was going to be lulling her to sleep, and soon.

"She was just an all-around lovely woman," Barkuss continued. "Never hurt a hair on a Graespur, loving, caring, what more could you want? And she always gave kisses for our cuts. But they were magic. I swear, I'd come home from the Alley, cuts up and down my hands. Momma would kiss em' and POOF, magic! All better." He paused. "You missin' your momma?"

Through the deepening of his voice, she sensed a lump welling inside his throat, dying to burst free in the form of hot, streaming tears.

"My mother was a shrew, Barkuss! After I got my Life Job, she held all kinds of protests. She wrote letters to the Council, too, but her circus sideshow actions were never really for my benefit. She was obsessed with publicity, drawing more attention to her clothing line than to my rescue, which I think was her point."

Barkuss frowned. "Self-indulgent attempts at nothing."

"Exactly."

She'd replied with fervor, but her head was swirling. The grulish was clouding her mind, allowing her to openly share something rarely mentioned between them, removing inhibitions so that no subject was taboo. "Mother" was a touchy subject for both of them, but Barkuss, not truly paying attention, simply made a humming sound. "Momma never whipped us kids or nothing like that," he said in a faraway voice.

His statement took Ember back to the time she was ever reprimanded so harshly. Carole was gentle and patient, and had only raised her hand to Ember once. Once had been enough. There'd been that smell of the color gray in the air, and the snow was more like warm summer slush on the ground. Ember had been wearing pink rain boots with yellow polka dots on them, using them to stamp through the slush puddles in the Nessie Fruit Grove.

Nessie Fruit was the mainstay in most elves' diets. The tall trees blossomed in a variety of colorful flowers, bringing fruit whose flesh eventually ripened into a dark ruby red. The meat of the Nessie Fruit was thick and succulently sweet. They were used in just about all dishes and delicacies: as glazes on cakes and cookies, as sweeteners in cocoas and teas, squeezed as a straight juice, mashed into chutneys to be served with fish and meat, seeds toasted and salted for a snack, skins peeled and used as ointments, meat dried and ground as spices. But it wasn't just the plethora of uses this fruit had that made it so special.

Nessie Fruits were *powerful*, an ancient magic that gave all the elves their longevity and vitality. It was through this power that all elves were kept alive.

The morning after the Big Night was the time when Nessie Fruits ripened in mass quantities. The happiness of human children acted as magical fertilizer, and suddenly, there they were—deep red, plump and juicy, ready to be gobbled by the hard working elves at the Pole. The circle of life was clear: happy children equaled plenty of fruit, equaled long-living elves, equaled happy children....

Nanny Carole had been gingerly gathering Nessie Fruits for the week in her beige-cotton apron, when one of them bounced off her knee and onto the ground. "Little Ember," barely four elfyears old, had scampered over to the fallen fruit, picked it up, and was about to raise it to her tiny lips when she felt Nanny Carole's swift, hard hand crashing across the side of her cheek.

"Don't *ever* do that!" Carole had screamed in her small face. "Don't ever, ever, *ever* eat it once it touches the ground! Do you understand me, Ember?"

She'd rubbed the bruise that was quickly forming under her eye, her response insolent. "No? Why not?"

"Why?" Carole's green eyes had flashed with anger. "Why? I'll tell you why. It'll kill you! You'll die, Emmy!"

The angry words had alarmed and unsettled her for the first and only time in her young life, but that had been long ago. Why was she even thinking of it now? Oh, yes… Mother.

She must have been dozing off because she finally realized Barkuss was cleaning up the kitchen and getting ready to leave.

"What are you…?" Her words sounded strange, incoherent.

"Shush! Shush!" he commanded. "You get your rest. Let the grulish work its magic. I'm gonna wait till you're asleep, then I'm gonna go talk to Banter, clear you for work tomorrow, and I'm gonna come back and check on you tomorrow night."

Random thoughts took over her mind. She was suddenly bombarded with a rapid-fire onslaught of images and phrases and, most of all, questions. It was as if the grulish had opened her mind to clarity and truth and….

She struggled to formulate a complete thought, mumbling fragments of phrases and half-words and garbled sounds. For six elfyears she'd not been able to come to terms with the "why." Why was she here? Why was she a Miner? Why did she deserve this?

Clearly there were those who had other life purposes. What in the hell was *hers*?

Finally, she managed one coherent sentence. "Have you ever met the Boss?"

Barkuss's eyes widened. "No." His abrupt reply sent a quick chill up and down her spine.

"But you've seen him, right?" It was a half-question, half-statement.

His face suddenly became a mask. Gentle but sad eyes just gazed at her. This was not the Barkuss she knew.

After many moments, he just shook his head back and forth.

What, no? Never? Could that be?

An odd sensation of dread ran its icy course down her spine once again. Then she lost her battle with consciousness.

Chapter Four

COAL ELVES SET THEIR CLOCKS EACH DAY BY THE DEPARTURE AND ARRIVAL of the Graespurs. Being so far underground, no sunlight ever reached the rocky caverns; the Graespurs were the elves' only indication of night and day.

Graespurs were nocturnal creatures that dwelled in the Underground. With a wingspan of about eight inches and bodies covered in grey velvety fur, these harmless insect-eaters flew out of the caves at sunset, scavenging for food. Aboveground. At the first hint of dawn, they instinctually retreated back to their dark, damp nests deep within the caves. When leaving each evening, they made a sound like the thunderous hum of a steam engine, rich bass tones pulsating everywhere. Upon returning, they sang a happy song of triumph, their soft little bellies filled with grubs and other creepy-crawlies.

Ember awoke to the deafening hum of the Graespurs' arrival, as she did every day. The effects of the grulish had begun to work its magic, for she no longer felt the heaviness in her chest. She rubbed her eyes, removing grit from the corners, and stretched her arms high above her head while a long, satisfying yawn took its time finding a way out of her mouth. Then she rocked her head from side to side to shake off the couch-cramps and pop her neck bones. *Crack-crack-crack* filled her ears and she smiled, ready to start the day.

She sat at the oak vanity table in her oversized bedroom, where the elf in the large central mirror stared back at her, and began her daily routine. Although she was sixteen elfyears, she looked much older. Her time in the Mines had not been kind to her appearance. Gone was the soft visage of innocence and happiness and in its place was a hardened face of anger and near-desperation.

Her once-blonde hair had been permanently marred with coal dust and had an ashy-black color. The coal dust had also masked her face, and no matter how many times she scrubbed, the thick blackness encircled her almond-shaped eyes like heavy black eyeliner. No longer was her skin a porcelain-white hue. In its place, a soft fog color was imprinted on her flesh.

As an elfling, she'd dressed in vibrant colors—fire engine reds and brilliant Kelly greens were among her favorites. She'd once had a glorious teal pinafore with purple flowers stitched throughout—until she'd outgrown it. The only color to wear that made any sense now was gray or black. She'd also been self-conscious about her long, pointy ears, but there was no one to impress now, not in the Mines.

Sighing, she put on her black jumpsuit, went to the closet, got her supplies, and was off to work. This time she'd take Barkuss's advice and ride the trolley car to Onyx Alley instead of walking, but something was unusual. She was the only elf waiting for the Catta-car at the platform. Usually there were other elves humming and mumming about, busily talking about their day and all the work that needed doing, complaining about this or that, grunting and groaning.

There was no one at the platform; she was alone. The creeping feeling of the grulish making its last rounds through her body relaxed her, and the silence of the cave kept her at ease, so she decided to sit on the ground, crossing her legs at the ankles.

I've been doing this for the last six elfyears! How the hell have I even made it this far?

Coal Elves were there for the long haul. There was no going Home—no more Aboveground for her. This was it; this was life, for now and always. It had begun that fateful day she first arrived at the Mouth of the cave. The arriving elflings shuffled out of the carriage into a silent, single-file line, some wiping their noses from their last bout of hysterics, some wearing a glazed look of surrender, while others were shaking in terror. In contrast, she'd been relaxed, calm. Like she was right now. *Everything is going to be all right, everything is going to be....*

Apprentice elflings were greeted by Master Elves who filed out through large iron gates, one by one, approaching their new charges in a very official manner. The Mouth was a very menacing-looking area, with two large elf guards, positioned on each side of the entranceway, each as still as a stone statue.

In her case, she'd thought she would be greeted by one of the older female elves, a female Master who'd train her in the ways of cooking in the caves and laundering and sewing and healing. She'd visualized a soft-face, one aged with lines of wit and wisdom, smiling at her with knowledge beyond compare. Perhaps it would be a robust little elf, with wisps of gray hair framing rose-colored cheeks, speaking words of comfort and advice—much like her very own Nanny Carole.

And what about her new living quarters?

Her daydreams had been interrupted by the arrival of a gangly, emaciated elf named Corzakk. How odd! *He* was going to teach *her* to cook and sew?

Everything that followed was a blur. Corzakk instructed her quickly, in a rapid-fire kind of way, making her head swim. The black jumpsuit she was forced to change into was sackcloth material that grated against her flesh and made her legs itch. Corzakk was her Master and she'd be *his* apprentice. She'd work under him for the first year, and upon completion of her exam, would assume the responsibilities of Coal Miner.

After the rushed formalities, he barely spoke another word, grunting when he wanted her to turn left and nudging her a bit when he wanted her to turn the opposite way. They were going deeper and deeper into the darkness ahead. Surely this was not the way to her new cave, the place where she would take care of all the workers' needs... was it?

He's taking me into the Mines! I'm not supposed to be a Coal Miner. He's confused me with someone else.

Fear dug its rocky claws into her chest when she first ventured into the dark and dusty caverns. The elves there were... well, they were really strange. She'd never seen the likes of them before. And the Mines were peculiarly warm, the way it felt when Nanny Carole started the fire in her sweet and cozy cottage—except for the smell! A horrific odor permeated her small nostrils, not one of cookies baking or apple cider singing in the kettle. This was the smell of burning dirt, and it engulfed her.

"Wait, there must be a mistake," she blurted. "My father said—"

Corzakk's stare stopped her in mid-sentence. He gave another grunt to keep moving. A wave of anxiety suddenly crashed over her.

"Everything's going to be all right… candy canes and lollipops… everything's going to be…." She repeated the words to herself, almost out loud this time, to help combat her growing uneasiness.

As she walked through the cavernous hallways, hardened eyes stared at her with empathy, remorse, and even a bit of wonder. Was it because so few coal miners were girl elves? Was *this* what she'd become?

"Will Santa be here for the induction?" she'd asked her lanky guide.

His answer was a chuckle. "Induction? No darlin', there ain't no induction, and the Boss don't come 'round these parts!"

She tugged on his sleeve. "Excuse me, I think you're confused. Father said that—"

"Look," he huffed as he pulled away from her grip. "I don't know what your poppa told you, but the Boss has nothing to do with this. Sure, he chose you, one name pulled from his cap. There's no induction. There's no *nothing*. The Boss don't ever come around these parts." He had rolled his eyes and started off again, but she'd stopped walking to digest the words he spoke, to decipher them like a foreign language.

"Out of his cap?" she finally repeated.

"Yes, ma'am. A *cap*!"

She gulped, letting the words sink deep into her heart. "And he don't come here, ever?"

"Ever."

She'd swallowed hard. The knot from her belly had now worked its way up into her throat, and was slowly strangling her to the point of suffocation. It became hard to breathe. The weight of her father's lie now became a boulder on her chest, and she desperately fought back tears.

The Boss is not coming? Help is not on the way?

It was at that very moment she realized that she did not want to spend the rest of her life in this deplorable place! There had to be some way of getting out of this. There just *had* to be!

She tugged harder on his sleeve and her voice became wild and frantic. "Excuse me, but when do I get to go Home?"

He stopped in his tracks, and his face had twisted in a way that made her think he didn't understand what she'd said. She opened her mouth to repeat her question, but saw a crazed grin spread across his dusty visage. His eyes widened a little bit and he began to shake.

A new wave of terror crashed over her as she witnessed his bizarre display. Was he sick? Should she call for help? But then she'd heard a low hiccup sound coming from his quivering belly; it rose up through his chest, to his throat, and out his mouth in uncontrollable laughter. She took a confused step backward and waited for her Master to settle down.

After a minute or so, he was able to get a grip on his laughing fit. He breathed deeply, wiped the tears from his face (which left cobweb-like streaks across his cheeks), coughed a few times, then put a grimy hand on her shoulder. Peering deeply into her sapphire eyes, he whispered, "Child, you *are* Home!"

Home. This cave. This darkness. This stench.

Her mind shifted back to the present. She realized that a good fifteen elfminutes had passed. No Catta-car. Strange. Had she missed something? Was there some sort of meeting going on, or some sort of... *emergency?*

This is dumb! Exactly why I never ride this thing! I'm just gonna walk it.

She stood, and as she turned around to make her way to the station steps, she heard the chugging sounds of the Catta-car's wheels. The bright headlight of the trolley shone from around the bend. "Scratch that idea!" She headed back to wait for the car to pull up.

The trolley stopped at its usual position, and she hopped over the metallic gap between the car and platform. Tannen, the trolley driver, the reason she walked, poked his head out from the driver car window and called to her.

"Hey!" he shouted. "What are you doing?"

She was puzzled. What else would she be doing? "Um... going to *work?*"

Tannen's eyes sparkled. He didn't start the engine back up. Instead, he moved his body from his trolley seat and made his way back to the passenger carriers. Tannen was twenty elfyears old, with what would have been sandy blonde hair and emerald green eyes. His cheeks were slightly sunken, like most of the Coal Elves, but there was still color in them. He was taller than most elves, a sign that he was from the Trayth Clan, the longtime descendants of the Tree Elves from Aboveground who were the ones who designed, built, operated, and maintained the Catta-car system.

If it had been another time, another place, Ember would have smiled flirtatiously at the handsome Tannen, but this was now. She purposefully purged any of those types of thoughts from her mind. There would be no happiness in her slavery.

He approached her carriage and extended his hand. "No work today for you, Em!" he said with a half-smile, and beneath the coal dust and dirt, she felt the heat of a blush upon her cheeks.

She jumped down from the carriage and hopped onto the platform trying to catch her balance with her free hand. "Oh, great. Barkuss got to you, too?"

Tannen's brow furrowed slightly in confusion. "Uh, no," he stammered, "not sure what you mean by that, but the alarm sounded last night. Sturd suspended all work for today."

Alarm? She must have slept through it. *Man, that grulish was something good!* "What happened?"

"Not sure. Rumor has it that it's a Defector. I'm just riding the rails, tellin' anyone I see that there's no work today. So, you can go on home and relax." He smiled again as he walked to the driver cabin and jumped in.

Was that a wink she saw? Did Tannen actually wink at her?

Tannen turned the light of the Catta-car back on, revved up the engine, and threw his hand out the window in a goodbye wave.

Defector. Another forbidden word—in *all* Coal Elves' vocabularies. While the urge to run away was always there—usually in the elves that were brought to the Mines from Aboveground, and usually in the first year or so of service—it didn't happen often. Not many Ceffles attempted to run away; they were usually content with the life they led, like Barkuss. But the ones brought down from Aboveground...

that was a different story. They were the ones who let the darkness of the Mines invade their hearts. They were the ones who let the coal dust cloud their minds with a layer of sadness and resentment. They were the ones who ran.

The majority of the time, Defectors were caught and punished. Every now and then there would be a story of one actually making it out, but those stories were few and far between. The consequence for Defectors was severe, and she remembered Corzakk schooling her on the issue when she'd threatened to run away from him not long after arriving in the Mines.

"I'll just run away! You can't make me do anything I don't wanna do. I'll just leave and go back Home!"

"Is that right?" he had hissed from beneath the cup of cocoa he was drinking.

Her naïve, ten-elfyear-old head bobbed up and down furiously. Her crown of golden curls was just starting to accumulate a permanent layer of black dust.

Unfazed, he continued to sip his drink. "Your insolence will get you in trouble if you don't watch yourself."

She snarled. "Can't get in trouble if you can't catch and find me, now can I?"

"I'm warning you, girl. Watch that tongue of yours."

"Yea? Or what?"

"Defectors are severely punished," he said matter-of-factly.

She folded her arms defiantly across her chest. "Defector? What's a Defector?"

"A Defector is a naughty little Coal Elf who runs away from his or *her* duties. The alarm sounds, the hunt begins, the Defector is caught and dealt with."

She paused, giving thought to his words. "Oh yeah? And how are they *dealt with?*"

Without moving his head, he'd raised his eyes and looked up at her from his cup. "Banished. But that's rare. Usually, they're killed."

Spellbound by his words, and with defiance giving way to morbid curiosity, her body had shifted forward as her mouth gaped open. She hung on to his last syllable.

He raised the cup to his lips again. "Or eaten."

ഔൽ

Not happening. Not going Home. Go Home? To do what? Sit and twiddle her thumbs? Sit and think about her life before this life? Sit and scribble her endless dreams and worries in her journal? Sit and spiral further down the slope of depression? No. Not happening. Not going there.

Regardless of the orders given, Ember headed straight to the Mines. Nowadays, work seemed like the only thing to take her mind off what her life had become. Bizarre as it may have sounded, concentrating on the physical work distracted her of her thoughts of her former years, her life before the Mines. It seemed like a temporary escape in a twisted way. Alone, she collected her thoughts and tried so desperately to piece together some sort of meaning to it all.

Heave.

Break.

Heave.

Smash.

All day. Every day. For the List. Chosen by the Boss. Summoned by the Council. Hacking away at cave walls.

Did the List really exist? Or was that just more lies, lies, lies to beat them into submission, make them work all day, every day. The List? Light List, Heavy List, Naughty Kid List. A fantasy. A hoax. A *trick.* A LIE!

Heave.

Break.

Heave.

Smash.

Barkuss was different. He was *born* here; this was all the life he knew. But this *wasn't* life.

No. Life was snow banks, and snowmen, and snowflakes, and cookies, and toys, and cheerful songs to ring in the Big Night.

Not *this*. Not darkness, and dust, and Coppleysites, and Graespurs, and solitude. This wasn't life, this was *existing*. She knew what real life was like.

Of course Barkuss could love it down here. He had never seen the sun, had never seen the snow, never smelled the pine trees or saw them glittering with a thousand twinkling lights. He didn't know any better.

She soon started to feel as if there were shackles on her hands and feet—shackles that bound her to the caves and this job for the rest of her life.

Heave.

Break.

Heave.

Smash.

"...the Boss don't come 'round these parts!"

Heave.

Break.

Heave.

Smash.

"...Your mother and I had hoped you wouldn't end up o'er there in them mines, but apparently the Boss has got it all figured out...."

Heave.

Break.

Heave.

Smash.

"...there ain't no induction...."

Heave.

Break.

Heave.

Smash.

And then, as if the cave walls themselves were crashing onto the very soft spots of her brain, she had a wild revelation. All this time and she'd never figured it out before—the true purpose, the true meaning to all of *this*. Through all of her self-assessment and remembrances of past conversations and deep introspection, she thought she had finally figured out *why* she was brought down here.

But now, she finally understood!

The thoughts and emotions intertwined and took root in her soul, and slowly, very slowly, like an Alcanthia blossom coming into full bloom, it unraveled. There was a moment of blissful clarity.

She stopped working and dropped her axe beside her. She needed a minute to absorb the gravity of her epiphany. What if they *all* thought like this? What if she shared her theory with all of the other Coal Elves? What would the Boss do about it then?

Before she had time to fully process her new thought, something hard and cold hit her on the back of her head. Flashing speckles of light danced in front of her eyes, and for a split second, she was dancing in that butterfly garden back Home Aboveground. Her neck soon became wet and sticky, and she was thrown off balance and swayed to the side a little bit. She didn't fall to the ground; she had the sense to realize that something had purposefully struck her, nearly knocking her unconscious. Her eyes went out of focus for a few seconds and when she was able to get her bearings she saw what had happened.

Sturd!

She should have known. Seconds before the whack to her head, she had smelled his putrid odor. He was just too fast for her to react.

She rubbed the back of her head. "What the…."

He shrugged his shoulders as he made an empty apology. "Oops. Sorry."

"Wanna watch where you're going, Sturd?"

"You're lucky I didn't catch you from the front," he hissed with a grin. "I might have taken out those pretty little eyes of yours." Sturd made two clicking sounds with his tongue. "Coulda popped those suckers right out with my axe. You really need to be more careful."

She glared at him. "Yeah, I'll take that under advisement." She picked up her axe and sauntered over to him. She eased closer, each step deliberate and graceful. He stood there, the menacing grin still a mile wide on his face as she pressed her pickaxe on the inside of his

left thigh. "Never miss a chance to sneak attack me, do ya, Sturd?"
She tilted the sharp point a little harder into the meat of his thigh.

His eyes widened just before he quickly shoved her away.

She fell to the ground, her axe sliding across the rocky floor. Still
off balance from the dizzying blow to the back of her head, she began
to rise. But he stood over her, preventing her from getting up. Worse
yet, he pressed his foot in the sensitive crevice between her legs. She
groaned as she stared into his dark red eyes.

Corzakk. Sturd's eyes were like his father's. Not the color, but the
shape and the size. It was about the only thing the two had in common as far as physical appearances went. And as she stared deeply
into those menacing eyes, she thought she saw a flash of sadness, of
peace, of remorse and regret, an intense combination that puzzled
her for a moment.

She had lived with Corzakk and Sturd during her apprenticeship, and from the word "go" it had been a tumultuous relationship
between the young elves. She was afraid of his odd appearance, his
weird animal transformation that got progressively worse as the year
went on, and of his explosive temper that had the tendency to blow
at any given moment. She had felt his anger and hatred while she was
being trained by his father, and yet, that hadn't stopped her from trying to reach each out to him. On one occasion, she had mistakenly
asked about his absent mother, sending him into a tantrum, and ending in a shoving match between the two. It was often that way—ver-
bal and physical confrontations, with no intervention from Corzakk.

It was no secret in the Mines that Sturd hated girl elves. His own
mother had defected from his family when he was an elfling, leaving
him with a slow, black rage and a vicious loathing of all females. But
there was something in his eyes—right here, right now, that Ember
couldn't quite put her finger on. Was he completely unredeemable?

"You've got a lot of nerve addressing me in such a way! You've got
a lot of nerve disobeying a direct order, too! Were you not informed
that mining was suspended today? All elves are to be on watch for the
Defector!" Sturd scolded.

Thinking nice thoughts about Sturd was useless. He was nothing more than a vicious animal, just as she'd always believed him to be. "What, so we can catch him and cook him up real nice with our Graespurs?" she hissed.

Sturd mashed his foot deeper between her legs as she fought back a cry. "All these years, you would have thought that a great Master like my father Corzakk could have gotten you to fall in line with the rest of them! What a shame. You'll get what you deserve, though."

"Yeah? And what *do* I deserve, Sturd?"

He spit at her. "What every female elf deserves! You're disgusting. I said from day one that it was a mistake to bring someone like you down here, but no one wanted to listen to me."

"'Cause you're a psycho!" She grabbed his ankle and shoved him away. "Get over yourself, Sturd. You act like you're all high and mighty, but let's face it: you're barely a day older than me. The only reason why you have the job you have is because of your father. If Corzakk wasn't a Master Elf, you'd have no privileges. Nothing. You'd be a regular worker like the rest of us. If you can't see that for what it is, then I feel sorry for you!" She stood up and dusted off the bits of gravel from the back of her jumpsuit.

"*The rest of us*," Sturd sang sarcastically. "Get one thing straight, missy, you'll never be like the *rest* of us! Simple biology!" He laughed. "And I am *above* you! And that's all that matters down here, isn't it?"

"Please. You're just jealous that your poppa saw more potential in me than in his own son!"

Enraged, Sturd rushed at her and violently pushed her back to the ground. She fell backwards on her bottom and skidded a few feet, her hands scraping along the rocky floor, flesh curling up like soft wood under a chisel.

She returned his diabolical smile. "Typical. When you can't respond in words, you respond with force. You're still a little boy, Sturd. A little, lost boy!"

"Pick yourself and your axe up," he snarled through his gritted teeth, "and get yourself Home. I will deal with you later. The Council will not be happy when they hear what I have to say about you."

"Tell them," she said, rage giving way to apathy.

"What?"

"Tell them. I really don't care. Actually, Sturd, *they* won't care."

"What?" he repeated.

She gripped the back of her bloody head and began to stand up. The Coppleysites were starting to act up again and she coughed a few times. "The Council. Doesn't care. They won't care if I gut you like a fish, as long as they get their coal quota for the month. They don't care about any of us, including you. And you know what? I wouldn't doubt it if the Boss himself didn't care either! So go ahead. Tell them. Tell them I hit you first if you want to."

His beady red eyes twinkled as he gazed at her. He carefully licked his thin lips, his weasel tongue darting rapidly back and forth in an obscene way. "I beg to differ, filthy girl elf," he boasted as his eyes flashed. "I *have* the List. Right here. Right now."

She paused. Trapped. Motionless.

Did he just say he has the List? The List? No, no, no, it's impossible.

"I... I... don't believe you," she stammered. "You're lying. There's no way you have the List on you right now...."

But, as if to silence her, he reached into his back jumpsuit pocket and retrieved a small golden scroll held together with a red ribbon. He untied the knot and the scroll uncurled to the dirty ground, and silence her, he did.

Billy Anderson, Corinne Bauman, Gary Canfield, Madison Little....

She could make out name, after name, after name. A lot of Brittanys and Tylers and Taylors; it was never-ending. Thousands of names hand-printed in bold calligraphy—girls in red, boys in green—like a delicious candy cane swirling with yummy goodness for her eyes. She was mesmerized as the scroll rolled beyond her feet. In slow motion, the names danced before her in a hypnotic twirl.

Here was her answer! This was what her work was about!

Above any and all, even surpassing the law and power of the Council, this List was the commander of every Coal Elf in existence. Its mysterious existence gave her and every Coal Elf their drive, their purpose. She was enchanted as she tried to memorize each and every child's name on the parchment.

Kaden Peters, Jacob Robard, Clarissa Salazar, Tori Youngblood....

The big revealing theory she had formulated ten minutes earlier felt like years and years away, a distant memory. And that didn't matter anymore. Her epiphany now a speckle of cave dust floating aimlessly over black rock. All that was in focus was the List. All that mattered was the List. It was real. It was *real.* And it was *there* in front of her, teasing her, tantalizing her, hypnotizing her.

Her hand instinctively moved to touch the aging scroll. *If I could just hold it for one second....*

With a quick flick of his wrist, the List curled back up and disappeared in Sturd's ferret-like paw. His eyes narrowed again and he smirked. She ignored the throbbing in her head and the growing pain in her chest, and kept her focus on his hand, hoping to glimpse the sacred document again.

He tucked it away back into his pocket, glared at her one last time and commanded, "Go! Now!"

As he huffed off into the shadows, Ember's trance was broken.

Chapter Five

WHEN SHE REACHED HER HOME, SHE HEADED STRAIGHT FOR THE BATH-
room to doctor the wounds from her encounter with Sturd.
The cut on the back of her head had stopped bleeding, but she
still wanted to put some medication on it to avoid infection. The
Apothecary Elves were adept at making tinctures and other healing
products, and the Medic in charge of the Miners' health always made
sure the workers had a steady supply of ointments and other rem-
edies. Her hands were cut up something awful, too.

She reached for a bottle of holly berry and kissle leaf salve, knowing it would do the trick, and winced as the medicine came into contact with the exposed flesh of her shredded fingers. Her whole body
ached now, a combination of being sick and her encounter with Sturd.
The pounding sensation in her chest was slowly, but surely, making
its way back, and she noticed she was coughing a little bit more.

*Damn Coppleysites got me good this time. Damn Sturd got me good,
too.*

Sturd.

The very way his name sounded nearly made her wretch, and now,
knowing he had physical possession of the List sickened her even
more. Why would the Boss entrust him with that divine document?
Why would Sturd, above all elves, be given that power over every
Coal Elf in the Mines? Sturd was cruel, more animal than elf! He
hated everyone and everything, and actually took pleasure in inflict-
ing pain in others. So why in the hell would he be given the privilege
to even *see* the List? Was he just the Boss's "muscle?" Unless....

...unless the List Sturd had was a fake.

That possibility now injected itself into her mind. A fake. It
was the only plausible explanation. A fake List constructed by the
Council and handed to the most wretched elf to keep him thinking he had some sort of power, and this thought, this false sense of
authority, ultimately made him behave. If there was any logic to this

life, it would be logical to have Sturd control a doctored List (either knowingly or not).

Give him control—the worst, meanest elf in all of history (who probably only got coal himself every Big Day); make him maintain order by force and intimidation; have him flash around that dummy List to reinstall hope. And that made sense. If he wasn't muscling the other elves around with his so-called clout, then maybe he would be doing other dastardly deeds and creating a plethora of *other* problems. And he would be none the wiser—just bullying other elves and taking notes on the collections.

Ultimately, the List went back to the Boss, anyway, so He could deliver the coal to the bad kids of the world. Sturd would never know if his List was the real one or a fake!

It sounded logical to her, but the question that gnawed on the soft spot of her brain was this: *why?* Why would the Council even *dream* up such a plot, if such a plot truly did exist?

The Boss's Council was an ancient order. They were the direct link to Him, the Boss, the Big Man, the Head Honcho. Since the beginning of time, since the beginning of anything, the Boss and the Council went hand in hand. Made up of five elves, the Council oversaw most everything—they formed the laws of the North Pole, managed the specifics and logistics of the Big Night, assisted in Life Job distributions, and most of all, kept the Boss as "hands off" as possible, shrouding His Excellency with facts, figures, legends, and suppositions. Ultimately, the Boss had the last say in any decision ever made, but the reality was that the Council controlled the leg-work.

Thinking this only made her feel worse about her situation and status. Thinking this only made her feel like coughing. Coughing, and coughing, and more coughing.

Coppleysites!

Hoping there was some leftover grulish from the night before, she sauntered into the kitchen.

Before opening the icebox, she noticed a note attached to the door by a silver metallic magnet. It was from Barkuss:

E,

Waited until you passed out last night. Don't worry about work for the next few days. I'll talk to Banter. Get your rest. I made some more grulish. Be careful, though, it's extra strong. Be by tonight to check in. Go back to bed!

Tootles,

~B

She frowned. She had missed this note before she left for work today and Barkuss obviously didn't know she had gone to work this morning!

She crumpled the pink piece of paper and tossed it on the floor before opening the icebox. *Stupid Barkuss.* But the grulish *did* look awfully pretty in its yellow plastic container.

Extra strong, eh? And her heart started to pound furiously in her chest as a macabre plan began to take shape in her mind:

Extra strong. Extra sleep. Everyone on Defector watch. Barkuss probably not coming back tonight because of all the craziness in the caves. Extra strong. Extra sleep. Extra strong. Extra sleep. Extrastrong. Extrasleep. Extrastrongextrasleep. Forever sleep? Escape. Escape. Escape. Esca....

"Get that thought out your mind, right now!" she said to herself, but as she said the words, her eyes gazed lovingly at that yellow container in her hands and got lost in the berry-colored liquid within.

Hopelessness. Like she saw on the faces of the elves at the Quarterly Meeting. Like she felt in the pit of her stomach on a daily basis. Mining life was hopeless. There was no escape for her. There was no going Home to family, and snowmen, and frothy cups of hot cocoa. Her Home was here, and she hated it. There was no escape for her, except maybe at the bottom of that yellow container, or within the swirling depths of the elixir. Maybe a good long sleep would remove her from her misery. Maybe....

After she twisted off the cap, her hands shook anxiously as the thought of drifting off into a deep slumber enticed her. She knew if she drank the entire potion at once, she would fall asleep for days. She whirled this possibility in her mind over and over. The swoon of sleep was a thought that made her weak in the knees—especially a sleep that could possibly last forever and be her ultimate release! There was no more thought behind it, just the act. She put the lid to her mouth and cocked her head back full force, allowing the sweet grulish to caress her lips and coat the back of her throat with its thick syrupy texture.

Barkuss wasn't kidding, this batch was strong! Almost immediately she began to feel the hazy sensation behind her eyes and the numbing sensation of pins and needles in her joints. The plastic container fell to the floor with not a drop to be cleaned up later. A dream-like fuzz enveloped her mind as she languidly glided to her bedroom and collapsed on the bed. Images and sounds started to engulf her, and she let the deepness of the medicated slumber carry her away....

...Mother is a pretty elf. Her soft white locks fall over her shoulders in tumbles of curls that cascade down to her waist. Her ears extend high above her head and are curved, not pointed like most elves. This gives her a glorious distinction among other lady elves, especially when she affixes glamorous jewels and crystals that dangle from her lovely ears. Other girl elves are jealous of Amalia Skye, and with good reason.

Father is a strong elf. A handsome elf. A by-the-books elf. Elden spends countless hours huddled over his blueprints at his desk, feverishly drawing up new and exciting toys to go into production every following year, and making sure that all the Toy Makers are "on-point" or "in check", as he likes to say.

Ginger is a capricious little thing. Her carrot-colored crown is cropped to the nape of her neck. Older by one elfyear, she teases Ember in natural older elfsister fashion by plucking the corncob pipe out of Ember's Frosty puppet, or disabling Rudolph's light-up nose on Ember's Rudolph blankey. Ginger's leaving next year to be a Designer Elf, like Mother. Her Nanny, Mintha, is going to be re-assigned to the new elfbaby in the Grubbins family. Ember doesn't really care because she never liked Mintha very much, but Ginger is clearly upset about this.

Nanny Carole is a kind elf. A sweet elf. She has round rosy cheeks and short stubby fingers. She is the epitome of comfort and safety. Ember knows she is well protected with Nanny Carole.

The house is warm. The fire dancing in the hearth casts shadows on the parlor walls. The warmth not only comes from the fire, but from the love felt in this family. It's dark outside. Dinner is over. Mother, Father, Ember, and Ginger have just gorged their elfish bellies on cakes and pies made from the Nessie Fruits, and are now sitting on the candy cane striped sofa sipping hot chocolate with white fluffy marshmallows billowing from the tops of their mugs. Nanny Carole and Nanny Mintha are hurriedly cleaning up the remnants of the meal while singing traditional elfish songs about family and love. "All on a Summer's Eve" is Ember's favorite, and she hums the melody quietly to herself as she catches glimpses of the Nannies' smiling faces while they swish from room to room. Their lavender and green Nanny aprons rustle across the white marble floor of the dining hall and the plush azure carpet of the parlor.

"An old family recipe? Am I right, Nanny Carole?" Mother inquires as the clan simultaneously sips the hot beverage.

"You certainly are, madam!" Nanny Carole calls from the butler's pantry.

They all smile at each other. Father wraps his right arm around Mother. Ginger rests her head on Mother's shoulder. Father pats Ember's head. Life at the Pole is good, charmed.

Mother suddenly shifts on the couch. She raises her head and cocks her elongated ear to one side as if sensing something audible, yet far away.

"Did you hear that?" she asks in her silver bell-like voice.

Ember turns her head slightly then shakes "No." Father's lower lip protrudes out as if to say "I don't know." He shrugs.

"It was like a banging noise," Mother continues.

"Maybe it was just some kids throwing snowballs outside," Father says calmly. "Besides, your super sharp ears can hear sounds miles away!"

Ember and Ginger giggle. Father gives the girls an "inside joke" look, as if he and his daughters have spent many hours discussing the length of Mother's ears (at her expense, no less). Mother still has a perplexed expression on her face.

"You're probably right," she says with a nervous chuckle.

Father chuckles. Ginger chuckles. Ember chuckles, but is a little bothered by her mother's tight-lipped expression.

Mother cocks her head again, but says nothing. Ember knows her mother has heard that banging noise again. This time, Mother's eyes widen in terror.

"Did you hear it again?" Ember asks.

"No," she slowly replies with a hushed voice. "I heard something different."

Ember, curious little Ember, stares at her mother for a few moments, scanning her face as if she were trying to read an encoded text in the ancient Elvish tongue.

"Well then," Father jovially interjects, "if ya didn't hear a banging sound, whatd'ya hear now?"

Before Mother answers, the entire Skye family hears the sound. An awful, terrifying sound, as if one thousand screaming elves were being ripped in half at once. The sound freezes the family. Ginger throws her hands to her ears to stifle the horrid cacophony to no avail. Ember looks to her mother for some comfort and reassurance, but the tears are already streaming down Mother's porcelain cheeks. Father is no better. His small mouth is opened as wide as it can go. Ember can see the pink color of his tongue and the white specks he calls teeth.

"W-w-w-what in Claus's name was *that?*" Father mumbles.

Ember buries her face in Mother's arm. "I'm scared," she says in a muffled voice. She has never felt fear before and the feeling is gripping her belly. She feels like her dinner wants to come up out of her mouth. An acidic sensation creeps up her throat, and she turns her head from Mother's arm and faces the floor of the parlor. She can't hold back the feeling any longer and a liquid substance spews from her stomach onto the blue carpet.

She cries the word like a pitiful mewing kitten. "Mommy!" *Mommy.*
A word she has never used before, but somehow, at this very moment
in time, seems to be the only word to escape her lips.

Father turns his nose up in disgust when he sees and smells Ember's
vomit on the floor.

"Look what ya did now!" he scolds in a harsh voice. "It'll take me a
long time to get that up!"

Ember continues to cry. Mother embraces her.

The noise again.

Closer.

Screams and shearing and banging. Awful sounds. Terrible sounds.
Loud sounds. Animals-dying sounds. Women-and-men-elves-in-pain
sounds. Torturous sounds. Murderous sounds. Flesh-ripping-from-
bones sounds. Blood-rushing-through-veins sounds. Wind sounds.
Storm sounds. Ice-balls-against-glass sounds. Fingernails-scraping-
chalkboard sounds.

Closer.

Louder.

Closer.

Louder.

Ember grips tight to Mother's arms. Ginger is paralyzed with fear.
Father screams. The fire in the hearth extinguishes. All is dark. Cold.
Ember feels Mother's tears streaming down her own arm. Wet and
salty, but soothing. The manor shakes and rumbles. Nanny Carole
and Nanny Mintha are gone. Disoriented. Shadowy figures enter the
room. The noise is a constant sound in Ember's head.

Wide eyed, Ember awakens and screams.

"Relax, relax," a familiar voice said from above her. "It's okay, it's
all over now."

Ember sat up. Her eyes were slowly coming into focus, and Barkuss
was at her bedside with a bucket of water in his hands. Banter was
standing in the doorway with his miner's goggles on top of his head
and his stone cutting machine resting securely on his back.

Barkuss put the bucket of water next to the bed and laid his hands
on her legs. "You gave us quite a fright, girl!"

"W-w-what," she muttered.

"Somebody wanna tell me what the hell is going on here?" Banter demanded.

Barkuss ignored his brother with a dismissive wave of his hand. "I'm so sorry, E! I was supposed to come check on you last night, but there was that whole business with the Defector, and I got wrapped up in all *that* drama. I just figured you were resting and doing like I said. So tonight, I'm all like 'let me check on E!' I knocked and knocked, but your door was locked, and I got scared! I got Banter to get the stone blaster and we ripped the front door off your den. And I'm all calling and calling for you, but you didn't answer. Then I see the empty grulish bottle on the kitchen floor and knew something was *not* right! So, I go to the bedroom calling and calling. Your bedroom door was locked too, so that had to come down!"

She put her head in her hands and furiously rubbed her eyes. "I can see that!" she replied in an aggravated tone.

"Oh, sweetie, we were lucky we found you when we did! One more day and you could have slipped into a grulish coma for sure! Why'd you drink the whole bottle? I told you it was strong!"

She glared at him for a few seconds. Was it possible he really didn't know? Was he truly clueless? Must be! Sweet, and caring, and concerned, but utterly clueless. Or perhaps in denial....

She glanced over at Banter as he eyeballed her up and down. *He* knew. He knew exactly what she was trying to do when she drank all the grulish, and he was not shy about letting her know he was well aware. There was a glint in his eyes, a glint of *knowing*. A glint of "I've-seen-this-before-and-you're-not-getting-away-with-it." With his hard look came a shake of his head from side to side as if to say, "Come on, kid, what am I gonna do with you now?"

A sickening feeling of guilt bubbled up from her stomach and came spewing forth in an arch of pink vomit. Luckily, Barkuss's slop bucket was able to catch the sweet-smelling goo. She wiped her mouth with the back of her hand, leaving a pink streak across her face. Then she turned back to Barkuss and asked, "How'd you get me out of it?"

Barkuss stuck out his tongue and crinkled his nose in a "yucky" face. "Um, I don't think you want to know." He held an empty glass vial. "Let's just say, this is what made you throw up the first time. The Graespurs clear their system so you can clear yours...."

Another wave of sickness threatened more vomit. "All right!" she yelled as she waved her hand in front of her face. "I don't need to know anymore!"

Barkuss patted her face down with a cool, wet rag. "I'll take care of the cleanup for you and everything will be as good as new!" he sang. "But no more grulish for you, young lady! Besides, I think you drank so much, you won't get Coppleysites for a few years!"

She let out a little huff of a laugh. She was too groggy and weak to say or do much else.

Barkuss comforted her the rest of the night while Banter reattached the doors in her den. Barkuss went on and on, telling gossipy stories about other Coal Elves they both knew. He forced her to slowly sip water, and occasionally she managed to chuckle at Barkuss's outrageous tales, all under the uncomfortable eye of Banter, who went about his work in silence.

"So," she said when her strength returned. "What about the Defector? Y'all seem like you were so busy and wrapped up in that. What of it?"

Barkuss narrowed his eyes. "Oooo, child! You really don't want to know."

"No, I do," she replied. "Did they catch him?"

"*Her*, baby, it was a *her*."

"And?"

"Let's just say, it was not pretty. Thank Claus you were in that deep sleep! Lots of yelling and commotion and hootin' and hollerin'...."

She paused. "Is she okay at least?"

Barkuss's voice dropped a notch in volume. Even Banter stopped working for a moment to hear the end of the story. "Corzakk was there. And Sturd. Does that answer your question?"

Chapter Six

COPPLEYSITES. GONE, BUT CERTAINLY NOT FORGOTTEN. A FEW DAYS HAD passed, and Ember's infestation cleared. No more coughing fits, no more blood puddles. Finally, she was almost Coppleysite free. Not entirely, though. Every once in a while, a metallic taste would tinge her saliva and pool in her mouth, or a deep breath would hurt just a little bit more than normal. These were signs that, although the Coppleysites were gone, they would never truly go *away*. More painful reminders of the toll the Mines took on the Elvish body; painful reminders that the damage done by three back to back bouts had left its permanent mark.

After much insisting from Barkuss, she had taken the last few days off from work. Banter was fine with the arrangement, more so after witnessing her "accident" firsthand. After she saw that look in his eye, that look of knowing and disappointment, she knew she would have to eventually face him and explain; the thought made her queasy. With every fiber in her body, she wanted to avoid the barrage of questions: "how?" and "why?" But most of all, she dreaded Banter's cold, hard stare.

She usually walked to work, mostly to avoid Tannen, the trolley car driver. There was something so magnetic about him, something that enthralled every one of her senses. The butterflies in the pit of her stomach went wild every time she saw him, spoke to him.

However, after battling Coppleysites the way she had, she figured riding the Catta-cars was probably the best way to go. "Rest, rest, rest!" Barkuss's words blared in her ears. In her mind she made up some trivial justification about preventing more Coppleysites if she rode the rails and didn't expose herself to all the coal dust. But who was she kidding? When the trolley pulled up to the station and Tannen's head poked out of the driver's car, she felt the butterflies stirring in her stomach and tried desperately to ignore them.

"Morning, Em!" he cheerfully called above the roar of the trolley engine.

Her stomach knotted up, and she felt her throat start to close with anticipation. "Morning, Tannen," was all she managed to respond, but her voice was so low and the Catta-car was so loud, she doubted he even heard.

Em. He was the only elf who called her that. She was basically "Ember" to everyone else who ever knew her. Barkuss had given her many affectionate nicknames over the years, Nanny Carole would call her "Emmy," and her father had thrown in a "kiddo" or "sweetie" once in a while, but that was about it. Tannen always called her "Em." If it had been anyone else, she would have scoffed at the stupidity of it, but coming from Tannen, she found it sweet and endearing.

When the trolley pulled up to the platform at Onyx Alley, Tannen stuck his head out and announced their arrival in his official "trolley-car-driver" voice. She hopped off the carriage, minded the gap, and threw her hand up in a small wave at the driver's car. Her cheeks flushed with embarrassment as she hurried down the platform stairway. Was he watching her walk away? And was it her imagination or did it seem like the Catta-car took an extra-long time to start up again?

When the trolley was finally out of sight, she inhaled deeply and took in her surroundings. *Onyx Alley.* Of all the areas she'd mined over the years, Onyx Alley was, by far, her favorite place to work. The wooden staircase wound in a circular fashion and led to one of the deepest caverns in the Mines. The rocky walls glistened with jet black crystals; behind the beauty of the walls lay the soft coal. The walls of Onyx Alley were hard to penetrate, and most Coal Elves grumbled if they were assigned to work there, but not Ember. She enjoyed the mysterious gloom of the cave, the twinkling of the black crag, and the wonder of hidden corners and treasures.

Once she found a Graespur nest hidden in a rock shelf. Five baby Graespurs were waiting patiently for their mother to return with food, but it was daytime, and their mother hadn't come back from her nightly wanderings. The Graelings were velvety pink and couldn't have been more than a week old. She knew they would have died without assistance, so she filled her canteen in the cool spring, found some grubs and kissle leaves and helped the babies survive. She marveled at how they grew strong and independent. She was amazed at how their fur turned from bright rose pink, to a dark salmon color, to a lavender berry shade, to the deep gray hue of all adult Graespurs. They had survived because of her and were ready to begin their adult life. Each day after, she would come to check on them while they peacefully slept. One, Two Three, Four, Five all nestled in their kissle leaf bed on the jet black rock shelf. Then one morning, Five was missing. One, Two, Three, and Four seemed agitated in their sleep without their brother. Then a few days later, Three was gone. Then Two. Then Four. Then One. Then the next week, Sturd came to work with a new pair of boots, brown leather with gray velvet trim.

Sturd! Another elf she hoped she wouldn't see today. She prayed to Claus she would much rather endure the curious and reprimanding stares from Banter than to have to look into the wild ferret eyes of Sturd!

She found an untouched ridge near the cool spring that ran through the Alley and decided to start hacking away at the crystalline rock. She had barely raised her axe when she heard the high-pitched voice of Barkuss calling to her from above the terrace.

Here we go!

He was running and huffing and puffing so hard, it looked as if he was going to pass out. "E! E!" he frantically called to her in his effeminate way. "Girl, you need to put that axe down and getchour lil' self over here *now*!"

"Seriously, Barkuss," she called back, exasperated. "I just got here, and I just wanna get some work done…."

"Now!" he interrupted. "Banter's office! There's something you really oughta see!"

She dropped her axe and exhaled, shoulders slumping downward in defeat. The whole Catta-car ride over, she had purposefully *not* thought about a confrontation with Banter. She had hoped to avoid all contact with Banter. But it was no use. This was the inevitable. She knew it was time to face whatever it was she had to face. Banter was her Supervisor, and she had to rise to the call.

Banter's office was a trailer perched next to the Catta-car platform. It overlooked a jagged cliff, giving him an unobstructed view of the Alley. There he could keep watch over the Coal Elves as they heaved and hacked away at the onyx. The view was glorious—the rock shimmered with the frost-like crystals and created a dazzling reflection in the cool spring that could only be seen from his office window. She had been in Banter's office from time to time, filling out paperwork and making coal deposits, but this time was different. This time she had been called for, summoned, and she knew the consequences of her actions would soon befall her.

Banter sat at his desk scratching his stubbly brown beard, the short brown hairs whitening at the roots. His face was focused on a stack of papers before him, and he peered up from his glasses as she and Barkuss entered the room. Banter was Barkuss's older brother by ten elfyears, and if one had to judge by personality alone, there was no resemblance between the two whatsoever. Banter was Barkuss's polar opposite – no real sense of humor, no flare for entertainment and gossip. Banter was all business, all the time. He had been appointed Supervisor of his own crew at a very young elfage, and that large responsibility was taking its toll on his young elf body. His shaggy long hair was thinning at the top, and there were deep-set lines around his eyes like creases in old paper. He looked old. He looked tired and worn. Years spent Underground hardened his appearance, and his personality.

He eyed Ember up and down then pointed to a chair opposite his desk. "Sit," he instructed. He looked at Barkuss and motioned to the door. "Leave," he ordered. Banter was an elf of few words, but he was quite effective in getting his point across. Barkuss obediently turned on his heels and left the trailer.

She sat in the black swivel chair in front of Banter's desk. Unable to reach the floor, her feet dangled back and forth. Quickly, she crossed her legs, taming their swing, and making them appear somewhat lady-like. She was unsure as to how to present herself. Banter's presence was always so commanding, so intense, and not knowing the reason she was being summoned by him was enough to make those butterflies in her stomach eat her alive.

He waved his hands above the pink and yellow papers that were scattered about. "Listen," his voice boomed in the small office. "Do you see these papers on my desk?" His hands were cracked and wrinkled; his hands alone gave the appearance that he was far older than his thirty elfyears.

She nodded her head. "Y-yes, I can explain," she mumbled. "I swear, Banter, I swear to Claus that it was an accident. Really. Truly. I didn't mean to….." She felt herself fighting to hurriedly get the words out, but Banter's piercing brown eyes stared at her so intently that she stopped speaking.

"I've never seen these types of papers in my life before," he continued. "And I had hoped that I never would. But here they are. And we have to deal with it."

"What are—" she started again, but Banter's furrowed brow of annoyance silenced her. She figured it would be best to keep her mouth closed and let Banter do all the talking. She figured whatever it was to make Banter say this much in one sitting must be extremely important.

He removed his glasses and wearily rubbed the insides of his eyes. "What I have to say, let me say. You'd best listen closely."

She nodded.

"You," he continued, "you're a good worker, a hard worker, one of my best. Something about you. Your spirit, your fire… you've always reminded me of my mother." His voice stammered in a way that she had never heard before. Banter was cold and calculating and told it like it was, but now, she felt as if there was actual emotion in his voice.

She nodded her head again because she had always had much respect for Banter; he had taught her well and took care of her, even after her apprenticeship with Corzakk was complete. At times, she had looked up to Banter as being the tough older brother of sorts – silent and strong.

"But, the fire is gone, Ember. You're lost. You're on the wrong path. I can see that. And after that little stunt you pulled the other night, well, others see it too."

Others?

He cleared his throat. "You... you did a bad thing. Barkuss, he knows, he just denies. He's not dumb, ya know. He just thinks that if he ignores what happened, it'll go away and fix itself." He drummed his fingers on top of his desk, the thudding sound muffled by the papers littering the top. "I don't know what's goin' on with you, but I'll tell you this... you're not the first elf to try to hurt himself." There was that "knowing" glint reflecting in his eyes again.

He shifted in his chair and continued. "I don't understand it, and I don't attempt to try to either. I do know this: you're a good worker. Hard worker. Strong worker. Stronger than you think. Stronger than you know." He inhaled. "Is it fair what the Boss did to ya? I don't know. His plan is his plan, and ultimately, we all have to fall in line. The hierarchy, the chain of command, has been in motion ever since before the oldest elf can even remember. Boss to Council. Council to Masters, Enforcers, Managers. And so on down the line.

"And you know what you did was bad. We need to fix this. Now. Can't have ya goin' all nutty on us again. Bonkers. Crazy. Throwing a precious life away. Why? Cause you're angry? You think you're the only elf that's ever been angry? We all get angry. Even us Ceffles, the ones who were born here, raised here. Anger is a real emotion, and we need to just deal with it."

Deal with it? Deal with it? How can you say that when you have no idea what the other side is like?! But, she held her tongue as she promised and let Banter continue.

"The Defector from the other night was a female elf from the West Valley."

Yes, that was the rumor that was going around.

He picked up a bright yellow sheet of paper from his desk and began reading. "The elf's name was Pepper Brightly. She completed all her training and exams with flying colors. A good student with no flight risk. Female elves of the West Valley are considered apprentices for a year. After completing their course, they remain in their Master's care for another year, practicing their trade, while their former Master prepares for them to be matched with a partner. Miss Brightly was informed on her twelfth elfyear celebration that she would be transferred to Welfort Den and matched with her future elfhusband."

Welfort Den? Sturd lives in Welfort Den.

"The night after this information was imparted to her, Miss Brightly took it upon herself to flee the West Valley, and was subsequently deemed a Defector. The actions that followed thereafter are to be sealed in the records. There are no remains to be handled. Brightly's family in East Bank have since been notified of her *disappearance*," and he briefly paused, stressing that last word.

He placed the yellow paper down and lifted a pink one. "Do you understand, Ember? This is a copy of your 'accident' report." He waved the piece of paper in her face. "As your Supervisor, it is my duty to document and report any activity of my workers. Of course, I didn't come out right and say what I knew you were doing, but there's no sugarcoating it, Ember. The higher-ups saw right through the notes."

Her body twitched. Pepper Brightly's story was much like her own: a scared and frightened girl trying to get away. Was she scared and frightened? No. More like angry and *done*.

But am I considered a Defector now, too? Do they look at my "accident" as running away?

"I thought the worst," Banter continued, "but then I got this." He dropped the pink accident report and lifted a cream-colored envelope.

Great, it just keeps getting better, doesn't it?

He breathed in deeply and on his long exhale he finally continued, "You got a Pass."

She quickly looked up. "W-w-what do ya mean, 'a Pass?'"

"A Pass. A Pass," Banter repeated as if his mere repetition would bring understanding. "Ya know. A *Pass*," he said again, this time strongly emphasizing the word.

A Pass? A Pass for what? What did all this mean? Aren't I going to be punished, banished, hanged, eaten?

"You lost me," she said, bewildered.

Banter was starting to get upset. He fidgeted in his chair, apparently unable to understand what *she* didn't understand. He was obviously frustrated and began to stroke his beard to calm himself down.

She knew he was aggravated, but her curiosity needed to be assuaged. "Explain to me what you mean," she said gently.

He deeply inhaled again, opened the envelope, and began to read the contents of the letter within. "'Banter Dwin'nae, you are hereby summoned to escort Miss Ember Skye...'" he read, but the words sounded like Graespur hums to her ears. She was lost in them, drunk. Banter's mouth was moving and there were sounds coming from his lips, something about his directions on how to get her to the Mouth of the cave, something about his duties as her escort: follow the map as planned, adhere to Code 739, and something else that she didn't catch. Each word paralyzed her in disbelief that she truly didn't absorb all the fine details.

"'... to go Home,'" he concluded.

She sat, completely frozen. The room felt like it had spun a few degrees, similar to the false motions of a grulish-trip, and her hands were soaked with the sweat of anxiety.

That day, that day, that awful hurtful day of her arrival replayed over and over in her mind. Corzakk had laughed, so hard and diabolically. *"Child, you* are *Home!"* he had mocked. Home? What was Home?

"But aren't I...." she stammered to Banter as her consciousness slipped back to the present.

He pointed his forefinger in an upward motion. "Home, up there. You got a pass. Forty-eight elfhours."

"But Sturd!" she argued. "Sturd hates me! He would never let me leave!"

Banter shook his head. "You're right, he wouldn't. Sturd doesn't like anyone. He's a jealous little elf."

"So how did I...?"

"This isn't from Sturd."

Her face twisted with a puzzled look.

Banter took out from the envelope a piece of silver paper that was folded in half and handed it to her from across the desk. "It's from the Council, under strict direction from the Boss."

She unfolded it slowly and gently as to not rip or crease any inch of it. "Ember Skye" was written in deep red block letters at the top. Mystified, she held it in her hands for a few moments, examining each corner and fold.

"This pass entitles the recipient, Ember Skye, Coal Elf #7390, of Ebony Crag, to attend a 48-elfhour retreat to Tir-La Treals under the Seventeenth Provision of Regulation 12," she read. There was other writing below that and a few signatures and dates at the bottom, particulars she quickly glanced over. Her focus mainly stayed on the first line of the Pass – 48-elfhour retreat to Tir-La Treals. She smiled. Her lips spread open, teeth clenched tightly together, and her nose scrunched into a tiny ball on the center of her face. Her eyes sparkled with sheer joy and excitement. She was going *Home*.

Home.

But just what exactly was Home now? The very definition of the word was confusing to her. Time spent in her rocky abode had distorted her original meaning of it. The lines had now been blurred, and both worlds she knew had taken on a strange significance in her life. Home. Aboveground Home. Underground Home. She suddenly thought of Barkuss. Would going Aboveground betray him? And just for a split second, a wave of guilt and nerves washed over her.

She set the paper gingerly in her lap. It was clear Banter was not pleased with this decision. This puzzled Ember slightly, but her joy was so overpowering, she scarcely gave it a second thought. If it was a direct order from the Boss, it really didn't matter how Banter felt about it.

"Listen," he said in his firm tone, "you're happy. I see that. But I worry about you. It's been six elfyears since you've been there. Just be careful."

She exhaled. "Oh, Banter! This is the best, the absolute best!" And with that, she flew from her chair and embraced him where he sat.

Bending close to his stubbly cheeks, she slathered him with fifty kisses.

He winced from the outpour of emotion. "All right, all right," he replied, agitated as he tugged away from her grip. He stood up and walked to the door. "Pack a bag. I'll take you to the drop-off point tomorrow morning. Take the rest of the day off. Go!" He signaled for her to leave as his body shuddered, like a dog shaking off fleas.

Barkuss was waiting for her outside the trailer. His smile was just as large and bright as hers. "Get packin', crazy girl!" he said cheerfully.

She nodded and ran straight to her den, her smile never once leaving her face.

Home, Nanny Carole, Father, Mother, snow, sunshine, fresh wind, candy canes, cookies. Everything she remembered flooded her consciousness so vividly that all the sights and smells that had felt like a thousand years ago were once again in her reach. This retreat would be exactly what she needed! Sleep was certain to be an impossibility. There would be little if no sleep tonight as all these thoughts and images raced through her mind. Soon she would be back Home!

Home.

Home.

HOME!

Chapter Seven

W HEN SHE HEARD THE GRAESPURS MAKING THEIR NOISY RETURN TO THE
caves, those butterflies went wild again in the pit of her stomach. Morning had now arrived, and Banter would soon be there to
take her to the drop-off, the place where she would be reunited with
her loving family and past life as a normal Land Elf: Aboveground!

The night had been wasted on tossing from side to side on her
bed with moments of forced sleep in between. Thoughts of seeing
her parents played continuously in her mind. What would she say to
them? How would they react to her? What would she tell them first?
And what about Nanny Carole? She would surely have to visit her at
her new home. Maybe Nanny would even bake her favorite cookies.
The wait was unbearable. She stood impatiently in her living room
as she wrapped the elastic on her drawstring bag tightly around her
wrist. She fidgeted so much that her fingertips were starting to feel
tingly and numb.

Then there was the hollow sound of the knock at the door booming throughout her den, making her jolt from the inside out—Banter
had arrived to escort her on the first leg of her journey. His deep
brown eyes were weary and greeted her with unspoken sadness when
she opened the door. It was clear to her that Banter hadn't slept either,
but that wasn't her concern at that very moment. She was too anxious
and excited to think about anyone or anything other than her trip.

"You ready?" she eagerly inquired.

He slowly nodded. "Make sure you have your Pass," he admonished.

She smiled. The very word "Pass" invoked so many different emotions within, it practically made her head spin. She slithered out the
front door, closed it tightly behind her, and followed Banter down the
dark corridors.

The walk to the Mouth of the cave was a silent one. She knew well
enough not to babble incessantly or to ask any frivolous questions,
although the butterflies that were going crazy in her tummy made
her want to rave about all of her feelings so very badly.

All Coal Elves had an idea of how to get to the Mouth, but very few had the need to travel there. The Importer Elves for the Mines made their way back and forth daily, receiving food and supplies from Aboveground. All other Coal Elves were forbidden to even travel close to the Mouth. There were rumors that trolls dwelled in the vicinity of the Mouth and that those trolls ate elves. At ten elfyears old, thoughts of elf-eating trolls did seem feasible; however, the real reason why most elves stayed clear was because of the Guardian Elves who stood watch at the Entrance Zone, wielding menacing looking spears, challenging anyone to dare try to pass.

Banter's instructions had notified him that the route to the Mouth would be shrouded in magic. His map was written in the ancient Elvish script, but Banter had a small device he squiggled across the paper every now and then to translate the text.

She guessed they were close when she felt a sudden drop in temperature and a sudden increase of light within the hall. For the first time in a long while, she was able to see remnants of her breath come from her mouth in smoky puffs. This was the oldest cavern she had ever been in; the rock wall glistened with a sheet of frost—*or was that fairy dust?*

Panic began to creep up into her chest when she first saw the two Guards. They stood in front of a wrought iron gate, one at each side, with their pointed spears criss-crossing each other. Their faces wore permanent scowls. Meekly, she tried to crack a smile as she nodded respectfully to them, but they did nothing but stare at her with their piercing eyes. She felt as if their eyes could have very well been the spears they carried.

"This is it. This is the Mouth!" Banter proclaimed as he motioned to the opening.

Past the iron teeth of the gate, she saw the sunlight shining through and could feel its warm fingers tantalizing her cheeks amidst the frigid open air. "I vaguely remember," she said through chattering teeth.

Banter grinned. "Then you must remember them," he said motioning to the Guards.

She rubbed her hands together anxiously and nodded.

"Your Pass," Banter prompted.

She tilted her head to the side and gave him a puzzled look, still in awe of her surroundings. Banter widened his eyes. "Pass!" he shouted to her.

As if snapping out of a trance, she flung her drawstring bag from around her shoulder and snaked her tiny hand inside. Feeling around for a moment, she finally produced the paper and extended her arm to hand it to Banter. He shook his head from side to side. "Not me," he said calmly as he pointed to one of the intimidating Guards. "Him."

She slowly inched to the Guard and hesitantly gave him the silver paper. He glared at it, scowl intact, held it up so the other could have a look at it, turned it around a few times as if to examine it, folded it tightly, and gave it back to her. The Guard at the other end closed his eyes and gave a hint of a nod, one that barely registered a "yes" on the body-language scale. She took back her Pass and slipped it into her bag. There was a heavy silence in the cavern that made her desperately uneasy.

"Now what?" she called to Banter who was now behind her.

He glanced hesitantly at his instruction sheet, and he quickly brought his hand down with the translator so that all she could see was the curvy design of the Elvish letters. "That's it, I suppose," he said.

"It?"

He nodded. "Listen, this is all new to me, too. I'm just telling you what this paper here says," he said, frustrated.

She looked up at the Guard who had held her Pass. She noticed he was much taller than most Coal Elves, nearly human in size, or was that her mind playing tricks on her in the presence of such a powerful being? "Can I go?" she asked, her voice barely bouncing off the cave walls.

The Guard's eyes narrowed downward. Then his lids closed, he gave one of those "barely-there" nods, and both lifted their spears toward their opposite shoulders, the metal grating against each other with a scraping, clashing din. The Guard at the far end made a hand gesture and the wrought iron gates lifted. She looked over her shoulder at Banter as she began to shuffle forward into the sunlight.

Banter looked down at the map again, "Says here that transportation back here has been arranged. There will be a coach waiting for you at the town square of East Bank by five tomorrow evening."

She was still unsettled. She glanced out into the white open space and back at Banter.

He pointed to the opening. "Don't worry," he grunted.

She fidgeted with the drawstring of her bag again as she inched closer and closer to the opening. She looked at Banter one last time and said nervously, "See ya in two days!" He nodded again, and with that, she passed through the gate. As soon as she was through, the gates slammed closed with a vicious metallic *thud.*

The sun was bright and hot, its light blinding her sensitive, unadjusted eyes. She needed to violently blink for a minute before she was able to adapt to the now-unfamiliar light. The snow was wet and frigid on the cuffs of her jumpsuit pants and against her leg, but the feeling was so glorious she vowed to remember it always.

She rubbed her eyes a final time and gazed at the mountain and gates. Iron and rock. Then she outstretched her arms, breathed in the cold crisp air, and exhaled with an "ahhhh." After one last look at the beauty around her, she headed for the town, specifically her parents' Home in Tir-La Treals.

Tir-La Treals was a small suburb of the city of East Bank. It was a quiet little town with friendly neighbors who were always willing to help each other out. Her Home was Skye Manor, a sprawling compound on a hill that overlooked the suburb. It was nice to live there and be away from the large city, and yet be close enough to all the hustle and bustle. East Bank was particularly fun around the time of the Big Night. She remembered how her father hitched up his team of chocolate-colored reindeer and took the family to see the tree lightings, skating competitions and the other fun activities of the season.

She would have to travel through East Bank in order to get to her Home, and this time of year was the best! The chaotic aura of the Big Night was not yet in full swing, but late August brought many

harvest festivals and the outdoor flea market! Not only was she going
to be reunited with her family, but she was going to be able to enjoy
the sights and sounds of the city she loved as a child.

Finding her way was easy. As an elfling, she had ventured many
times to the outskirts of the city. She and her friends of yesteryear
had often played "Good Elf, Bad Elf" in the white woods. The map
inside her mind's eye unfolded before her, and soon enough she was
on the edge of town. She immediately recognized the smell of the
roasted chestnut street vendors, and the faint whiff of black toy lacquer from the numerous toy-making shoppes. Her nose twitched as
she breathed in the familiar odors, and a smile spread across her face.
East Bank was just the way she remembered it. It wouldn't be long
before she arrived Home.

She passed the Fish Market where the Fishing Elves were working.
Behind the building, they were hauling large nets from the river onto
the dock, many of them tying and singing away with great fervor. It
was a busy scene; the Fishing Elves worked so diligently, yet there
was a sense of happiness that was in stark contrast to the labor she
steadily endured as they tied up their fresh morning catches of Swee-
Swee. Her mouth watered at the thought of grilled Swee-Swee fish
marinated in Nessie Fruit sauce and slathered in a honey lemon glaze.
Add a side dish of marshmallow-dipped turnips, a glass of sparkling
cider, and that was enough to make *any* elf's mouth water. What elf
could resist *that*? Perhaps Nanny Carole could prepare such a meal for
her tonight. Of course Nanny Carole would make it for her. It would
be the perfect homecoming feast!

But what if she doesn't have any fresh fish?

"I'll just have to bring some Home with me!" she exclaimed out
loud.

The elf at the Fish Market who wore a yellow jumpsuit, was obviously the head of the guild. She could tell by his deep voice and
serious demeanor that he was the one who took care of all business
aspects. She approached him happily, practically singing her request
as she got closer.

She smiled. "Excuse me, sir?"

He glanced over at her, did a sort of double take, and then looked away. She noticed the expression on his face had changed drastically when he had briefly made eye contact with her. He ducked his head down and began scratching his pointy nose as if to distract himself from her presence. "Excuse me?" she repeated naïvely, raising her voice a bit as she moved closer toward him.

He fidgeted, and he refused to catch her gaze, even though she could see him eyeing her with his peripheral sight. She was now close enough to read his name tag on his jumpsuit, and she addressed him by name in hopes of forcing him to acknowledge her presence.

"Smitty Fishworth? Head of Operations? May I have a word, please, sir?" she huffed as she came right underneath him and extended her hand. "I'm Ember Skye, pleased to make your acquaintance," she beamed. "I wish to buy one your biggest, sweetest Swee-Swee, preferably a blue one as I'm more partial to the vanilla undertaste."

His eyes passed her up and down like fingernails over a chalk board. His uncomfortable glances made her wide grin diminish like a balloon slowly deflating. She retracted her outstretched hand.

"What *are* you? And what are you doing here?" he finally growled at her. "What do you want with us over here?"

"I... I... I just w-want.... "

He continued his assault. "Yeah, yeah, yeah, I know whatcha want! You want to rob me blind, don'tcha? Where do ya even belong, you filthy thing? Are you even an elf?"

Filthy thing? Coal dust. Caked on.

She desperately fought back the tears forming in her eyes. She reached in her bag, took out her silver letter, and waved it in Smitty's face. "I'm a Coal Elf, sir!" she barked defiantly. "I'm here on holiday. Here is my Pass signed by the Boss himself. I just wanted to buy a Swee-Swee, but if you're refusing to sell it to me, I–"

Smitty grabbed the notice from her hand. It was genuine, all right! Signed by the Boss himself, just as she had declared! Quickly, his demeanor changed. As a sign of good faith, Smitty gave her his biggest, bluest Swee-Swee, free of charge, and threw in a bag of turnips, profusely apologizing the entire time, albeit behind his disgusted smile.

The rest of the walk through the heart of East Bank was pretty much the same. Elves stared her down; Nanny Elves hid the eyes of the elflings in their care as she walked by; workers in store fronts gawked; shoppers whispered. Everyone seemed wide-eyed and open-mouthed. Was her appearance *that* revolting, or was their ignorance *that* abundant?

Finally, she traversed through the heart of the city and arrived at the foot of the hill to Skye Manor. The road to the gate was winding and steep, but she was determined to make the climb Home. The large iron gates glowed gold as they towered around the perimeter of the property. The *S* emblem that held them tightly shut glittered in rubies and emeralds. The landscaping was as impeccable as ever; large topiaries and green hedges surrounded the grounds with splatterings of colorful flowers to accent the greenery.

When she approached the wooden guardhouse, the elf who stood watch tilted her head in surprise. "Who are you? What business do ye have at Skye Manor?" she said in her flat, no-nonsense voice.

"I have a Pass, ma'am," Ember responded, flashing the paper. "I'm a relative come to visit."

The guard glanced over the paper, back at Ember, and back to the paper a few more times. The guard narrowed her eyes and gave Ember a final suspicious look before saying, "Looks legit. All right then. Go on in." She slammed her tiny hand on a red button that opened the gigantic gates. Ember sprinted through as soon as the opening was wide enough to fit her body.

Beyond the gates was exactly as she had remembered! *The garden maze, the butterfly chamber, the hammock and swing.* The sights and sounds of the Manor filled her mind, and memories of her childhood washed over her in excited waves. *The circular carriageway, the rose bushes, the pond and waterfall.* One after the other like sensory overload!

She approached the front doors, and they, too, were as she remembered. The majestic glass panes were frosted in silver dust and framed in the finest of gems. A large *S* and *M* were etched in the glass, and a gold woven rope hung to the right. Her hand shook as she gripped it and gave it a delicate tug. The chimes played a merry tune, and within seconds the door was flung open.

She was greeted by an unfamiliar elf, and she felt the smile on her lips start to melt from her face. "May I help you?" he asked, rather disgusted at the sight of her, but curious all the same.

She fumbled with the Pass. "Yes, um... I'm here to see my family. I'm Ember, Elden and Amalia's daughter."

The man's eyes flashed wide in disbelief for a second. "W... w... wait right here," he said in hushed tones. He turned his head slightly, and in the same confused and whispered voice called down the hall of the foyer, "Ginger, there's a girl here who says she's Ember, your sister."

"Ember?" It was Mother's voice from the parlor. "Ember?" she repeated again, as her voice got closer from within.

"Mother, go back to the parlor," the elf coaxed as Mother's body manifested at the door. "I'll take care of this."

Mother pushed passed that young man. "Ember?" she repeated as she came into full sight.

Mother's eyes were weary, dark circles pouched under her lids, and black makeup smudged her entire face. Her hair was fully grayed and disheveled. She wore a pink fur robe and had a glass of cider in her hand; the contents of the glass wobbled with every unsteady move she took.

Ember dropped the bag of food and exclaimed, "Mother!" She out-stretched her arms for an embrace.

But Mother stood there, motionless. "Ember?" she said again in disbelief, examining the girl.

"Yes, Mother! It's me! I'm on a Pass. On holiday! I've come to visit you and Father!"

Mother's mouth turned downward in a menacing frown, and she squinted her eyes as if to get a better look at her. "What are *you*?" she hissed, still struggling to see through the coal dust caked on Ember's face, still trying to recognize this unfamiliar creature before her.

Ember froze. Had her own mother forgotten her?

"Get off my property, you... you... *imposter*! My daughter is dead! You're just... just... a... a... a... *monster*!"

Mother turned away and stumbled back into the parlor. Ember heard Ginger's voice say, "It's okay, I'll handle this. I'll get rid of her," before appearing at the door.

And there was Ginger, her orange hair flowing over her shoulders, much longer than the last time Ember saw her. "What's going on here, Vonran?" she asked the male elf.

"This girl, here," he began, "she has a Pass from the Mines. Says she's your sister."

Ginger peered from behind him and came into full view at the door. Ember saw her pinafore dress poking out from her midsection like a round ball. Ginger looked aged as well.

She looked Ember up and down, and finally recognized her sister from underneath the coal dust. "Why are you here?" she snapped.

Ember stammered. "I have a Pass. I wanted to see.... "

"Six elfyears later?" Ginger scolded. "Six elfyears of *nothing* and then you just pop up?"

"You don't understand, I couldn't—"

"No, *you* don't understand," Ginger interrupted. "Things aren't the same, Ember. Father is gone. There was an accident."

Ember was still in shock. She and Ginger had always had a love/ hate sibling rivalry type of relationship, but even in her wildest nightmares, she had not envisioned this to be a proper "welcome-home" greeting. The mention of her Father made her ears perk up even more, the word "accident" dangling invisibly in the air before her. "W... w... what do you mean? Accident? What do you mean, 'Father's gone?'"

Ginger inhaled deeply; annoyed she had to retell the story again, as if she had told it a million times before. "Dead, Ember. He died. A few years after you left." Her voice was cold, matter-of-fact.

Ember's head swam at the news and the ground beneath her felt as if it had shifted. Her knees started to shake and buckle inward, and she consciously had to plant her feet on the ground to keep from falling down.

Father? Dead? How could this be? How come no one ever told....

Ginger callously continued, "Mother didn't take Father's passing too well. Vonran and I had to move back here just to take care of her. She believed you were dead, too. Quite frankly, we all did, and we were all fine with that idea." She began to turn away, but Ember took a step forward and placed her hand on the door.

"Ginger, can I please come in? Can you please explain what's happening?" Ember begged.

Ginger huffed, her shoulders and bean-bag belly heaving forward as she noisily exhaled. "You're not serious, are you?" she hissed. "You've clearly upset Mother! Who knows if we'll be able to calm her down now?"

Ember heard a crash from within the parlor and Mother yelling something incomprehensible. "Ginger! Please!" she desperately pleaded. "I don't have much time, maybe I could just...." She pushed a little harder on the door and took another step forward as if to push her way into the home.

Ginger's eyes flashed in anger as she pushed the door back with a force that made Ember stumble onto the walkway. Ginger's sarcastic laughter filled her with memories of childhood tauntings. Decapitated dollies, unstuffed teddy bears, dirt-covered lollipops. Ginger's reign of sisterly terror had left its permanent imprint within her. She shuddered on the inside as she caught her balance.

"Now I have to pick up the pieces. Again!" Ginger complained. "You should have never come here. Go back to the Mines, Ember. Go back to where you belong!" And with that, Ginger stormed into the parlor to assist Mother.

Tears began to well in her eyes. "Wait!" Ember protested. "Where's Carole?"

Vonran stood there in silence for a few seconds until he heard Ginger calling to him. "Sorry," he finally said hesitantly, "but you really should go." It was apparent he didn't know what else to say.

"Go? Go where?" she sniffled. "I have no place to stay. I don't get picked up until tomorrow."

"Vonran!" Ginger screamed.

"Listen," Vonran said to Ember, "I run the Inn in East Bank." He took out a piece of paper from his pocket and scribbled something down. "Show them your Pass and this note. The Inn Keeper is an elf by the name of Slarrett. He'll help you. You can stay the night until you need to go. I'm really sorry about all this."

"You're... you're helping me?" she asked in disbelief.

"I had a brother. He was sent to the Mines. I had always hoped to see him again, but I never did." He gave her the paper and before shutting the door he whispered, "Carole is at Stixx Manor."

She stared at the paper for what seemed like forever. Finally, she heard Vonran saying, "She's gone. She's gone," from behind the door and she knew that was her cue to exit the premises. She turned around and walked back to the majestic gates, down the winding road, and back to the heart of East Bank.

Chapter Eight

THE SNOW BEGAN TO FALL GENTLY IN FLUFFY FLAKES, AND SHE FOUGHT hard against her childhood instinct to extend her tongue to savor the frosty particles. All around her, the sky was turning from blue to gold, signaling the end of the day was close at hand. She wandered through the villages observing the beauty she had once held in such high regard, but no matter how hard she tried to catch that nostalgic feeling, it seemed to escape her at every given moment. The snow-capped evergreens reflected the warm yellow light from the setting sun, and it made her think of that old man-made poem, the one about the Boss visiting some family on the Big Night: *'Twas the something or other.* Even still, the majestic illumination of the trees paled in comparison to the wondrous depths of her caverns and the obsidian walls of Onyx Alley refracting the light from her worker's helmet and casting mysterious shadows down hallways and hallways of darkness and ash.

She sighed. The weight of the Swee-Swee and turnip bag now made her shoulder ache. Her fruitless encounter with her family had sparked a fire of longing in the pit of her belly, and she realized she wanted to go back to her den Underground.

But not before adding insult to injury.

She was headed to the Inn in East Bank, the one her brother-in-law, Vonran, had told her about. Why he would take mercy on a filthy Coal Elf when her own blood family wouldn't was beyond her, but she was in no position to scoff at any amount of hospitality. Before making her final trek to retire for the night, she took another piece of information her kind-hearted kin provided: Nanny Carole—at Stixx Manor.

The Stixx family was wealthy, just like the Skyes. They had their own private manor in Tir-La-Dunes, the neighboring parish from her parents' Home. Cynnamon was one of their daughters who, at one time, had been a very good friend to her, but that was an old story, and she wished not to revisit that tale.

If what Vonran had said was true, then Nanny Carole would be there taking care of the youngest member of the brood. They probably would be outside making a snowman at this time of night, and Nanny Carole would probably be reciting the old elf poem, "The Mists of the North", while her charge danced in ceremonial circles around the newly formed Mr. Snow Frost.

"The mists of the North come rolling by,
As I spot them from the corner of my eye.
Changing yellow, to pink, to purple, to black.
I hope they soon would roll on back."

The poem was so embedded in her memory, she found herself mouthing the words in time with Nanny Carole. But this wasn't a memory, and this wasn't a daydream. There was Nanny Carole on the front lawn of Stixx Manor, singing "The Mists of the North" to a small elfling who was ceremoniously circling a newly formed snowwoman. The elfling's fire red curls bounced wildly under a pink knit cap as she wrapped a candy cane striped scarf around her creation's neck.

This scene haunted her with thoughts of her own past, as this could have very well been a page in her own book of memory. Nanny Carole was dressed in the same lavender smock, and the wind-rash cheeks of her charge stood out brightly against her pale white skin. The song, the ritual, the dance, it was already there, already written. And as if on cue, Ember practically recited the next line of dialog as she continued to watch from behind the Stixx's reindeer topiaries.

"Oh, Juniper!" Nanny Carole sang out in with her bell-like voice.

Only, ten elfyears ago it was Ember's name ringing out in sing-song tones in the frigid air.

Little Juniper giggled with delight, knowing all too well the next part of the game.

"Oh, Juuuuniperrrr!" Nanny Carole continued, raising the pitch and volume of her voice a notch.

Juniper's giggles increased. "Yeeessss, Nanny Carole?" she sang back as she ducked behind the snowwoman.

"Who wants a Brimmle Brummle Bushell Borg?" Carole continued with a mile-wide smile spread across her face.

Juniper tried to contain her laughter by holding her pink knit mitten over her mouth, but it only muffled her chuckles.

"I saaiiddd, who wants a Brimmle Brummle Bushell Borg?" Carole repeated as she slowly crept up to the snow figure.

Juniper, who was in full blown hysterics by now, popped out from behind the snowwoman, arms outspread for a warm embrace, and squealed, "Borgie Blushy Bots!" And with that, Nanny Carole swooped down for the hug, picked up little Juniper, and spun her body around and around, her tiny elfling legs dangling horizontally in mid-air.

Ember could barely stomach it. "Brimmle Brummle" was a game *she* had played with *her* beloved Nanny Carole, but now another child had replaced her. This display of rehearsed affection stabbed Ember deeply.

Rehearsed. Nanny Carole had done this all before. The snowman, the dance, the song, the game. A play, an act. How many children had Nanny Carole played with in the exact same way? How many before Ember? Was Ember's entire upbringing a lie? Was it all part of a script? Were there ever any real feelings of love and devotion, or was all this really "just a job" for Carole?

Ember toyed with the thought of approaching her former caregiver, but decided against it. Instead, she watched the two play the silly, nonsensical game until the sky turned to a dome of black ink and offerings of hot cocoa and peppermint Nessie crescents were made.

Being on the outside for so long made looking at things on the inside a lot different. She had thought for so long that the ash and dirt and dust of the Mines had clouded her mind and darkened her thoughts, but maybe it was the snowflakes and sunshine of her youth that had blinded her to some truths she hadn't been willing to confront.

Speaking of snowflakes, the falling snow began to come down a little harder and the wind picked up a notch or two. Her jacket pockets were not enough to shield her scrawny fingers from the lick of the frigid air.

She lingered on a few minutes longer, watching the two figures in the kitchen lovingly talk over their tasty snack. Finally, Nanny Carole turned out the light. "Let's get to bed now, Emmy," she beamed at the child as she tousled her blond curls.

Only, this time, it was "Junie", and Nanny Carole's fingers were swept away in a sea of red locks.

Chapter Nine

E MBER SLAPPED HER PASS AND VONRAN'S NOTE ON THE INN KEEPER'S DESK with a heavy sigh. She was done. Enough. The stares, the looks, the *oohs* and *ahs*. The harsh blow of reality went straight to the middle of her chest, and she was more than over it. All she wanted now was something to eat and a place to rest her head.

The Inn was located in the town square. It was a large, two-story building with a red brick façade. Beyond the Inn Keeper's desk was a narrow wooden staircase that led to the guests' rooms. She took note of the rich décor—the elaborate and intricately woven tapestries made from the finest threads that hung on the walls of the entrance-way; lovely embroidered pieces that depicted scenes of ancient Poleonic lore. Only the finest museums had pieces like these!

Slarrett, the Inn Keeper, didn't give her a second look. He picked up the papers in his chubby hands, read them through, and nodded as if in agreement to a set of unspoken instructions. "Miss Skye," he said in his peculiarly high-pitched voice, "come this way. Mr. Verthar has reserved the High Court Suite for you."

She sighed again. High Court Suite? Right now she would settle for a blanket and worn-down mattress if it meant getting some rest. Being treated to luxurious lodgings was certainly not high on her "I Need" list at the moment.

He led her up the wooden staircase to a narrow hall. There were doors on each side, many rooms for many traveling elves. He stopped at Room 23 and reached into his pocket for his key ring, and after flipping the numerous keys around for a few seconds, he found the right one with an "Ah-ha!" and opened the door.

Once the door was pushed fully ajar, she let out a tiny gasp of amazement. The room was spectacular! Nothing short of its name! The wood floors shone with a newly waxed glean. And the bed was dressed in a thick purple comforter with gold velvet curtains draping the wooden spindle bedposts. There was an antique writing desk in the corner, and a matching nightstand with an iron oil lamp already lit. Every accent, every detail was of rich and royal splendor—from the elaborate carvings on the nightstand legs, to the intricate details on the dresser drawer knobs. This was old-school elf craftsmanship, a dying art, so she had once been told.

Slarrett's eyes closed as he grinned a closed-mouth grin. "Mr. Verthar said you were to have this room as a special courtesy," he proclaimed. His nose shifted upward, revealing the tiny little hairs in his nostrils. He was beaming with pride over this room as if it were his greatest creation. Slarrett was an Inn Keeper; he had spent his whole adult elflife accommodating others, and it was obvious this lavish room was his crown jewel.

"It's very lovely. Thank you," she half-heartedly gushed, because at the end of the day, when all was said and done, this room would be a distant memory, clouded by soot and coal dust.

He walked in the room examining every inch to make sure there were no dust specks to be found. "I can have the chef bring up something for you to eat if you like."

She held out the package of Swee-Swee and turnips. "Oh, no, that's fine," she said still gazing at the room with mild astonishment. "I have this."

Slarrett walked over and took the bag from her. Her pulled open the drawstring and looked inside. "Can't eat raw fish! I'll have the chef fix this up for you right away!" And before she could protest, he was out the door.

She flopped onto the soft bed. Her body melted into every crease of the heavy comforter like warm butter filling the crevices of a freshly baked Nessie muffin. Her head sunk low into the fluffy pillow, and the billowing ends came up over her pointed ears and blocked out all sounds around her with a muffled din. It had been so long since she had been in a bed as luxurious as this one, if ever. *Fine. At least I'll get a decent meal and some rest.*

The whooshing quiet engulfed her as she began to drift off to sleep, and she barely heard the gentle tapping at the door. It was Slarrett with her meal. When she finally realized someone was knocking, she called out, "Come in," from the bed, and she heard him fumbling with his key ring again before he entered. Slarrett was followed by another elf who carried a large tray packed with food. She sat up in the bed as the elf set the tray over her lap.

She bowed her head in gratitude, "Thank you."

Slarret clasped his hands together with a tiny clap. "If you need anything else, Joona will be right outside your door. Call for him when you're finished so he can clean this up. Enjoy!"

The two elves exited the room and she sat in awe at the feast before her. There were heaping plates of fruits and warm breads, a small pitcher of cider, and a covered dish with the Swee-Swee and turnips. The delicious aromas tantalized her and made her feel comforted. Each different smell played upon a different note in her stomach's song of hunger. While savoring the glorious scents, a growling noise rose up from the depths of her belly.

Utensils were not an option as her little hands savagely tore hunks off the grain bread. She stuffed whole chunks of sweet Nessie Fruit into the sides of her cheeks, letting the sugary flesh saturate her mouth. She gulped draught after draught of the bubbly cider without stopping for air, and when she let out a burp of relief, her belly was ready and clear for the main course. Blue Swee-Swee, grilled to perfection, with a light Nessie sauce glaze and a side of candied turnips. A feast fit for a royal elf.

After she had furiously gorged herself, she called for Joona and he swiftly wisked the tray away. She was full! For the first time in six elfyears she could see the little pouch of her stomach extended. With one last burp, she rose from the bed and made her way to the large window seat. The window overlooked the entire city. She perched herself on the long sill and watched the elves hustling and bustling below like a hawk observing the forest from his highest treetop. A street choir of apprentice Chorus Elves approached the main intersection and burst into song. Their Master waved her arms frantically to and fro as the apprentices worked so hard to remember their lines and their harmonies. She smiled to herself as she detected a few bum notes throughout the tune, but overall they sang well—not a bad start for apprentices.

Everything beneath her seemed good from up in the High Court Suite. Sunshine, snow, lollipops, and puppy dogs. But this was not where she belonged. Not anymore. She slipped away from the sill, ears still fastened to the song being sung and made her way back to the bed. The song continued on, but she curled up to the side and drew the covers as high as she could so the sounds came to her in muffled tones, like the echoes in a dark and dusty cavern where each breath taken is deep and labored. *Sounds of Home.*

The next morning she showered and decided to check out early. And of course, no matter how many times she scrubbed, no matter how many gels, and oils, and loofas she used to lessen the caked on dirt and grime, she still managed to appear a ghastly shade of Coal White, a muted gray hue permanently adhered to her body.

She thanked Slarrett many times for the wonderful hospitality. "No, no, thank you, breakfast won't be necessary, still full from last night's meal. Oh my stars, yes! The room was unlike anything I've seen before. Yes, yes, I will recommend your lodgings to other elves along my path."

Blah, blah, blah. Formalities and niceties.

There was still time to kill before she would be picked up in the town square, so she decided to do some window shopping and explore her old stomping grounds. A gentle morning snow began to fall, and before she realized she was doing it, her tongue extended to taste the icy flakes. Just like she remembered! Each frigid drop on her tongue made her giggle like an elfling again. But she wasn't an elfling. Catching herself having this moment of enjoyment made her snap her tongue back into her mouth and push her hair from her eyes. *No more of that. No more.*

She wandered the city aimlessly for a few hours, stopping here and there to smell the freshly baked cookies from the baker's shop, or sample peppermint sticks from the candy store. Slowly but surely, the realization that this was an alien life began to overtake her. Slowly but surely, she wished her ride to come as fast as possible.

Before making her way to the town square, she passed a large field with a house and stable on it. The field was enclosed with a wrought iron fence, and there were many trees and shrubs decorating the landscape. It was the Reindeer Stable, and she knew this place well. As an elfling, Nanny Carole would take her to watch the calves train. It was always funny to her to see the little ones try so hard to fly over a set-up obstacle course and stumble and fall, and as she would laugh at them, she remembered Nanny Carole scolding her and telling her to be respectful. "You never know which calf might actually be chosen for the Boss's team," she would warn. Ember rested her arms over the fence and placed her head in her hands, and waited to see if the calves would come out to train.

Within moments, a plucky girl elf came from the barn pulling three calves behind her on a cracked brown leather leash. The reindeer were striking creatures. The first on the leash was larger than the other two. He had a shiny white coat, broad shoulders, and enormous antlers. It was apparent he was the elder of the calves, and was probably on his last leg of training before making it up to Headquarters. The next was a very small female with tan fur. Her antlers were miniature compared to the first, but she was lean and strong. Her muscles rippled under her taut coat, and she walked with a determined stride out onto the field. The last was a male, medium-sized, with dark fur – the darkest fur on a deer she had ever seen. His hooves were thick, and she could hear heavy clanking noises with each step he took. He, too, was an older calf and his sheer presence was so alluring that she was immediately drawn to him.

The Trainer Elf called to the team as she freed them from her leash. "And... up!" The two males immediately took flight, but the female hesitated. "Viella," she commanded, "up!"

The reindeer reared back on her hind legs and hoisted her front end into the air. She was wobbly, but soon righted herself into a smooth transition. The males circled the female twice before she fell into formation. The white one led the group as the Trainer issued commands from the ground. "Left. Right. Twist. Sink." One after the other, she called simple words, and they followed her instructions. The female deer called Viella made many mistakes, but she managed to keep up and hold her own. Ember noticed a few times the darker male had tried to get in front of the white one. His form was much better, and his glide was smoother, prettier. It was as if the two were jockeying for position. The Trainer Elf also noted this and had to tell them to "Get back," or "Whoa, Zyklon! Easy, Asche."

Ember watched the entire session perched upon the fence. When it was over, the Trainer Elf tied up her team and walked over to her.

"Like what you see?" she asked Ember with her smoky breath.

"They're beautiful!" she raved. "They did a very good job, too."

"Thank you, they're really working hard. I'm Kyla Plumm." She outstretched her hand.

Ember grasped Kyla's hand in a friendly shake, the first she had since coming Aboveground. "Ember Skye."

"Nice to meet you, Ember." Kyla pointed to the white deer, "That is Zyklon." She motioned to the dark one, "That's Asche." And finally to the female, "And that's my baby girl, Viella."

Ember smiled. "They really are amazing. My Nanny used to bring me here when I was a kid. We used to watch the Trainer have his morning sessions."

Kyla smiled back. "That was my dad! This is a family business, ya know. My father used to be head trainer, and his father before him, and his father before him. You know how it goes!"

Ember let out a small "hmmph" in mock agreement. *How it goes, all right.* Had that had truly been the way, then she would have been assigned as a Teacher Elf, or a Fashion Designer Elf, or even a Toy Maker Elf, not as a Coal Elf!

"Any of your deer make the Big Team?" Ember asked, making small conversation.

Kyla exhaled in near frustration. "Loooong story," she huffed. "It's been a very long time since the Council had approved any changes to the Boss's Team. Besides, there are other stables we compete against, and the fact that the Council is not so eager to mess with their current lineup makes it hard to get your 'hoof in the door,' so to speak. But Blitzen was born, trained, and bred here. That's the Plumm family claim to fame!"

Ember smiled at Kyla's enthusiasm for her line of work. A flash of envy flushed into her face, but drained as soon as the snowflakes descended onto her cheeks.

"Zy and Asche are going for their final tests soon," Kyla continued. "I'm hoping the Council sees their potential. I know Zyklon will have a good showing, but he can be cocky at times. Asche has a great presence, too, and he's much more workable than Zy, but I know they probably won't even give him a second thought. Coloring's too dark. The Boss supposedly is afraid the darker ones will get him lost during the Big Night, so Asche here might be hanging out with me for a long time to come." Kyla shook her head.

"How's that fair?" Ember naïvely asked.

"You tell me, Coal Elf," Kyla slyly responded with a wink.

"Touché," Ember quipped back. "We all have our place, don't we?"

Kyla lowered her head and drifted into the distance between them. "Yes we do, yes we do," she said in a faraway voice.

Ember jumped down from the fence. "Well, it was nice to meet you, Kyla Plumm. I have a ride to catch in a little bit. Good luck with your team."

"Fare thee well, Ember the Coal Elf," Kyla said, waving with one hand as she led the reindeer back to the barn.

Chapter Ten

CORZAKK.

Of all the Coal Elves that could have possibly come to pick her up, why in Claus's name did it have to be *Corzakk?* Ember's heart sank into her stomach when she saw him turn the corner. He snarled at her when they made eye contact, and when he reached her, he grabbed her by the arm, practically forcing her to the ground. Claus, how she couldn't stand him!

"Let's go!" he barked. "Hope you enjoyed your little vacation!"

She glared at him and jerked away from his grip. "Always trying to torture me, right, Corzakk?"

His hand latched onto her wrist again. "Be quiet!"

She had something clever to say back to him, but bit her tongue. He was walking quickly ahead of her, practically dragging her behind him. She thought Banter had said "transportation?" And yes, while walking is a form of transportation, this was not what she had expected.

Actually, this whole wasted trip was not what she had expected. Could that have been the Boss's plan all along? Could it have been possible the whole meeting with her family had been an act? Maybe it was a set-up to make her *want* to go back to the caves. *Doubtful.* Why would the Council go through so much trouble just for *her?*

They walked south for a good half hour when they finally came to the Mouth. It wasn't the area she had passed through at the beginning of her sojourn, but it *was* a familiar sight. This was the place where she was brought as an elfling. This was where she met the deplorable Corzakk for the first time.

The entire trek, Corzakk had been blathering on about work and the Mines and the Defector, which was very un-Corzakk-like. She thought she heard the word "delicious" in there somewhere, but she couldn't be sure, as she wasn't paying him much attention. Normally, the old screw provided his usual grunts and groans, followed by some sarcastically biting remark. Now, he seemed a little jittery, a little more on edge, a little bit *happy?* Regardless, she was trying hard to

block his incessant chatter out as she was mentally preparing herself
for entrance back Underground.

The cave was quiet. Usually there were machine sounds and
coughing coming from every corner of the cavern, but now there was
an eerie silence that blanketed her surroundings.

He clapped his hands together and mysteriously announced,
"Looks like we made it back just in time!"

"Time for *what?*"

"Sturd has a big announcement to make. *I'm* not even sure what
it's about. Apparently, he has some radical plans. We need to get to
Sandstone Shelf as soon as possible to hear the news!" There was an
unfamiliar hint of giddiness in Corzakk's tone that made her uncomfortable, and her new suspicions of everyone and everything led to
believe this was a set-up.

*He thinks I'm a Defector. He's leading me into a trap. They're going
to kill me, or worse….*

Sandstone Shelf was beyond Onyx Alley. It was the only section
in the Mines that wasn't connected by the Catta-car system, and the
only way to get there was by crossing the Ignis River. After they
passed the twilight zone of the cave, he led her to the rafting station
and motioned for her to get onto one of the small water crafts. She
hesitantly lowered her body onto one of the rafts, and he followed.
He unraveled the tethering rope, and the raft jerked into the river
where it picked up the current and headed downstream.

As they got closer to their destination, she could hear the voices of
many elves echoing back and forth on the rocky walls. It was as if the
conversations were repeating on a never ending loop, and she could
make out bits and pieces of doubled-up phrases and sentences. He
tied up the raft to the bank, and motioned for her to hop off.

Great. A public execution.

But she was wrong. Sturd soon appeared from a high ridge and
waved his arm for silence. Lanterns and candles cast shadows in the
cave, creating an eerie aura. A rumbled hush worked its way through
the crowd as all elves tilted their heads upwards to get a glimpse of
Sturd's lord-like visage. He was larger than life way up there; his own

shadow danced back and forth like a giant gangly monster. The crowd stood, jaws widened in reverent fear and awe.

She surveyed the crowd, searching for a familiar face among the blackened despondent ones before her. Soon she located Barkuss, who was standing by himself, and waved her hand quickly back and forth until he noticed her. He smiled and he signaled for her to join him at his spot. Corzakk was enthralled with his progeny. A smile of complete pride was spread thinly across his face which made it easy for her to slip by him.

Once she was out of Corzakk's earshot, she jogged over to Barkuss as he opened his arms for a friendly embrace. "How'd everything go?" he asked.

She shook her head side to side.

Barkuss frowned, his thick lips puckered out in a puppy-dog-sad-face. "Oh, not good, sugar? We'll talk about it later, okay?"

"Okay," she whispered unenthusiastically, because she had absolutely no intention of reliving her experience Aboveground. She pointed up to the ledge where Sturd was standing. "So, what's all this about?"

He shrugged his shoulders. "Dunno! We were finishing up a little early today and the siren sounds. Darn near scared me half to death! Then my brother gets on the loudspeaker announcing that we need to congregate in Sandstone Shelf for some major announcement!"

"Wait!" Ember said confused. "Banter called this meeting?"

Barkuss shook his head back and forth; there was very little ash that puffed out and strands of orange and red hair peaked through atop his head. "Not *that* brother," he said very seriously. "My other brother up there," and he motioned to Sturd high on the ledge.

She gave a puzzled "huh?" face, but Barkuss continued rambling on. "I swear, E, I'm just about gonna burst with all these declarations and announcements down here! Have you ever seen this much action in the Mines?" He was genuinely excited. She knew he really hadn't seen this much action in all his life, but then again, neither had she.

"Does seem kind of odd, doesn't it…" she began hesitantly, but she stopped talking when Sturd cleared his throat with a deep "ahem".

"Coal Elves!" Sturd finally cried out when there was almost complete silence. "I have much to tell you. First, we are saddened that one of our... sisters," and his voice trailed the word as if vomit had gurgled up to his throat, "made a horrible choice. Runaways are not tolerated lightly. We all have crosses to bear, and it is our responsibility to adhere to our commitments as needed! Defectors are traitors—traitors to their Clans, and Guilds, and Masters, and fellow workers!"

The crowd began to get riled up. Some of the elves were hooting out "Yeah!" and someone shouted, "You tell 'em!"

Ember and Barkuss glanced at each other, raising their eyebrows in a knowing look.

Sturd extended his hand again for silence and the noise died down. "These times for us have been dire."

"*Dire?* When would Sturd ever use a word like that?" Barkuss whispered into Ember's ear. She shrugged.

"There is much unrest among our ranks," Sturd continued.

"What the—? Is he for real? Do these elves actually think he's saying these things on his own?" Barkuss whispered. She nodded again, unable to vocalize to him how she really felt—*this has got to be a set-up!*

Elves all around them started bobbing their heads up and down in agreement to Sturd's words. They started humming and mumming again in unison.

"The horror stories are coming more and more frequently. Something has to change!" he shouted as he pounded a fist into his opened hand.

More elves hooted, more elves cheered, and again, the raised hand of Sturd beckoned the crowd to calm down.

When he was absolutely sure he had the full attention of each and every Coal Elf in the Mines, he reached his hand into his back pocket and pulled something out. It was a little golden scroll tied tightly with a red ribbon, and when Ember saw it, she nearly lost her breath. Apparently, so did the other elves, as not a sound could be heard throughout the Shelf.

"This," Sturd shouted as he raised the scroll high into the air, "is the List."

There was a collective gasp in the crowd. Barkuss let out a small squeal. For most, it was the first time they had even seen the document.

He slid the red ribbon off and let it float gently to the elves below. One of the older female elves extended her boney hand to try to catch it, but she was bulldozed by a much younger, stronger male. Sturd flicked his wrist, and the parchment spiraled downward like names tumbling head over heels to the ground. Ember watched, as if in slow motion, the names tumbling toward her, and once again tried to commit to memory the swivel of the candy-cane colored ink.

Various degrees of "ooohs" and "ahs" rose up from the crowd in a mystified din.

"This List," Sturd continued, "has driven us, worked us. We've lived–" he paused for dramatic effect "–and died by this List. This List has driven some of us to do great things, and led some of us down a path of destruction."

"Seriously? Is he reading cue cards?" Ember whispered to Barkuss, but it was no use; he was in a deep trance.

Sturd's plastered grin widened, giving him a demonic clown face in the shadows. "I've been in control of this List for some time now. The Council has given me specific instructions each year. The Boss has personally entrusted me with this knowledge, which eventually affects all of you and the work we are doing down here."

We? There's no we in Sturd's vocabulary.

"So now, in these dark times, with the Big Night less than four months away, I have made a decision that will shake the very fabric of our being."

Oh, please stop with the dramatics!

"This List is no more!" he cried over the speechless throng. "So why should we bother with a Light List this year? I think *all* children will get presents on the Big Night. Good. Bad. There is no distinction! For this year, the List is abolished, and all work in the Mines will cease. AT ONCE!"

The congregation of Coal Elves paused in disbelief for a few seconds. Even Ember's sarcastic mind-dialogue stopped, frozen, as the reality of Sturd's words took root in her mind. The elves stood, mouths agape, eyebrows raised, paralyzed with confusion and understanding, and maybe a little bit of both. Barkuss slapped his hands onto her shoulders, his fingers gripping her flesh tightly, shaking Ember back and forth in disbelief. Within seconds, a roar of sheer joy and excitement rocked the cave. The chaotic howls of delight from the masses reached its way throughout the twilight and dark zones, up to and beyond the Mouth.

Ember was speechless, unable to process the news. Did Sturd actually have the power to make such a decision on his own? Was he *that* trusted by the Council?

She was confused, disturbed. What would become of them now? What ramifications would a decree like this impose on the human world? She started to remember Nanny Carole, started to remember the connection, like the balance scales....

Amidst the frenzy, Sturd still held the List in his hand, shaking it back and forth, while screaming something inaudible over the echoing boom. Then, Sturd's ferret paw of a hand curled over the side of the List and began tearing the parchment down the center. Like a nightmare, Ember could only watch as the red and green names halved in the middle.

When Sturd got to the end of the spiral, he put the two pieces together and tore through it again. And again, and again, over and over until there was nothing left of the List but fragments of colored letters. With pieces bunched in his hands, he gently blew on them, and they descended to the crowd below like gently falling leaves. The crowd was in such complete hysterics by now that the majority of them didn't even notice that the List had been destroyed.

But Ember noticed. From the moment Sturd had revealed the List to the time it was ripped before her eyes, she knew *exactly* where it was at any given moment. Frantically, she jostled her way through the elves and raced to catch every last shred of paper.

Barkuss was lost in the crowd; a swarm of elves engulfed him in their frenzy. "What are you doing?" he roared when he saw her bent over the shards of paper. But she ignored his question.

Chapter Eleven

THE MOMENT SHE'D SEEN STURD RIP AND TEAR AT THE LIST, HER INSTINCTS had kicked into overdrive and propelled her body into motion, which is why the tiny bits of paper now were spread across Ember's kitchen table like hundreds of pieces in a jigsaw puzzle.

Barkuss stood next to her, observing the pieces of paper while shaking his dusty head from side to side. "What are we gonna do now?" he asked, his tongue making that *click click click* sound it made when he was anxious.

She sighed. "I don't know, Barkuss. I'm so confused about everything."

"Can Sturd really do that?"

She shook her head. "Your guess is as good as mine. The fact is, he did it."

"And there it is." He pointed to the table.

"Yep. There it is," she replied as her forefinger followed in time with Barkuss's.

"You know, E, if Sturd finds out that you.... "

"I know. I know. So let's just make sure that he doesn't, okay?"

Barkuss bobbed his head up and down. He feared Sturd just as much as everyone else. He knew what Sturd was capable of, and did not wish to see his best friend come under Sturd's wrath.

She began to move the pieces of paper around, just as if they really were a giant jigsaw puzzle. "It just doesn't make sense, Barkuss. Doesn't make sense that he would destroy it. Ya know, Nanny Carole always told me our worlds are connected – us elves and the kids in the human world – by Nessie. I never believed her. Never believed we could be bound together through magic fruit. I mean, how stupid does that sound? But what if it's true? What if she's right? What if the stories about the Nessie Fruit are real?"

Barkuss glared as she fit the pieces together. "Then this would be kinda bad, don't you think?"

"Kinda? I think more than just *kinda*. Barkuss, if Sturd is acting on his own, then it's possible the Council doesn't know about this."

"Yeah, but don't ya think they'll get suspicious when the Coal Collectors from Aboveground come looking for the sacks for the Boss's ride and we ain't got nothin'?"

She closed her eyes tightly. "I don't know! I don't know!"

He hesitantly reached towards a piece, and then drew his hand away. "What if you went and told the Council about it?"

Liking where Barkuss was going with his suggestion, she slowly opened her eyes and sat down, "Hmm." she thought out loud. "That sounds like a great idea!"

"I'll go with you if you want," he offered.

Even better.

"We can't," she said abruptly. "We don't have Passes."

He raised his eyebrows and smiled wide. "Sweetheart, who needs a Pass when you got the List? THE LIST! Ain't no magic guard go'n say no to *that*!"

It was a brilliant plan. "You know you're helping me put this thing together!" she exclaimed.

He frowned. "I figured you would say that. I was planning on going to some parties, and.... "

"Bar-kuss!" she said, deepening her voice in a kidding way.

"Yeah, yeah, yeah! Can I ever say *no* to your sweet face?"

For years now, she had struggled with her beliefs and questioned her life on many different levels. As an elfling, there were no questions. There was just family, and playtime, and carefree moments with candy canes and lollipops. The Boss just *was*, and blind belief in everything that was good and jolly was predicated on what her parents and Nanny Elf and other elders told her. No questions, no inquiries, no resistance; just like the Laws that governed the Nessie Fruit. They grew in the North Pole because the children in the human world had that very same sense of wonder and mystified belief in Claus. They were what kept the elves alive, essentially, and the circle of life played on and on year after year. No questions. No resistance. Just faith and hope, but for her, the lines of faith and hope had blurred, changed. Had *been changing* for some time now.

What was faith to her, anyway? She no longer believed the higher power, the Boss, Claus himself, to have greater purposes or grand intentions. She no longer believed in a "plan." She no longer had faith in the all-knowing Council. Life was random, hit or miss, and Ember knew the choices she made in her life had no bearing on anyone or anything else. *Like drawing a name from a cap.*

And there was one question with which she still needed to reconcile: *Why had she scavenged the fallen List?*

Why had she collected the torn scraps? And why was she sitting here now, after several days of organizing and sorting the fractured pieces of the once almighty List, holding a roll of tape in one hand, looking at the remnants, and slowly piecing them back together? Was it hope? Was it faith? Was it her constant quest for knowing? Was it fear?

She couldn't answer for sure; the pit of her belly gurgled to her that there was just something completely wrong in its destruction. Never mind Sturd's manufactured oration. Never mind the clamoring of the "freed" elves. She had felt a connection to the List. It actually invoked a physical reaction deep within her. The sight of it, the smell of it, the dazzling names written upon it put her into a trance, made her swoon, made her *feel.* These years of struggling with her faith suddenly seemed empty in the presence of the List. The List filled a gaping void within, awakened her spirit, and raised her pointed inner ears up a little with the thought of *what if this all isn't for naught?*

Her struggle had now become a bit more complicated. This dichotomous war between ultimate hope and faith, and the absence thereof, weighed heavily on her very soul. She had no idea what putting the List back together would accomplish, but a driving force inside her said it had to be done.

Barkuss maneuvered the ragged pieces of paper across the table. "This is gonna take a while," he complained.

She breathed heavily. "I suppose so. I...."

Then they heard a heavy knock at her door. They gave each other a panicked look before quickly scooping up all the pieces of the List. They dumped them into one of the pull out drawers underneath her kitchen's countertop, tucking the precious scraps safely away from anyone's sight.

"Come in," she called.

Banter made his way into her den. "Ember?"

"In the kitchen!"

"Hey, I was wondering if you… oh, there you are, Barkuss. I was looking all over for you."

Barkuss gave a nervous half-smile.

Perceptive Banter suspiciously glanced around the room. "Uh, you guys busy or something?"

She huffed out a small laugh as her eyes shot briefly to the secret drawer and nervously back again at Barkuss. "Yeah, right! Who *is* busy these days?"

Barkuss caught her eye and began circling away from the drawer, towards the door, to distract his brother. "I'm sayin'!" he agreed. "Ya know, it is kinda nice and all, having all this free time to myself, but there's a slight part of me that is kinda upset we're not working. Like, it almost doesn't feel natural. Does that make sense?"

"Yeah, I guess it does," Banter responded flatly.

Barkuss fluttered his eyelashes at his brother. "You said you needed me?"

"Uh, yeah, I have some furniture I needed to move and…."

"Oh, my dear, say no more. Let's go!" Barkuss sang as he began ushering his brother out of the kitchen and to the front door of Ember's den.

Over his shoulder, Barkuss looked back at her and gave her an exaggerated wink. She let her shoulders relax a bit as she was certain that Banter hadn't suspected anything.

After they left, she made her way back over to the drawer to continue her work of reconstructing the List. But as soon as she touched the knob to pull the drawer out, there was yet *another* knock at the door.

"Santa Claus!" she muttered, composed herself, and then sweetly asked, "Who is it?"

"Tannen," the voice replied.

She froze. Tannen? *The* Tannen? Tannen Trayth of the Tree-Elves? At her door? Now?

"Um... um..." she stuttered. "One minute!" She made sure the drawer was securely closed, brushed her hair back with her hand, and made her way to open the front door.

"Tannen!"

"Hey, how are you? Haven't seen you around much. Can I come in?"

She stepped aside, allowing him to enter. "Oh yeah, sure, sure. What's up?"

"Things are getting pretty wild down here! I've never seen so much going on here in my life!"

Of course Tannen was referring to what appeared to be an atmosphere of utter lawlessness. Coal Elves throughout the Mines were causing all types of havoc and running wild during their three-plus months of "freedom." But it didn't stop there. All Elves in the Mines, no matter what their trade, took an extended holiday. It was said Elves left and right were getting Passes to go Aboveground, parties were being held in multiple dens every night, mischief was increasing. The only thing that was operating as usual was the Catta-cars, and they were being used just to transport intoxicated elves from one lavish feast to the next.

"So, what have you been up to, Em? Haven't seen you out and about lately," he said as he sat at the kitchen table.

She chuckled. "Yeah, you mentioned that!"

A pink hue flushed in his cheeks beneath his ash smeared face.

"Eh," she continued, not trying to embarrass him any further, "I'm not one for that wild scene, ya know? I've been lying around, reading, writing in my journal, that kind of stuff."

Reading? Great. He is never going to believe that!

Tannen just smiled. "Well, I don't know if you're interested, but they released the details of the Defector situation from a few weeks ago."

She sat down across the table from him, perched her head in her hands and leaned forward. She didn't have the heart to tell him she already knew the details of the case; she really just wanted him to leave so she could get on with her task of reconstructing the List, but his voice was so dreamy and intoxicating she knew she just had to let him stay and tell her whatever it was he wanted to tell her.

"So," he began as he lowered his voice to a mysterious timbre, the "oh" sound fluttering upward to increase the intensity. "You know she was from West Valley, right?"

Pepper Brightly, her name was Pepper Brightly.

"She was a good elf and all. Never gave anyone any problems. Trained well. Well liked. From Aboveground.... " Tannen's voice trailed, and he slightly raised his eyebrows as he changed the subject. "Em, didn't you ever ask anyone why they never sent you to West Valley? It's a very nice place. All the girl elves go there. Why not you? It's a little weird that you're not over there with the others. Girls, I mean."

She stiffened up. Her muscles tensed at his sudden firing of questions. Noticing her quick and uncomfortable mood shift, Tannen continued with the fervor of his gossip and abandoned his curious side story.

"So, this girl," he started–

Pepper Brightly.

"–never got into trouble, never caused any kind of stir among the ranks. That girl was going be someone's elfwife. But the kicker is this: she wasn't going to be just anyone's elfwife, she was going to be *Sturd's* elfwife!"

"Well, I guess if I was assigned to be Sturd's elfwife, I'd run away too!"

Tannen laughed. It was a deep, genuine chuckle that came from the pit of his stomach. She giggled a little, too. "And that got me thinking," he continued when they had both settled down. "Ya know how the girls in the West Valley are being trained and all to be given away to someone? Do you think they're training some boy elf to be given to you?"

"No."

"Hmm," he huffed, puzzled at her abrupt response.

"Why? You know, not all elves are paired up down here. Do you think *you'll* be assigned an elfwife?"

Tannen shrugged. It was his only response. "Seriously, though," he picked up, "could you imagine living with Sturd and having to take care of him and having little elfbabies with him?"

"I know, right? Would they even *be* elfbabies?"

"Good Claus! What a scene that would be! I don't even want to think about it!"

They both were in hysterics at this point.

"And who would even consider Sturd for husbandhood?" she managed to get out through her laughter. "I mean, is he *really* the model candidate? He hates everyone and everything in existence. So, why does he qualify to have an elfwife, and not someone like say, Banter?"

Tannen's laughter was coming to a close in short labored pants. "Ah well, you know how that goes," he said as he stood up from the table. "It is what it is, I guess. Some want, some get. We go with it like rolling dice." He paused for a moment, and then began nervously rubbing his hands together. "Oh, well, the Nim'sim brothers are throwing a big bash in a few hours. Do you think you would like to go with me?"

She wanted to say yes so very badly, but there was work to be done. "No," she replied abruptly, the quickness of her answer making his face fall in disappointment. "No, thank you," she said more gently. "You enjoy. I'll come another time."

He looked defeated. "Oh, okay. Maybe some other time." And with that, Tannen stood up and made his way to the door.

She exhaled in relief. Finally, she was alone, and determined. She swung around to the drawer, pulled it open, and marveled at the job that lay before her. An instinctual, almost primal sensation engulfed her, and she began to work. The sea of greens and reds that flooded her table made her eyes want to cross. She had no clue where to begin, and no clue how this was going to turn out. She wasn't even sure if she had all the strips of paper!

She took a deep breath. Like anything else, the only place to start was at the beginning. She sifted through the rubble, found strips with black lettering, and turned them upside down. Then, she fastened them together with the clear tape she held tight in her hand, the edges crumpled and worn. After that, she turned her doctored paper over and read the heading. It read "The List," scribbled in black calligraphy.

It was a start.

Chapter Twelve

TIME BLURRED. SOUNDS AND LIGHTS AND DARKNESS AND MORE SOUNDS blended together. Sleeping and eating were done out of necessity, and there was very little need for any of that. Day after day (or was it night after night?), Tannen came knocking at her door asking her to join him in some adventure, and night after night (or was it day after day?), she kindly refused with various excuses of various degrees.

My head hurts.

My stomach hurts.

I'm enjoying my night alone, thank you.

Oh, I just made some peppermint swirl cocoa! I'll catch ya next time!

My clothes are still wet from laundry day.

I'm at a really good chapter in my book.

I'm writing in my journal tonight was her latest alibi, and after the words left her lips, she got to thinking about her once trusted confidante. Her long neglected journal sat in her nightstand next to her bed. How long had it been since she had scribbled down her inner most thoughts and secrets? It actually didn't seem like a bad idea to take a small break from the List and take a stroll down memory lane.

She propped herself up on her bed and caressed the leather cover. Its tough ridges were like Braille bumps; she closed her eyes as she ran her fingers over the surface, and breathed in deeply as the memories started to flood her mind. She clicked open the magnetic latch and began thumbing through the pages, catching glimpses of words and phrases of days long ago.

"It smells gross down here. I think I'll die from the smell alone," she read from one of her very first entries.

She read through the sad times, the happy times, and her dark-self remembering the light from Aboveground. The longing, the wanting, the need to go back Home to her family. All meaningless now. All wasted wishes that didn't come true. Time blurred.

Her last entry from weeks ago made a mention of Tannen. "I never gave much thought to being an elfwife, but I swear if I had to choose someone it would probably have to be Tannen Trayth. Descendant of the Tree-Elves, Tannen. Catta-car operator, Tannen. Blond hair, rosy cheeked, I-could-kinda-like-you-if-I-wasn't-such-a-miserable-girl-elf, Tannen...."

She crinkled her nose and shook her head. That was before her sojourn Aboveground; that was before her encounter with Sturd, and that was significantly before her love affair with the List. She barely even recognized the girl-elf who wrote that entry about elfhusbands and possible dreams of happiness. In a matter of weeks, she had significantly changed.

Her eyes blinked heavily and she knew it was now necessary to rest for a bit. Before succumbing to the woozy embrace of sleep, she reached for a pen and wrote one last entry. Sleep had firmly rooted its welcoming grip, but she had managed to jot down a few ideas before the book and pen fell lazily at her side and her head rolled back onto her upright pillow:

The passage of Hope raises questions of days gone by.
Fear knocks down my door with his wild eyes and magic breath.
There, he tells me lies in the circle of my brethren.
I was lost for far too long
And he's come to collect his winnings.
When Fear expands and collapses my lungs, I'll be but a memory.
On pages left in shambles.
I wish for sublime restitution, like a kiss from an enslaved heartbeat.
But Fear knows not my will
And his blackened mind hates my theories.
A feverish hand beckons me sleep.
And I quiver with the thought that I am truly alone.
                                        ~E.S.

Chapter Thirteen

C HAOS.
    All was now the way Sturd liked it. The smell of chaos—
like burnt embers from a wild forest fire; the taste of chaos—like
Graespur meat over an open grill.

All was chaos in the Mines right now. Chaos he'd created, and
chaos he continued to control. Because of him, the List was no more.
Work had stopped.

It was playtime in the Mines, and Sturd was Law. His ascent to
power had come all too easily.

Sturd clearly remembered the day he was called to his fate. He had
been playing in an old, dusty mine shaft while his father, Corzakk,
dissected the walls of Diamond's Row, mining the most valuable
coal. It was dark this summer afternoon, as they were deep in the
Mines. The lights from their hardhats danced off the cave walls, giving Diamond's Row a twinkling, twilight-like feel.

He and his father had awoken even before the Graespurs came
back to the Mines from their nightly jaunts. He had come with his
father in hopes of catching one to add to his collection. At the age of
seven elfyears, he had been adept in construction work and had built
an elaborate habitat, a graeviary, next to his mother's night-blooming
garden. He had been raising a family of Graespurs, with his mother's
help, of course. The Graespurs were free to come and go as they
pleased, and he provided them with the finest of cave bugs to gorge
themselves on, and plenty of kissle leaves for their comfortable nests.

Life in the Mines was good for Sturd, charmed.

His father was one of the best miners Underground. Corzakk
was well respected by the community and soon would be a Master,
training many apprentices in the ways of the Coal Elves. He was of
the Ruprecht Clan, one of the oldest and most revered throughout
the Pole. The Ruprecht Clan extended beyond the Mines and even
beyond the Heavens!

Mother, too, was of a high-ranking clan, the Melithoro. Her
foremothers were born and raised in the West Valley for many a

generation, and produced some of the finest elfwives.

Sturd and his Mother were inseparable. They often spent time out-side of their den, and Mother taught Sturd many things. There was a night-blooming garden where the purple petals of the Alcanthia flower grew in great abundance. In a corner of the fenced-in rock-yard they kept an elaborate graeviary where they spent countless hours raising orphan Graespurs. Yes, life was indeed good; it was charmed... but there were things beneath the seemingly perfect sur-face that were dark and abominable, because no matter how hard she tried to love him, I'len Melithoro Dwin'nae Ruprecht could not love her son. *Not this one.*

For as long as he could remember, Sturd always knew Mother had been "assigned" to his father. Not in the usual "elfwife" way, though. Father had had an elfwife before Mother—many years before Mother. Then there was an accident in the Mines, and his father's first wife was killed. In an attempt to make up for Corzakk's loss, the Council made the decision to assign him a new elfwife; however, in doing so, they tore Mother away from her already established family, including her five young sons. Sturd always knew the special situation of his family, and that he had older brothers in the Mines, but he never was able to fully comprehend the magnitude of how things came to be.

Perhaps he'd never understood the longing and pain in I'len's heart as she was ripped away from the arms of her husband, Borthen Dwin'nae. Never understood that his five brothers, Bommer, Banter, Balrion, Bulder, and Barkuss, had cried endlessly each night, praying for their Mother's return. Never understood that Corzakk had forced himself upon I'len numerous times in hopes of her bearing a child of their union, thus forgetting about her children. Never understood the abuse and suffering Mother had experienced at the hands of his father throughout his first seven elfyears.

When he and his father returned back to their den that day, it was apparent something had gone terribly wrong. Mother was not there, and any trace that she had ever been a part of the Ruprecht family was gone. The only thing she left behind was a cryptic note – it read, "I'm sorry."

Sturd couldn't understand. Why had Mother left? Where did she go? Had he done something wrong? Salty tears streaked his ashen face before his father called out to him in his "serious" voice, the one that stopped his crying and commanded his attention immediately.

Corzakk sat Sturd on the rock bench in their living room, hung his head low, and growled the news in shame and disgust. His yellow eyes stared deeply into Sturd's. "Your mother had a life before us, you know this," he stated matter-of-factly. "And that's where I assume she's gone back to. I always knew it would happen one day."

And that was that.

The one thing Sturd could understand for sure was that even he, her own child, couldn't make his mother forget her other sons. He was smart enough to figure out that Mother didn't love him enough to stay.

Sturd had been brought up to believe and obey, to never question (as all elflings were), and to trust in the comfort and safety of his family. Now, his father told him there *was* no family?

Sturd Ruprecht had just been informed he was without a mother, and no one could fix it. He had to accept it. What else could he do?

Such was the cruelty of the Mines.

That night as he cried himself to sleep, noises in the caves began to ring out. Elves were shouting and gathering outside his den. Father's voice could be heard booming over the crowd. Torch flames cast shadows through his bedroom window. He could make out the exaggerated forms of elves carrying pickaxes and other weapon-like tools. They looked like monsters to him on the wall, and their voices echoed wildly in his head.

"Find the little wretch…."

"No stone unturned…."

"She'd be a fool to try to get Aboveground…."

"…back alive…."

"…considered a Defector…."

Then an alarm sounded in the distance, a sound he had never heard before. It grew louder and louder, and closer and closer, rallying the elves into a chaotic frenzy. He listened to their voices as they echoed down the cave hall until all he could hear was a humming sound.

The next morning, he asked his father what had happened.

Corzakk smiled cheerily. "Never you mind about that." He placed a lavish serving platter on the kitchen table for breakfast. It was Mother's favorite serving dish, bone white with holly berries hand-painted in the corners; it was filled with succulent meat, hard boiled golden goose eggs, homemade Nessie Fruit bread, and peppermint crescents. "Now, eat up!"

Sturd's eyes widened at the delicious display. "It's not the Big Night, Father!"

A deep hearty laugh rose from deep in Corzakk's stomach. "No! It certainly is not, son! But there's much to celebrate! Now, dig in!"

Sturd filled his plate to the top. The breakfast feast was fantastic, and for a split second, it almost made him forget his mother had left him. The peppermint crescents were his favorite, and the hunks of meat were so juicy and tender. It was the sweetest meat he ever did have. What did Father say it was? There was enough to last a few days, and the two happily feasted at every meal until there was nothing left.

But when the feasting days were over, reality set in, and his world changed dramatically. During the elfyear that followed, he fell into a deep sorrow that was blinding. Once the meat was gone, he'd stopped eating altogether, and his body grew frail and weak. The bones in his hands grew twisted in a peculiar way. He'd hoped news of his grave condition would make his mother feel guilty and bring her back to him, even though he knew in his heart that would never, *could never* happen now.

In his fragile condition, he would play recklessly in the caves without his hardhat light as his eyes strained to find his way around in the darkness. Often he would weasel his way into chinchi holes to hide from his father and disappear from the world. Over time, the constant exposure to the dark took its toll on his eyes, making them adapt with a curious red hue. The constant ducking in and out of the chinchi holes, coupled with the lack of nutrients, arched his back slightly and gnarled his body in an unnatural way. His appearance morphed into something quite disturbing, and his spirits were so gloomy, Corzakk feared this depression would usher his son to an early grave.

Corzakk's anger was beyond compare. Not only had I'len left him, but she had forever destroyed the emotions, and appearance, of his only child. "Your mother was a deplorable creature!" he lectured. "But your suffering will not go unnoticed or unpunished. Do not let the choices of a filthy womanelf effect you... *ever*! A child should not be without a mother, and there will be restitution for your pain, I promise you that!" He touched Sturd's shoulder. "The Boss must have great things planned for you! If you can survive this dark time in your life, I'm sure you will be rewarded greatly!" he continued as he raised his fist. "Women are below us, Sturd! Remember that! Remember never to trust one or get close to one. They are vile and have one purpose: to serve *us*!" He took a deep breath to calm his rage and then smiled as he patted Sturd's hair.

Sturd threw himself onto the floor at his father's feet, curled his knees to his chest and sobbed uncontrollably. "But I don't understand! Why is this happening to *me*! Did I do something wrong? Am I a bad elfling?"

"Sturd Ruprecht," Corzakk commanded, "get up right now! Listen to me! Of all the elflings, the Boss will choose you... *you*! This has been the promise made, and this will be the promise kept. You will be the One!" He gripped Sturd's shoulders and brought him back to his feet. "Stop your crying right now. You have to be strong. Do you really think the Boss is going to allow someone so young to go through so much? Do you really think he would let an innocent elfling endure the horrors of abandonment without *some* sort of recompense? Trust me! You are strong and from a well-respected clan. You must do us proud! Become what is in your heart and you'll have the world at your feet! Now wipe your eyes. There, there. Go and wash yourself off. We'll be having supper in a bit."

Obeying his father, he retreated to the washroom to clean up. In the bathroom mirror, he stared at himself for what seemed like an eternity. His reflection was barely recognizable and he hated the visage that stared back at him in the glass. Who was he? What had he become? What did his mother *make* him? His desperation and confusion was a lot for his eight elfyears, and at that instant, from deep within his chest, he felt a rush of warmth work its way up and throughout his limbs. The sadness that had overwhelmed him for so long was slipping away and transforming, much like his body had done. The numbness of his mother's abandonment was leaving, leaving, leaving and he was now feeling, feeling, feeling! With each passing second, the warmth grew stronger and stronger until it felt as if his body was on fire. He righted his hunched back and snarled at his counterpart in the mirror, the image slowly becoming more familiar, more awake, more alive. A conquering surge of power rocked his body as the heat from within reached its pinnacle, boiling his elfish blood. He clenched his animal-like fist and punched the mirror, the shards sticking out of his knuckles, blood trickling to the floor, but the feeling of physical pain was absent from the act. He swooned with this newfound power! It was unadulterated rage, and he embraced it!

Corzakk was startled when he heard the commotion from the bathroom. "Sturd?" he called. "Everything okay in there?"

With that, Sturd raced passed him, a piece of broken glass in his hand, and out the back door. Concerned, Corzakk followed him outside.

Sturd had taken care of I'len's night-blooming garden the whole elfyear. It had been sacred to her, to them. They had bonded many days taking care of it, and he had maintained it well in hopes that upon her return she would be proud and thankful. But in a flash, it was destroyed. His footfalls stamped out any remnants of life in the garden bed. On his hands and knees, he ripped the Alcanthia flowers from their roots and viciously cut the stems with the broken glass. He sliced open the violet petals and smeared them across his face, allowing their toxic poison to wash over him and seep into his pores. He jutted his head back and forth with macabre twists, and released guttural cries and howling screams as the poison slowly worked its way into his veins.

When he finally opened his tightened eyes, and released one last groan and grunt, he spotted the corner of the rock yard. The graeviary. The Graespur family he had been taking care of was asleep in their nest. Without further thought, he opened the small wooden latch, reached in with the broken glass, and hacked away. Each slice went deeper, each stab went wider, and each rise and descent of the broken glass made him *feel*. Power. Slice. Vengeance. Stab. Power. Rip. Enlightenment. Tear. Power. Hack. Life. Release. Becoming... the Graespurs' screams gurgled in their helpless throats. Their innocent blood splattered on his shirt and arms and face as he silenced the defenseless creatures one by one.

When the deed was done, he removed his arm from the nest and wiped the back of his hand across his mouth. The Graespur blood tasted sweet as it trickled against his lips, and he wanted more! In one last act of defiance, he held his bloodied hands in front of his face and licked them clean, like an animal over a fresh kill.

Corzakk stood silent and still at the back of the house, and watched his son's murderous rampage.

When Sturd settled down, he noticed his father staring at him. Sturd stared back, his red eyes locking with Corzakk's in a "so-now-what?" stance.

Finally, Corzakk broke the silence with a wicked grin. "Becoming what's in your heart, son?" he asked, without reproach.

Sturd paused a moment, as if being snapped out of a trance or a daydream. He looked down at the gore that decorated his arms and clothes, and the realization of what had just happened filled up in his body and was released with a simple sigh. "Suppose so."

Corzakk's grin spread wider across his cheeks as if they were being pulled at the sides by an imaginary string. "Welcome Home, my boy. Welcome Home!"

Now, nearly ten elfyears later, Sturd oversaw the happenings in the Mines, had been in charge of the now-defunct List, had moved up the ranks faster than any other, and was anxiously awaiting the assignment of a new elfwife. He was hated by many, and feared by all. He knew his destruction of the List would be the destruction of the way of life as they all knew it. He marveled at the lawlessness that had overcome the Coal Elves, and knew he was in charge of that, too.

Chapter Fourteen

STURD TOOK OUT HIS NOTEPAD. ON IT WAS SCRIBBLED THE NAMES OF EVERY crew member under his watch, and since he was Operations Manager of three divisions of Coal Elves (a responsibility not had by any other), there were a lot of elves who needed to be kept under strict lock and key.

Now that mining was at a standstill, it was still his duty to keep tabs over his crews. Normally, once the Big Night was over, the elves would have their two elfweek holiday, and then immediately begin production for the next year, but this year, due to their extended lay-off, he planned to decree that work would commence immediately following the Big Night festivities. He needed to make sure his crew members were not getting completely out of hand.

At the heart of it all, he was a true competitor, always fighting for prestige over the other Managers. He insisted that his crews should work the hardest and be the best; he made sure his coal production numbers were always the highest each month. This drive and desire added to his status and did not go unnoticed by the Council.

He put a deep red check-mark next to a name in his booklet. "Carson Blithe. Not too much action going on, likes to explore the caverns, doing well." Another name, another check-mark. "Jaffert Jolley. Hurt his hand in a rafting incident, should be okay by January."

Then he came to the next name on his list that nearly made him vomit. "Barkuss Dwin'nae...." His voice trailed as his face twisted in disgust. "Jollier than ever, acting foolishly, non-stop gallivanting throughout the Mines. Hoping he gets pummeled in a rockslide."

Barkuss. Brother. Half-brother.

He shuddered to merely think those words. Barkuss was two elf-years older than him, and Barkuss had barely had enough time with I'len, their mother, to know her like he had; however, Barkuss's elabo-rate stories and engorged memories would lead one to believe he and I'len were "oh-so-close." Sturd knew the truth. Barkuss could barely even say the word "Mother" when I'len was cradling baby Sturd in Welfort Den.

Sturd remembered one time Mother had even suggested a friend-ship be formed between the young half-brothers, but Corzakk had been so adamantly against it that it never came to pass. In Sturd's mind, a friendship of any kind would have never worked out. Barkuss was just so strange and different in his eyes and he could barely stand being in his presence for small amounts of time. Besides, Barkuss's "false" memories and flamboyant mannerisms were enough to turn Sturd's steel-cast stomach inside-out.

Below Barkuss's name was Sturd's *other* half-brother. "Banter Dwin'nae..." he sneered as his voice grew colder and sterner.

Banter was older, and his memories of Mother were probably the strongest. Banter had actually had ten whole elfyears to bond, and love, and be cared for by Mother. His memories were probably more concrete, more specific, but Banter never spoke of Mother. Not to the crew, not in public, not to Barkuss, not to anyone.

Even so, Sturd hated Banter for his age and the time spent with her. He wished so badly to be able to reach down Banter's throat and rip those years away, like pulling out some vital organs, and leaving him for dead. Sturd winced at the thought, unsure if he liked it or if he should purge such images. What would Mother think?

Then he came to a name... *her* name, and he frowned. "Ember Skye," he said slowly and thoughtfully. What *had* she been up to? No parties, no rafting trips, no requests to go Aboveground, no *nothing*. It was as if Ember had been holed up somewhere, in hiding. Red flags began to flutter in his mind—he did not like this at all. If Ember was being low-key, that meant she must be thinking an awful lot. And if she was thinking, she was scheming, and this did not sit well with him in the least.

Best I make my way over to Ebony Crag and pay Miss Skye a visit!

Ember was busy working on her project. Although it looked the worse for wear, the List was nearly complete. There were a few bits of paper that were out of place or needed to be assembled, but overall, it was almost finished. She beamed with pride with every piece she fit together. The names were glorious! Whoever said it was a "Light List" this year certainly was given some bad intel. The List was huge—name after name of bad child after bad child! She loved it. This legitimized her hard work in the caves. All these rotten, nasty children would be witness to her handiwork, her coal, her sweat, and blood, and tears. Their dismal and morose Morning would be her triumph!

Then she heard heavy knocking at her front door. Ember's stomach nearly lurched into her throat. The slow and steady ominous beat was borderline obnoxious with its rhythm and timbre. She quickly cleared the table, folding the document as neatly as possible and tucking it under a cutting board in her kitchen drawer.

She raced to the door, took one deep breath, and opened it. Her stomach turned when she saw Sturd standing before her with his mouth contorted in a smirk.

He made her skin crawl; she was utterly repulsed by his animal face and red glowing eyes. And his smell! It was a revolting scent, like rotting Graespur flesh sizzling on an opened flame. It was putrid. *He* was putrid! She rolled her eyes when he smiled at her, flashing his gnarled ferret-like teeth.

She loudly exhaled, showing her disdain. "And what do I owe this pleasure?"

"Oh, stop being so dramatic, Skye!" he exclaimed as he pushed his way into her den.

"Hey!" she protested.

Like an animal sniffing for mischief, he raised his pointy nose upward as he pushed his way into her den. "What have you been doing with yourself these days?" He began to prowl around her home.

"Excuse me? What the hell are you doing here?"

"Oh, just checking in. Making sure my workers are not getting into any trouble."

She defensively clenched her hands together. "You have no right to…."

"But I do, Ember, I do," he interrupted. "You work for me. You're in my crew, and I need to know what you've been up to so I can be prepared for next year's workload."

"Up to? I'm not 'up to' anything, Sturd!"

"Yes, precisely. That's why I'm here."

She questioningly tilted her head. Having him poking around here was certainly not good for her cause. If he found out she had picked up and was reassembling the List, there would definitely be a hellish aftermath! She casually made her way to the kitchen and positioned her body in front of the countertop drawer where she had hidden the List. She fought desperately to change her attitude. *Be cool. Be cool. Play along. Play stupid. Hold your tongue.*

"I'm not sure I understand," she said raising her voice in a mock sweet tone while twirling the ends of her hair.

He stopped in his tracks at her sudden shift in demeanor, and she took noticed of this. She had to play along, but the whole hair twirling was a bit too much. She quickly put her hands at her sides and rested her elbows on the counter. Quietly, she inhaled deeply and regained focus on being more *herself. Sassy, but not too sassy. Defensive, but not too defensive. Ember, but not too* Ember, *if that made any sense.*

"C'mon, Skye, I'm not an idiot. Everyone is out and about. Getting hurt, having a gay ole time, going on expeditions, mining for *fun*! And you? You're here all day doing nothing? Am I really supposed to believe that? So, be honest with me, what are you up to? You know I'll find out if you're lying, so just come out with it and tell me the truth."

"Sturd, I really don't know what you're...."

"OUT WITH IT!" he screamed as his eyes flashed and his contorted paws came crashing down furiously on her kitchen table.

She jolted upright, and without realizing she had, her eyes instinctually darted to the kitchen counter. Sturd, the ever-so-observant, picked up on this slight nuance, pushed by her, and made his way to the shelves.

She panicked. Her heart stopped and a gasp escaped from her mouth, and she raced up behind him. "What are you doing?"

He was eyeing the cabinets of her kitchen, his twisted finger dancing on the granite countertops. "Think you're so clever, don't cha?" he sang. "There's something here, I just know it!" His eyes lit up with fascination as he flicked a finger against the door of a cabinet above the sink.

Dishes, bowls, mugs.

She desperately tried to divert his attention. "You're sick, you know that!" she taunted.

"Hmmm," he muttered, "let's see what's behind cabinet... number... two," he taunted right back as he flicked open the next wooden door.

More dishes, pretty goblets.

"This is an invasion!" she screamed as she watched him move closer to the pull out drawer. "I should have you...."

He looked up to meet her eyes. "What? What should you have me? Punished?" He chuckled a maniacal sound. "You can't be serious, Skye." He turned his attention to the pull out drawers beneath the stove.

She grabbed at his arm, but he shook her off in one effortless jerk. There were three pullout drawers lined in a row, and he gripped the knob of the one on the far left. The List was in the right hand one, and it was only a matter of time before he opened it. She was beside herself with grief. Once he found it, she knew it would be all over.

"Like, what are you even looking for?" she growled with sarcasm.

He pulled on the first drawer. "Don't know. But I'll let you know when I find it."

Knives, spoons, forks.

His hand gripped the knob of drawer number two.

Tears of anxiety began to pool in the corners of her eyes. "This is the most asinine display of your stupid so-called power!"

"Why don't you just shut up?" He yanked the other drawer wide open. "You know how much I can't stand your...."

And he stopped.

And *she* stopped.

For when he opened the second pullout drawer of her kitchen set, he had expected to find mixing tools and icing wands, but instead he found....

A brown leather book.

He lifted the book high in the air. "What... is... *this?*" he gasped.

My journal.

"A diary?" he questioned with disgust. "You have a *diary?*"

She lunged at him, trying to snatch it from his grip. "Give that back to me right now!"

Moving his arms back and forth, he waved the book in the air until he got tired of the game and pushed her hard to the floor. She fell on her bottom, her back slamming into the leg of her kitchen table. She leaned forward and rubbed the lower muscle where the impact was made. She opened her mouth to protest, but stopped herself when she realized, *This is my "out."*

He was no longer interested in the drawers; he thought he'd found what he was looking for. "Let's see!" he sniggered as he began to fan through the pages. "Aw," he mocked, "little Ember keeps a journal! How sweet!"

She stood up. "Give it back to me!" she demanded. Her plea was a half-hearted one, but she knew in order to avoid any further suspicion, she had to play the part – poor, innocent Ember keeping secrets locked away in a journal, *boo-hoo.*

"'Nanny Carole was the sweetest Nanny Elf ever. I wish she would have been my mother,'" he read aloud in a high-pitched girl-elf voice from one of her earlier entries. He flipped through some more pages. "'I think he winked at me when I got off the Catta-car today. If I do have feelings for Tannen, I think I have to forget about them,'" he continued. "Touching, so, so very touching." He puckered his lips and put one hand to his heart.

"Stop it!" she barked as she clenched her fist.

"'And I wait for the day when I can truly be free from this life of slavery and misery.'"

"Stop it!" she screamed as she made a move forward.

Sturd recoiled. "Uh-uh-uh," he sang as he held the book tightly to his chest and wagged his deformed forefinger in her face. "I'm not done. This is compelling, truly compelling! I want to see how it all ends!" And he flipped the book to the back pages.

Her heart stopped again. She couldn't remember if she had written anything about the List. Did she mention it? Make reference to it? She held her breath as his brow furrowed while he read the last entry.

"'Fear knocks down my door with his wild eyes and magic breath? And his blackened mind hates my theories?'" What in the hell is *this*?" he yelled.

She lowered her head and shrugged her shoulders.

"You're pathetic," he sneered between gritted teeth. "And here I thought you were plotting some grand plan, but actually you were 'wah-wah-wahing' in your dumb book! Woe is me! Life sucks! You're a loser, Skye. I *over*-estimated you! Really, though, I shouldn't have expected any more from a *girl!*" He spat at her as he threw the book at her feet.

"Get out! Get out! Get out!" she screamed repeatedly, throwing her arms in the air and waving them back and forth.

"With pleasure!" he said with a smile. "But just keep one thing in mind, Skye, I've got my eye on you. Always. I'm watching."

He slammed the door behind him, and she threw herself onto the couch and let the cushions engulf her tiny body. A heavy sigh of relief escaped her lips, her chest heaving up and down in a long, languid release. *That was a close call!* She wiped small sweat beads from her forehead with the back of her hand.

She clutched her knees to her chest and gently rocked herself, trying to shake off the disgusting and dirty feeling from within. She had *let* Sturd see the most delicate pieces of her, and a part of her felt filthy and weak. Most of all, she felt violated, but allowing him to see that book was a small sacrifice she had to make in order to preserve the greater good. And now with his assertion that he was going to be watching her like a hawk, she knew getting Aboveground was going to be trickier than originally anticipated.

But, the List was what mattered most right now. She would not let his small intrusion affect her any longer.

There was still some more work to do.

Chapter Fifteen

KYLA CURLED HER KNEES TO HER CHEST AS SHE SAT ANXIOUSLY ON HER front porch. Her chubby fingers tightly gripped her knees, and through her heavy coat, she could feel the tiny pinching of her sharp fingernails. Her breath came in shivery puffs of white mist that danced in front of her face like miniature storm clouds. Every year around this time she was nervous. Today was Judging Day.

The carefree reindeer played in the open field. They were magnificent creatures with coats of shiny fur. Their muscles rippled against their taut bodies with each movement they made; sure signs of their strength and capabilities. She only bred and trained the finest of deer, and at twenty-five-elfyears old, she was a master at her craft.

The door to the house creaked open, and her sister appeared on the porch. It was unusual for elves in different guilds to live together, but Kyla and Tyla were twin elves, and their bond was so strong that even the differences in their Life Paths could not tear them apart. Tyla was an inch or so taller than Kyla, and a little less plump, but there were striking similarities: the blonde curly locks, the piercing opal eyes, and the flawless porcelain white skin.

They lived together with their parents (who were now retired elves) on the Reindeer Ranch. The Plumms were a long line of Reindeer Training Elves, and Mr. and Mrs. Plumm had naturally planned for their children to follow in the family tradition; however, what they hadn't planned for was twin elves, an extreme rarity at the Pole. Kyla, the elder by three elfminutes, was bestowed the honor of her family's guild, while Tyla had been assigned a different path—that of a Grove Elf who picked and packaged the Nessie Fruits. Their parents, while disappointed she couldn't follow family tradition, were happy their daughter had been assigned such a prestigious and important Life Job.

Tyla handed her a small round Nessie and smiled. "Hey sis," she said lovingly, "eat this. It'll make you feel better."

She bit her lower lip. "I feel fine."

Tyla smiled and shook her head. "Yeah, I know you feel fine, but you need to relax. Go on, take a bite."

She grasped the fruit with her two hands and raised it to her lips. Her miniature mouth opened as wide as it could, and she sunk her teeth into the crimson skin. The juices filled her mouth with a sickeningly sour taste and dribbled down onto her coat. She scrunched her nose at the flavor and swallowed hard to get down the chunk of fruit. She was not fond of plain Nessie Fruit, but this one was awful.

"Echhh," she moaned, sticking out her tongue.

"No good?" Tyla frowned.

She handed the fruit back to Tyla. "You know I can't stand plain Nessie."

"Well, don't get too nervous, here they come!" Tyla said, pointing to the approaching buggy. Tyla gave her sister a loving pat on the shoulders and kissed the top of her forehead. "Show 'em whatcha got, sis!" she coached with an encouraging smile. With that, Tyla turned around and went back into the house.

The buggy pulled up to the gates, and she walked down the steps of the porch to meet the judges. The two elves who approached were very short, and both wore black top hats and black wool pea coats. One had a red scarf and the other had a green scarf. They were brothers. *Twins*—older than Kyla and Tyla, but twins all the same. Her eyes widened in curiosity, for she had never seen another set of elftwins in her life before. Would this give her an advantage in the Judging? Should she mention that she's a twin, too?

The elf in the red scarf outstretched his hand when he reached her. "Good day, Miss Plumm."

She received his hand and returned his firm, but gentle, grip. "G'day." The elf in the green scarf nodded and smiled as he, too, reached to shake her hand to which she responded in kind.

"Are you ready for the Judging?" Red Scarf asked.

"Absolutely," she said with a nervous grin. "Please come in as I get the team together."

Green Scarf gave Red Scarf a frown as he took a notepad from his pocket. Red Scarf nodded at him as they entered the gate and followed her to the barn.

"Okay, guys," she encouraged the deer. "Do me proud!" The deer whinnied in delight and stomped their hooves on the ground.

Mastodon was her first deer to be evaluated. He was an oversized giant of a reindeer, hence his name. His auburn fur was shaggy around his belly, and his shoulders were the broadest of any deer she had ever trained. He was awkward and near clumsy, but what he lacked in gentle grace, he made up for in brute strength. Red Scarf grimaced as he made notations on Mastodon's shaky air performance, but Green Scarf smiled as he happily scribbled some notes concerning Mastodon's physical showing. Her directions were clear, concise and firm, but overall the reindeer lacked the confidence to perform. The Scarf brothers whispered to each other as they filled out check boxes on her evaluation.

Next was Flutter. She was a lean, gray deer with pale blue eyes unlike any deer the Scarf Brothers had likely seen. She was light on her feet and took her instructions well, only missing one turn in her list of commands. Kyla smiled as she called out to her and waved her arms in the air for guidance. Flutter was a proud deer, and Kyla was her proud trainer—it was obvious there was a deep connection between the two. Flutter's air exhibition was far better than her strength performance. She was barely able to push the forty pound crates in the regulation obstacle course. Kyla explained, "She's been trained as a back-end and not a lead." Some more notations, more grimaces, and more whispers from the brothers.

She then called for Zyklon, the snow white male with the impressive antlers. Zyklon made no mistakes. His intense air performance was superb, and his physical prowess was awe-inspiring. He had confidence, speed, stamina, and strength. *Check, check, check, check,* on the Scarf Brothers' report. Zyklon shone, and she knew it. The Scarf Brothers were nodding and smiling and whispering and "ooo-ing" and "ahh-ing" throughout his entire performance. She knew Zy would be chosen, but she also knew that he had a temper, a raging storm within him, that would prove to be detrimental if ever unleashed. Zyklon lacked control, and she needed the judges to see that, lest he be chosen and cause havoc in the future.

"He's a beautiful reindeer," she said when Zyklon was finished, "but I have to warn you about his disposition."

Red Scarf kept writing. Green Scarf raised an eyebrow.

"He can be," she said, stumbling for the best possible word, "naughty."

The Scarf Brothers kept their focus on their paperwork and chuckled, dismissing her comments. She sighed.

"Do you have any more for evaluation?" Green Scarf asked abruptly.

Her face lit up. This was her moment! She had been saving the best for last, and she knew the judges would be more than impressed with her final reindeer.

She gave a sharp whistle, and out of the barn flew Asche. Asche, her Shadow-Deer, her dark knight with the huge heart, impeccable skill, and massive determination. He looked like a mystical shadow racing against the blue sky and weaving through the air. She clapped her hands in delight, and he perfectly materialized at her side. The Scarf Brothers looked up from their papers and "harrumphed" simultaneously.

She knew it would take some convincing for them to even consider such a dark reindeer, so she began to speak frantically. "This is Asche. He is top of the line in the stables. Probably the finest deer I've ever trained. His thick hooves are powerful and he can complete the obstacle course in record time, as you will see...."

"Miss Plumm..." Red Scarf interrupted.

She wasn't about to back down. Something inside her demanded her to press on with the presentation. "He is of Blitzen's progeny," she boasted as she stroked his black collar fur.

"Miss Plumm..." Green Scarf interjected as he cleared his throat.

"He's the fastest, strongest, gentlest, most controlled..." she continued.

"Miss Plumm!" Red Scarf shouted, raising his voice over hers.

She stopped and took a deep breath, lowered her head to the ground, knowing the lecture that would follow.

"How long have you been a trainer, Miss Plumm?" Red Scarf asked rhetorically.

"And how many times has the Council selected a Shadow-Deer?" Green Scarf completed with the same condescending tone.

"None," Red answered.

"None," Green repeated, their voices sounding so similar, she had no idea which one was now addressing her.

"You know that Shadow-Deer are a liability..."

"And the Boss doesn't need any liabilities, now does he?"

"Certainly not!"

"Claus, no!"

"So why would you think that this here Shadow-Deer would be any different?"

"You just wasted your time."

"Wasted your...."

"But," she pleaded, "he's from Blitzen's line!"

"Doesn't matter...."

"Not in the least...."

"Please!" she begged. "Just look at him. Evaluate him. I know he would be perfect for the main team!"

The Brothers scoffed in unison. "What makes you think...."

"What makes you think...."

"He knows Elvish," she said, eyes still fixated on the ground.

The Brothers stopped and pulled back a little. Elvish? It had been many, many moons since they had come across a deer that could follow directions in the ancient tongue. Red Scarf and Green Scarf had been trainers in their former elfyears, and had advanced to judges along the way. *They* knew Elvish, but they certainly didn't know of anyone else who did, except maybe The Boss.... This was a piece of information that was worth at least checking out.

They looked at each other and nodded. "Proceed," they said together after a hesitant pause.

Her face was overcome with a smile. She patted Asche's hind quarters and yelled, "*Oontza ahnga*, Aschen!" And with that, Asche disappeared from beside her and materialized onto the obstacle course.

She continued to give commands in the lost language, and Asche maintained his focus and grace. The Brothers scribbled in their note pads furiously. Red Scarf wore down the tip of his pencil from writing so much!

When Asche's glorious performance was over, the Brothers walked away and pored over their paperwork. The two fell into a huddle with feverish chatter and barely audible whispers. A few times, Green Scarf straightened up and adjusted the brim of his top hat onto his forehead. Once or twice, Red Scarf crossed and re-crossed his arms over his chest. Kyla's palms were drenched with the sweat of anticipation. Finally, after almost an hour of deliberation, the Scarf Brothers came back with their decision.

"Mastodon," Red Scarf said.

"Not Team material," injected Green Scarf.

"Powerful, though. We'll take him. Hauler, lifter, loader. He'll be a good work deer!"

She nodded her head. She had surmised Mastodon had no chance of being selected for the main team, and she understood the rationale behind why they would take him now.

"Flutter," Green Scarf announced.

"Possible Team material," Red Scarf injected.

"We've selected her as an alternate. Won't be part of the permanent Team, but will be used if needed. Dancer and Vixen are getting up in age, and if anything happens to one of them, Flutter would be a good substitute. The Team position is just right, too."

She nodded again as she fought back the tears starting to well in her eyes. The thought of not having her beloved Flutter around saddened her, but she knew Flutter would do well, and she was proud of her girl.

"Zyklon!" Red Scarf announced proudly.

"On... the... team!" Green Scarf paused at each word for emphasis.

"Words cannot express our amazement!"

"No, they can't!"

"As a trainer, you know that it's not every year a Team member is replaced. In fact, it doesn't happen very often at all. In the last fifty elfyears there have only been three replacements."

"Dasher, Cupid, and Blitzen!"

"But Zyklon is something else. He is a deer we cannot pass up!"

"Zyklon is to take old Red-Nose's place immediately at head of the Team!"

"We are very excited at this new and wonderful prospect!"

"Excited and delighted!"

She nodded again. There was never doubt in her mind that Zyklon would make the team. She had suspected he would at least get Comet's or Donner's position, but Rudolph's? That was shocking even to her!

"And Asche?" she meekly inquired.

Green Scarf tightened his lips. Red Scarf shuffled his boots in the snow.

"Asche," Red Scarf declared.

"While we were impressed by his performance...."

"You're not taking him," she finished.

Red Scarf breathed deep and exhaled a thick white cloud. "No. We're not. Elvish or no Elvish. He's a Shadow-Deer...."

"And a liability to the Boss."

"As for your rating," Green Scarf continued. "Kyla Plumm, you are pending further evaluation as per the Council's request."

She looked up, puzzled. "Huh?"

"There needs to be an investigation, Miss Plumm," Red Scarf informed. "Elvish is an ancient and forgotten language. It needs to be determined how you, and your Shadow-Deer, learned it!"

Investigation? Council's request? What in the Claus were they talking about? It was just the two of them and some notebook paper! "B-but I told you already," she protested, "he's of Blitzen's line and—"

"That's not the point, Miss Plumm," Green Scarf forcefully interrupted.

"I–I don't understand," she stammered in confusion. "I'm a twin, too."

The Scarf Brothers gave each other a quick, knowing glance. Their lips puckered out and they both raised one eyebrow. For a split second, she thought what she had said had some meaning, some clout, and maybe invoked some empathy within them.

Red Scarf handed her an envelope as Green Scarf made his way down the line of reindeer. He tethered them together for transport back to Headquarters. "We will be in contact." They began to walk back to their buggy.

"I don't understand!" she shouted.

"Your position of Reindeer Trainer is hereby suspended until further notice. If you are caught breeding, raising, or training any animal, you will be brought before the Council and dealt with accordingly. As I said, we will be in touch. Good afternoon."

Chapter Sixteen

N   O, THAT GOES HERE."
          "No, it goes there!"

"Stop, you're blocking my view! I can't see. You know you're freak-ishly fat for a Coal Elf!"

"Oh hush, you! You're just jealous that I can work it!"

"Quit fooling around, and work *this!*"

"All right, all right! Sit tight! Move that skinny behind of yours and let me put this red 'a' with that red 't.'"

"No! *That* red 'a' goes with *this* red 't'. *This* red 'a' goes with *that* red 'r.'"

"Are you sure? I don't see how…."

"I'm positive! Just shush for a second and look! See how the lines are curved?"

"Ooohhh! I see it now! But what about this green 'p?'"

"Oh my Claus, Barkuss, that's not a 'p', that's a 'd!'"

"Whatever. Look, if you think it's best I leave, then…."

"No, stop with the dramatics, we're almost done. Just… a… few… more… pass me the tape. I need to reinforce this section."

"Wow, you really are a slave driver, E. I guess it's from all that time working under Corzakk and all."

"Har, har, har! Now pass me the tape!"

"One roll of tape, coming right up."

"And that piece over there. I want to see if it–"

"Fits that center-left section?"

"That's exactly what I was thinking. Look at the 'o', like it could be part of…."

"O'Donnell?"

"Yes! And then the capital 'J' for Johnson, which would connect the–"

"'K' for Kiki, as in *Kiki* Johnson?"

"Yes! Now you're talking my language!"

"I always talk your language, dollface!"

"Yeah, yeah, yeah. More tape!"

"Big or little?"

"Big. I got one… more… section… to…."

"E?"

"Yeah, Barkuss?"

"It's done. Look at it, it's done!"

"I need to stand on the chair. I need to see the whole thing."

Ember stood on the chair in her kitchen and propped her hands on the top of Barkuss's ashy hair. From her tip-toes, she was able to see the completed puzzle. The red and green letters of the names glinted in the lamplight of her chandelier underneath the layers and layers of clear tape. She breathed in heavily. It was a work of art. Swirls and curls of jagged-ended letters all neatly affixed and mended back to life. In its ruin, it was awe inspiring, hypnotic and trance –inducing. Barkuss stood there with his mouth hanging open in an "o" shape. In her excitement, she began rubbing his hair back and forth.

"We did it," she said softly at first. "We did it! We did it! We did it!" Her words got louder and louder each time she repeated the mantra, and soon he was bouncing up and down, chanting along with her in a frenzied tone. He turned around, lifted her off the chair and spun her around wildly, dancing to their harmonious cries of "We did it! We did it!" Then with one last squeeze, he held her firmly in his arms, off the ground, and hugged her fiercely. She threw her arms around his neck and squeezed back as hard as she could. The two were laughing and giggling as he nearly dropped her to the rocky floor, the both of them winded from their suffocating embraces.

"You know, Ember Skye, if I could choose any girl-elf in the world who could be my elfwife, it would most definitely be you!"

She blushed beneath the grime on her face. "Oh, Barkuss," she gushed as she put her hand over her heart, "that's so sweet of you, but we all know how you really feel!"

He stiffened up and grinned. "Don't you know it, sugar!" He wagged his forefinger through the air. "No elf, and I mean *no* elf, can handle *me*!" he concluded with his finger pointed at his chest.

She chuckled. "Ah, c'mon Barkuss! Don't cha want a nice little elfwifey taking care of you and having lots of little elfbabies running around?"

He stuck his tongue out and crinkled his face as if he had just tasted something sour. "Claus no!" he howled. "I like my life nice and simple, thank you very much! I got a good system going on, and I don't need nobody messin' that up for me! Besides, you're enough elfwifey for me to take care of without all the marital baloney that goes along with it!"

They continued to laugh for some time until the reality of the List came back to them.

"So, now what?" he asked in the silence.

She stared at the List and shrugged her shoulders. "I have no clue," she muttered.

"E, this List is very dangerous for us to have, ya know, and I was thinking that...."

"I'll keep it here. Don't worry. It'll be safe with me."

He nervously scratched his nose. "Good, 'cause I don't know what I would do with it." He gave a small sigh of relief. "What about the Council?"

"We need to get there and talk to them," Ember responded matter-of-factly.

"Yes, but think about all the steps involved."

She raised her eyebrows. "Why do I get the sense that you're backing out on me, Barkuss? First you suggest I keep the List, now you're all worried about 'steps involved?' What gives, man? Talk to me."

He shuffled his feet, kicking up some dust unto his boots. He kept his focus on the floor. "I... I... don't know, E. It was one thing to help you put the List back together and all, but the whole idea of the Council, and Aboveground, and maybe being called out as a Defector, it's just too much for me. I'm a Ceffle, ya know? Coal Elf for Life. Ain't never been up there. Don't think I ever wanna be, ya know?"

She tried to wrap her head around what he was saying. *He doesn't want to see the snow? He doesn't want to feel the sun beating on his face? I don't understand.*

She watched him shuffling a small pile of rock dust with the tip
of his boot. He was dirty, like she was; he was different, and weird,
and talkative, and misunderstood, and flamboyant, and she suddenly
realized he had enough trouble fitting in with his own people! There
would be no fitting in Aboveground. She knew it firsthand—had
experienced the hatred and disgust from the eyes of elves she had
once called kin. The grass wasn't always greener on the other side,
and for someone like Barkuss, who was good, and kind, and a thin-
skinned soul, he would *never* be able to get passed the stares and
ridicule—List or no List.

She gently put her hand on his shoulder. "It's okay. Not a problem.
You just keep my secret and help me figure a way out."

He smiled and touched her hand with his, giving it a gentle squeeze
as if to say thank you. "Well," he began, "it's not really a 'way' as it is
more a 'time.'"

She thought about that for a second. *Sturd.* It would be hard to
work around his prying eyes. "Ya know, I've had just about as much as
I can stand from that jerk! He's power hungry, maniacal—"

"Demonic!" Barkuss interjected.

"That, too! He thinks he can do what he wants, when he wants, to
whom he wants. The Council really ought to know what the hell is
going on down here. I know they probably don't care about us. Why
would they? We're filthy little Coal Elves who do their bidding, but
it's time that we spoke out!" She pounded her balled up fist into her
open hand.

"Love the fire, E!" Barkuss gushed supportively.

She smiled and curtsied. "Thank you."

The two laughed, but only for a moment because sometimes the
truth—the real truth—is no laughing matter.

Chapter Seventeen

THE DAY BEFORE THE BIG NIGHT WAS KNOWN TO THE COAL ELVES AS Adam's Day. Adam's Day was an ancient tradition among the Coal Elves, and was not something the elves Aboveground had even known about. It was a day of celebration when all Coal Elves stopped working, took a break, and marveled at the work they did throughout the year. Feasts were held, games were played, elves gathered together with kith and kin. The hustle and bustle of the Eve would be chaotic with last minute double checking and preparations. It was always very important that everything was in its proper place and ready to be delivered to the proper child. If not, they were told, there would be dire consequences that would rattle the very fabric of humanity and elfhood. Precision was the key in doling out the coal to the bad children.

However, this particular Adam's Day was different. The majority of the elves had spent the last three elfmonths partying like it was their last night alive, and on the day when there was supposed to be festivities and merrymaking of all sorts, there was an eerie silence hanging in the Mines. What would tomorrow bring when there were no coal carts to pick up shipments at the Entrance Zone? What would happen on the Big Night when every child on Earth was rewarded with gifts and goodies? As Ember sat at the bank of the cool spring in Onyx Alley listening to the low hum of quiet elves throughout, she knew everyone was contemplating the same exact thing with heightened anticipation.

She threw her head back and looked at the rocky ceiling above her. It had been months since she had gotten her Pass to go Aboveground, and already she was starting to forget the smell of fresh air and the sight of a blue sky. Those were things she had always thought would be emblazoned in her memory, but as the days passed, slowly but surely, those images began to fade. The stalactites on the ceiling hung like rocky icicles from the dark canopy above her. Every now and then they would drip their liquid substance like gentle tears splashing to the stony ground below. Through the lantern lights and reflection of the cool spring, the gloaming created in the cavern gave the rock-icicles the appearance of a thousand glittering stars, like being outside on a clear night.

She took off her boots and socks, rolled up the pant legs of her jumpsuit, and dipped her feet into the frigid water of the spring. She leaned back on her elbows and her hand instinctively gripped the pocket on her upper thigh.

She closed her eyes and smiled. The task was complete. She and Barkuss had been successful! She pressed the material of her jump-suit, feeling the crumpled up scroll within. With her mind's eye, she envisioned the List, now just a ruin of pieces of paper held delicately together with some clear tape, and she rattled off all the names she had committed to memory... *John Washington, Jocelyn Winters, Abigail Yost.* All those names—all those glorious names! With each petting motion she made over the fabric of her jumpsuit, she felt overcome with a sense of confidence and strength. To possess the List was to possess great knowledge and power. She knew now how easy it was for Sturd to become so filled, and corrupted, by this gift.

At that very moment it dawned on her—now would be the per-fect time to run, head out, make it to the Mouth, pass the Guards, get Aboveground. There didn't seem to be anyone around and what better time to reach the Council then on this day? But what would Barkuss think if she left without him? He did help her out some, and he was guarding her secret, and....

"A low-key Adam's Day, wouldn't you say?" a voice called, pulling her from her thoughts.

It was Tannen. *Descendant of the Tree-Elves Tannen. Catta-car operator Tannen. Blond hair, rosy cheeked, I-could-kinda-like-you-if-I-wasn't-such-a-miserable-girl-elf, Tannen.*

He motioned to a spot beside her. "Mind?"

She shook her head "no" and moved her body to the side to make room. He put down his fishing pole and bait box, removed his boots and socks, and sat down next to her. When his feet hit the spring, the water splashed up on her jumpsuit. She tilted her head to the side and he laughed. "Sorry," he apologized with a smile.

She smiled back. "Fishing?" she asked with a smirk. "I thought you were just a Catta-car driver."

"I'm an elf of many talents!" he boasted in jest. He baited his hook with a cave grub and threw the line into the water. "So what brings you out here? I thought for sure you never left your den!"

She smiled again. Actually, she hadn't stopped smiling since he sat down. Instinctively, her hand drew itself to her pocket, but she quickly pulled it away in fear of drawing attention to it. "Oh, I just came out to think and relax," she answered nonchalantly, which in all actuality was *not* a lie.

"Yea. Need a break from all those wild parties you're so secretive about?"

She snorted a little laugh. "No. Nothing like that. That's more Barkuss's scene."

He nodded in agreement as he kept his focus on the water. "Haven't seen you around much," he remarked.

"Haven't seen you around much, either," she replied in hopes of deflecting the attention from her secret doings. "I think the question is do *you* need a break from all *your* wild parties?"

He chuckled. "Well, I've been around." He tugged on the pole. "Still have to ride the rails, ya know? Not too much merry making on my end. Pretty much business as usual. The only ones who made out like bandits on this deal were you guys in the Mining Guild."

"I guess so."

He lurched forward as the line shook.

"Already?" she asked.

He struggled with the pole. "Let's... see... what... this... big sucker... is!" His voice echoed off the cave walls.

He pulled in the line and on the end was a hefty iridescent fish with cloudy blue eyes. Its fins were tattered, but its tail was a beautiful shiny blue fan. Its body thrashed and jolted a few times before all movement ceased and he released it from the hook.

"Fyarda fish!" he proudly announced, holding it in the air. "The hardest to catch, and the best to eat!"

She clapped her hands in delight.

"Thank you," he said as he wrapped the fish in plastic and put it in a steel container.

"Thank me? For what?"

"You're good luck. Do you know how long it's been since I caught a Fyarda? Months! This is prime eatin' right here!"

She looked at the ground and shook her head. "No, I don't think it has anything to do with me," she said, embarrassed.

"Of course it does! Then tell me why is it that I've been coming here almost every night since Sturd's announcement, and every night all I've gotten were some tiny Hi-Hies, or some squirmy Dakooms? No Fyarda. I see them; I hear them splashing, but none on my line."

She scrunched her nose and stuck out her tongue. "You actually *eat* Dakooms?"

He rolled his emerald eyes and huffed. "Please... don't get me started."

She giggled.

"Seriously, though," he continued, "explain to me that the *one* night I'm out here with you, I catch the biggest, meanest Fyarda? I think it's more than just a coincidence." He smiled at her, flashing his perfectly white elf teeth in a genuine grin.

She looked up from the ground, her eyes locked on his, and she smiled back. "Well," she said with sarcastic confidence, "it must be my sweet bell-like voice that drew him out!"

He laughed again. "Must be, must be." He baited his hook again and cast the line back into the water. "So, are the rumors true, Em?" he asked after a few moments of silence.

She clutched her pocket again. *Rumors? What rumors? Did someone know about the List?* Her heartbeat thumped a little faster in her chest.

"Huh?" she replied, trying to keep her calm.

"Ya know, the rumors... about you?"

"Um, honestly, Tannen, I have no idea what you're talking about. But if there's stuff going around about me, I'd really like to know."

"Well, it's just that the elves are talking. Word in the Mines is that ever since you got your Pass, ya know, to go Aboveground, things are different for you. Word is that after the Big Night, the Boss is going to release you and let you go back up."

"What?" she cried in disbelief. "Are you serious? That's some rumor! News to me."

"I don't know," he replied as he kept his focus on the spring. "You know how they all talk."

Ain't that the truth.

"Well," she said in a flat voice, "I'm not going anywhere."

A small smile crept slowly out from the sides of his mouth. "Did you at least find what you were looking for when you were up there?"

She held tight to the crinkled makeshift scroll within her jumpsuit. "You can kinda say that. And you can kinda say there's nothing for me up there anymore. I know that now."

His smile grew larger, and just as he was about to comment back, he was interrupted by the pulling and tugging of the line.

She jumped up in excitement. "Fyarda?"

"I... think... so...." He beamed as he battled with the pole. And again, when he reeled it in, there was another lovely iridescent Fyarda fish flailing for its last breath. This one was larger and more aggressive than the first. "This is unreal!" he marveled.

That's how the late afternoon played out: Tannen and Ember making small talk, playfully exchanging one-liners, keeping the mood light and spirited, smiling and beaming at each other, Tannen pulling up his line with a treasured Fyarda attached. No nasty Dakooms, no little Hi-Hies, just Fyarda—big, strong, and meaty Fyarda.

After the sixth one was caught, he stood up and started packing his gear.

"Six Fyarda!" she exclaimed, nodding her head. "I'm very proud of you!"

"Why, thank you," he quipped back. "I could not have done it without you, my fishing good luck charm!"

Ember chuckled. Tannen chuckled. Then she stood up and was about to say her goodbyes when he asked, "Hey, Em, what are your plans for tonight?"

Not really thinking about what he was asking her, she replied, "Nothing, why?"

"Well," he began, fidgeting a bit and tugging on his hair, "I just figured since you helped me out with the fishing that you would like to, ya know, join me?" His voice cracked a little on the last syllable. "I understand if you have plans or if you don't want to, I mean, you've turned me down so many times I'm starting to think that–"

"Yes," she said firmly, interrupting his mumbled speech, surprising even herself at her abrupt response.

His eyes widened in almost disbelief. "Yes?" he repeated as he gently touched her hand.

She nodded. "Yes. I would love to." She clasped her fingers within his.

Her quick response and sudden display of affection and emotion were not completely self-serving, however. Sturd said he would be watching her, and there was a gnawing feeling in her gut that told her she was being watched at that very moment. Of course, she wanted to spend time with Tannen, but she also needed to divert Sturd's attention, and if acting like a normal, giggly, teenage elf was the only way, then so be it.

Adam's Day. The day of the year when all Coal Elves stopped working, took a break, and celebrated the work they did throughout the year. This Adam's Day was very different from all others. This Adam's Day, the Coal Elves sat in their dens contemplating, waiting anxiously to see the fallout from the Boss's ruling. A hushed silence echoed throughout the Mines.

But not in Ebony Crag. In Ebony Crag, there was a blazing fire in the hearth, a scrumptious meal on the table, good conversation filling the room, and Tannen Trayth sitting across from her smiling the most handsome smile she had ever seen. Descendant of the Tree-Elves Tannen. Catta-car operator Tannen. Giant emerald eyes and gentle voice Tannen. The "I'm-telling-myself-that-you're-my-diversion," Tannen.

But I can't-allow-myself-to-fall-completely-head-over-boots-for-you, Tannen.

Chapter Eighteen

L ATER THAT EVENING, TANNEN RETURNED TO HIS DEN. IT WAS A VERY late night, indeed, as the two had chatted (flirted?) away the early morning hours. Even after he was gone, Ember found it difficult to sleep; her attentions divided between Tannen and the document that was now tucked away deeply in her bedside nightstand. It seemed the only thing that could lull her to dreamland was reciting the list of memorized names. *Hattie Lawhead, Debbie O'Connell, Matthew Powell....*

She slept until she heard the Graespurs humming again. The Big Night was now upon them.

There were no carriages to make coal pick-ups this year; no mad rush to check and double check; no triple checking, either. By midnight, many Coal Elves gathered in the Entrance Zone to listen for the sounds of the Big Night: the whooshing of the Boss's sled cutting through the sky, shaking the very ground upon take-off, and the roar of the Land Elves as they watched in awe. The Land Elves celebrated this night, the Big Night. They toasted with ceramic mugs filled with foamy hot cocoa, munched delightfully on fresh baked cookies made in the image and likeness of the Boss, and sang song after song about the Big Night and their seemingly wonderful lives. Once the "whooshing" and the rumbling ceased, the Coal Elves all made their way back to the dens without the pomp. Their party was now officially over, and life would be back to normal in no time.

On December 25th, mining resumed. The return of the Graespurs started the day, and she was glad to get back to some form of normalcy. Before leaving her den, she peeled off a notice posted on her front door. It was from Sturd, and it was her new mining assignment. She had hoped she would be staying in Onyx Alley, but according to the message, the Alley was no longer an option as the cool spring was filled with Fyarda fish and the Fishing Elves were going to make a run at it.

Yeah. Good luck with that.

Ember's crew, the former Onyx Alley crew, would join the Crystal Cave crew in the northern territory of the Mines. Sturd's third crew, The Raker's Cove crew, would remain there until further notice.

Crystal Cave? That's a stone's throw away from Tannen's den....

The notice also went on to say that Jaffert Jolley was still laid up with an injury, and it was unclear as to when he would be returning. And although mining was to begin again, a new List had not been drawn up yet. The higher-ups of the Council were still evaluating the effects of what was now being referred to as the "Coal-less Night." It was just too soon to tell.

Barkuss approached her front steps. "E! Baby girl!"

"Morning, Barkuss," she lazily responded.

"See you got our love letter!" he said, referring to the same notice that was posted on his front door. "Should be different in Crystal Cave, yeah?"

"Yeah."

"No List yet, either. Strange. What the hell do ya think is going on up there? Do you think Sturd got in trouble for what he did with the coal and everything?"

She gave him a raised-eyebrows look. "I'm not sure; things just aren't adding up. If Sturd was acting out on his own, then why didn't the Council intervene? Obviously, they let it happen. And now, there's no new List for this year, and they're 'evaluating' things? I don't get it."

"E, do you think they know about what Sturd did? Ya know, about ripping up the List?"

"I don't know. I don't know. If what Nanny Carole said is true, they would never let something like that happen! How could they?"

Barkuss lowered his head and drew closer to her. He cupped his hand around his mouth and whispered, "Do you think we're too late? Ya know, with *our* L-I-S-T? We finished it about a month ago and we haven't decided when we're going...."

"Shhh," she hissed at him as her eyes darted around the cavern. "I'll figure it out! Stop talking out in the open about it! You never know who's lurking around rocks down here, ya know what I mean?"

"Uh huh," he replied. "But it just feels like we should—"

"Barkuss, I swear to Santa Claus, if you don't...." she began to admonish, but Barkuss tightened his lips together and curled his hand over his mouth in a "locking the key" gesture.

She breathed deep. "Okay, you ready to go to work?"

"Yes, ma'am," he sang.

She threw her pick axe over her shoulder, and latched the fastener on her lighted helmet as the two of them began their trek to Crystal Cave.

Chapter Nineteen

KYLA WORKED IN THE KITCHEN, CREATING A MIXTURE OF OAT GRAINS and Nessie Fruit for her reindeer to eat. It had been a month since the Big Night, and still no word from the Scarf Brothers, or the Council concerning her revoked Trainer Elf status. She had been spending most of her time tending to the deer she was left with: two calves that were nowhere near evaluation, and her beloved and gifted Shadow-Deer, Asche. Unable to do her job—the one thing she loved and treasured so much—was torturous, and she didn't know how much longer she could last without going completely crazy!

But Zyklon's first ride was a big hit. Kyla's friends and neighbors fawned over her and treated her like a super-star. It was *her* stable that had produced a fine replacement for the Team, and that was a status that many envied. Now, she was known all over the East Bank as Zyklon's Trainer! Zyklon, the new leader of the Team! Zyklon, the Swift! Zyklon, the whitest deer in all the Pole! She knew there would be poems written and recited about him, and by the next Big Night, she was certain little stuffed animals bearing Zyklon's resemblance would be stocked on shelves both at the Pole and in the human world.

When curious elves asked her why she had "taken a break" from her training duties, she had a perfectly good story in place: *when you've got the best deer in town, you deserve a break, don't you?* This was followed by fake chuckles and pleasantries.

To make matters worse, Tyla, her twin sister and one and only confidante, had been working day in and day out. Tyla was always her "shoulder," her "lean-on gal," but lately, Tyla's days and nights were consumed by work. It was normal for a Grove Elf's workload to be doubled, or even tripled, after the Big Night; it went without saying that the happiness of the children in the world produced the finest and most abundant fruits, but for some reason, this was different. Tyla was on call at *every* moment of the day to pick and gather. She would have a few hours here to rest, or an hour there to eat and wash up, before being whisked away to labor under the swollen Nessie Fruit branches.

When Kyla was finished preparing the meal for her deer, she took the mixture out to the stable and filled their feeding containers. Viella, too young to sense her Trainer's sadness, wanted to play and fly the moment she saw her.

"Not now, Viella," Kyla said with a heavy heart, "not now."

She stayed with her deer until they were all finished eating, cleaned up, and made her way back to the house.

When she got back, she was surprised to find Tyla sitting on the plaid couch, rubbing a Eucalyptus balm into her raw hands. Her cheeks were sunken and red with wind rash, and her lips were dry and cracked. Dark circles outlined her opal eyes.

Kyla was appalled by her sister's appearance. "Tyla!" she exclaimed when she saw her.

Tyla looked up at her with weary eyes. "Oh, Ky! You don't know the half of it! It's terrible out there!"

"You look absolutely dreadful!"

Tyla put her hands to her face and began to weep. Kyla raced to the kitchen and wet a dishrag, and when she returned to her sister's side, she began to wipe the tears from her face.

When Kyla touched Tyla's forehead, she was shocked at what she felt. "Oh, Sissy! You're freezing. Your skin is like a sheet of ice. Please tell me you're not going back out there today!" she exclaimed in horror.

Tyla sobbed, "But I have to. They need me. I don't know what to do!"

Kyla patted the cool wet rag on the back of Tyla's neck. "What's going on over there?"

"You know I'm not one to complain, but it's just so chaotic. And so cold!" Tyla began to cough, and the rattling sound in her chest made Kyla wince with worry.

Kyla couldn't bear to see her sister so overworked and in such a state of despair. There was only one thing she could think of to relieve her sister's overworked agony – take her place! Of course, it wasn't the perfect plan, as Kyla hadn't the first clue how to work in the Groves, but for now, it was the only thing she could come up with. And if the situation was as chaotic and hectic as Tyla made it out to be, then who would notice? Pick the fruit. Put it in the basket. Dump the basket in the storage container. Don't let it touch the ground. Simple enough, right?

"Let me go back for you today," Kyla said as she rubbed her sister's temples. "You've done enough. If it's as crazy as you say it is, no one will ever know the difference. You need to go to bed and rest. Get some sleep. Warm up. Get better."

"Oh, no," Tyla gasped with a quiet voice. "That's not possible. I can't let you do it. The reindeer...."

"I'm not training, you know that. They've been played with and fed, and they will be just fine. *You're* what's important right now. A few hours in the Groves are not going to kill me, but I'm afraid if you stay out there any longer, it *will* kill you."

Tyla lovingly looked at her sister. "You're not going to take "no" for an answer are you?" she muttered with a small, forced smile.

Kyla shook her head. "No, ma'am."

Tyla stood up from the couch, and gave Kyla a quick, weak hug. "Thank you," she whispered in her ear, and went up to her room.

After bundling up, Kyla made her way to the Groves. Even though she and Tyla were identical, there was no doubt in her mind someone would notice a healthier appearance on the run-down Grove Elf, so she had done everything possible to cover up: she'd put on an extra scarf and wrapped it twice around her mouth, and a purple knit cap was pulled to just above her eyelids.

Kyla knew that there was something going on in the Groves that was unprecedented. The Nessie Fruits were growing at an alarming rate. Tree branches were weighted down and snapping, fruit piles were accumulating at tree bases. There wasn't enough elf-power to collect all the fruit the trees were producing, and if that wasn't bad enough, the storage containers were at maximum capacity. The Nessie Fruits were the Elves' life force, and if things went completely wrong... she shuddered to think.

Even so, the Groves were stunning to look at. The trees were lined up in rows, and the ground was clear of snow — something that she had never seen in her entire life. The branches of the trees touched each other in a frosty embrace, but the branches hung low to the ground, wrought with the weight of snow and overgrowing fruit. The Grove Elves hurried to and fro on small step stools and ladders, picking what they could. There were apprentices carrying tan woven baskets filled to the brims with Nessie Fruit. Some were trying to scoop what they could from the ground in hopes of saving the crop.

An apprentice elf frantically dashed by her, stumbled over her tiny feet, and took a nose dive onto the green field. Her basket spilled before her as she desperately tried to scoop up as much fruit as she could.

She tried to remain calm in the wake of the rising panic. "Relax, relax," Kyla tried to coax the girl as she knelt down to help.

"No! No! No!" the apprentice hollered. "Don't touch them! Don't help me!" Tears were now streaming down the girl's face. "It's no use! Once they touch the ground, that's *it*! They can't touch the ground, you should know that!"

Kyla nodded in agreement. She watched the young one stand up straight, pick up her basket, and run back into the groves, leaving the spilled contents of her previous rounds helpless in the grass.

"Maybe we should burn them?" she heard an elf yell over the frenzied din.

"We can't do that!" another voice replied.

"It takes five elfyears for one tree to mature and produce!"

"If we burn any down, we'll be depleting our overall quantities!"

She hadn't even realized it was nightfall until she heard a flock of Graespurs singing up above the icy treetops. She had lost count of how many trips she made up and down a ladder, and of how many buckets full of Nessie Fruit she had hauled to the storage unit. The Grove Elf Supervisor sounded a bell and announced that work was over for the day.

"Go Home. Get ready for tomorrow. It should be a little bit better," he declared as she blew warm air into her closed frigid hands and zipped up her coat for the walk Home.

When she arrived, she went straight to the kitchen. A foaming cup of cocoa with extra marshmallows and a peppermint stick stirrer was calling her name. After that, she would take a hot ginger-bubble bath to soothe her aching muscles, and then check to see how Tyla was holding up. She closed her eyes and smiled at the thought of pampering herself, but was startled when she saw her mother sitting in the darkness of the kitchen. A lit candle on the table cast shadows on her mother's worn-away face, making her appear menacing and almost ghost-like. Her mother's gaze remained on the candle light when Kyla gently touched her shoulder.

"Momma?" she asked as she bent closer to her face. "Momma, what's the matter? What are you doing in here by yourself this late at night?"

Her mother didn't respond. She just kept staring at the flame.

"Momma? Where's Poppa? Where's Tyla?"

Still no response. Kyla felt a wave of terror rise in her chest. She wanted to scream for her sister and her father; she wanted to scream for anyone to come and save her from this eerie scene, but she kept her composure and continued to question her mother's peculiar actions.

"Momma. Talk to me. What's going on? Why are you just sitting here alone? Do you feel okay?"

With that, Kyla's mother broke her stare and slowly shifted her head toward her daughter. Her opal eyes were bloodshot, and dark circles engulfed the skin beneath. Kyla was frightened by her mother's ghastly appearance.

"I don't feel so well," her mother finally said, but her words were garbled by the mouthful of blood that dribbled onto her pink nightgown.

Chapter Twenty

T HE SINGING AND HUMMING OF THE GRAESPURS' CALLS WERE A BLUR TO Ember, sounds meshing with sounds meshing with sounds. Work was the same. Heave. Break. Heave. Crash. Barkuss collected like all good Collectors do. Miners mined like all good Miners do. Status quo.

The higher-ups had announced there was a new List in the works, but it would not be released just yet. It was still in what they called "pre-planning stages" (*whatever* that *meant!*).

No List, eh? Not true. Ember had her List tucked away in her den, and that was really all that mattered to her at this point in time. Tucked safely away from Banter, and Sturd, and Tannen....

Tannen.

His very name confused her. It put her at ease, and on edge, at the same time. She was most comfortable around him, yet most guarded. She *had* been seeing a lot of Tannen in past months. In the mornings, she would purposefully ride his Catta-car line, even if it did take her ten minutes out of her way. After work, she would purposefully stroll by his den. Sometimes he was sitting on his front porch, sometimes not. Sometimes she went with him to the Ignis to fish (Onyx Alley was now off limits to recreational fishing), and sometimes they caught something worth eating and would feast together. Sometimes they would just talk all night as he walked her Home. And sometimes, she made the trek Home to Ebony Crag alone.

Due to all this time she'd spent with him, she'd learned quite a bit about him and his family. Tannen's family really was descended from Tree Elves. Many, many years ago, the Boss had sent for a handful of Tree Elves (from Aboveground) to come to the Mines. He had commissioned them to build the Catta-car system, and they were free to leave as soon as the task was completed. But, as things turned out, they never left. Apparently, they found something very appealing about the Mines, and decided they wanted to stay. Curiously enough, she also learned Tannen was not eligible for an elfwife. "Guess my name wasn't picked from the cap," he had joked.

In return, she opened up to him as well, and told him all about what life was like Aboveground. He was genuinely interested in all of her tales, but most importantly, he was genuinely interested in *her*. He asked her silly questions like, "What's your favorite color?" and "What's your favorite thing to eat?"—Trivial things that she had never even given much thought to.

However, through all of their discussions and heart-to-hearts, the one thing she did not reveal to him was her possession of the List. As she found herself getting closer and closer to him, the weight of her secret was like a blanket of guilt wrapped around her scrawny body. And even though it killed her inside to do it, she knew she had to halt their growing friendship. She made a promise to herself: until she could feel one hundred percent comfortable with letting Tannen know about her List, she would stop all communication with him.

So she did.

There were no more Catta-car rides. No more late night fishing. No more "story time with Tannen." It stopped. Ended. Over.

All in the Mines was status quo, except for the fact that in a recent and official announcement by the Council, it was mentioned that apprenticeships were being suspended this year, and any elfchild assigned to the Mines would take up their duties the following year. In plain terms: no new elves were assigned to the Mines this year.

No new elves? When had that ever happened before? They were already short elfpower, considering that Jaffert Jolley (who was "laid up with an injury and was due to return to work soon"), never did return to his post in the Mines. In fact, Carson Blithe hadn't been showing up to work these days, either. And come to think of it, where the hell was *Banter*? Things didn't seem to be so "status quo" after analyzing it.

And to top it off, Sturd was still keeping a very close eye on her. His red eyes were like pickaxes, splitting her spinal column into fragments of bone. He tried to conceal his presence, but his odor was so overwhelming, it was easy to know when he was close by. She caught glimpses of him watching her from behind giant rocks or in dark cave corners. And every time she thought she would be able to sneak away to the Mouth, Sturd would pop up and halt her plans.

It was as dark and hot in the Mines as usual. The day was coming to a close and the weight of her lighted helmet felt especially cumbersome on her neck. Crystal Cave was not like Onyx Alley in the least. There was no cool spring to sip from, or dip your head into, and the terrain was so uneven that one wrong step could send an elf plummeting into a sinkhole of broken crystal. This proved to be a great difficulty for the mining crew, with their heavy equipment and steel-toed boots. Fragile crystals adorned the entire cavern, and these precious stones needed to be preserved as best as possible for the Crystal Collectors to harvest, sell, or trade.

Her head ached. Her back ached. Her hands ached. She lifted up her pickaxe to descend upon a glistening hunk of flowstone when she lost her footing and wobbled into a quartz pyramid. A piece broke off from the highest point and pierced her elbow. "Claus!" she yowled in pain.

Suddenly, Sturd emerged from the shadows of the cave. "Better watch where you're going," he snarled.

She gripped her elbow tightly and exhaled in exasperation, "You've been following me all week. What gives?"

"Oh? I thought you'd be happy to see me."

"No. Not really."

He smirked. "Just keeping my eye on you. You *are* part of my crew. I need to keep watch over all my men… um, I mean, *workers*," he cooed, the sarcasm dripping from his tongue like slow rolling sap down the bark of a Nessie tree. "Just making sure you're not finding yourself in any kind of… trouble. You really ought to be more careful around those crystals, Skye, or the Collectors just might make you pay for what you break."

She had been trying so hard to keep her cool, but the stress of the day, the aches throughout her body, and the very *smell* of him turned her stomach inside out.

She threw her ax to the ground and unfastened the strap on her helmet. "That's it!" she yelled. "I've just about had enough of…."

"E!" Barkuss's voice echoed from the cave hallway, "E, let's go. Quitting time!"

She inhaled and stared back at Sturd just as the siren sounded.

"Your playmate awaits," Sturd said as he waved his hand in dismissal.

She bent down and picked up her equipment, but never once broke her stare.

Do you know how much I hate you? her eyes tried to say.

Just as much as I hate you, Sturd's hard gaze replied back.

She turned on her heel and walked through the hallway where Barkuss was waiting for her. He looked frazzled and distraught.

"Hey." She raised her hand in a small wave when she saw him.

"Hey," he meekly responded, "when in Claus's name is he going to get off your back? He's really putting a wrench in our plans!"

"I know. I know," she agreed. "What's going on?" she finally asked, sensing something wasn't quite right.

"Banter's sick. I'm not sure what's wrong with him."

"A lot of us seem to be sick these days," she replied as the two started walking back to their dens. "It's probably just Coppleysites. Trust me, if there's anyone who knows about a bad case of Coppleysites—"

"It's not that," he said, cutting her off. "It's not Coppleysites."

"Well, maybe he just has, like, a cold or something. Maybe he's overworked and run down? Would that be so unbelievable an ailment for one of us?" She wished she could offer more comfort to her friend.

"No. Not that either. I know it. It's something bad, girl. Something real bad." Barkuss lowered his head and his walk slowed.

"Then, what do you think it could possibly be?" She slowed to keep pace with him.

He just shrugged his shoulders and grunted something that sounded like "I don't know." The rest of the walk Home was a silent one, which was rather unusual for the two of them.

"Could you go check on him for me?" Barkuss asked when they reached the front walkway of his den. "I've been going every night since he got sick, but I gotta be honest with ya, E, I don't feel so hot myself."

"Sure. Sure. No problem," she promised as a feeling of worry began to creep its way into her throat. "If you want me to come back to check on you later, I could."

Barkuss gave a weak smile. His eyes were starting to get heavy, and he could barely keep himself standing upright in the doorway. "No, no," he protested, "I just need to get some sleep. Just look in on Banter. I'll see you at work tomorrow. Maybe tomorrow will be the day." He gave her a weak wink and shut the door.

She smiled back at him half-heartedly, then made her way to Banter's den just to see how bad the situation really was. Along the way, she noticed that a peculiar silence had fallen throughout the caverns. It was the first time she'd noticed it—now that the List and Tannen and Sturd and work were somewhere in the back of her mind—but there weren't the usual nighttime bustling noises, and most dens along the rock road had their lights out. As she approached Banter's den, she could see there was a low light coming from the back room window. Other than that, the den was dark and still, and she was afraid as to what she might find upon entry.

There was no need to knock at Banter's door, as it was unlocked. She cracked it open as softly as possible. The darkness was thick in the room and the quiet was deafening. She blindly felt the wall for a light switch and flicked it up furiously as soon as her finger fell upon it. "Banter?" she called out, but there was no response.

"Banter?" she called again as she approached his bedroom. The heavy wooden door was partially open, and she gently pushed her way through when she heard a slight moaning from within. Banter was balled up in his bed. A thick gray quilt was pulled up to his chin. His eyes were closed and his head was moving slowly back and forth on his pillow as he moaned softly.

It disturbed her to see him like this. "Banter, it's me, Ember," she said as she sat at the edge of his bed and touched his foot.

"Huh? What?" he managed to mumble.

"It's Ember," she repeated. "What's going on? Can you talk to me?" She had no clue what to say or do for him.

"Water," he moaned and motioned his head to the end table beside the bed.

She got up and grabbed the glass that was there. The water within was warm and almost stagnant.

"Let me get you some ice for this!" she said when she felt the warmth from the cup.

"No, no!" he weakly protested. "It's good warm. I'm so cold."

His hand appeared from underneath the quilt and he reached for the glass. As he grabbed it, her finger grazed his palm, and her eyes widened as she felt his icy touch. She bent down to touch his forehead with the back of her hand, and sure enough, his body was like a block of ice.

Don't sick elves get hot?

"You *are* cold!" she exclaimed, trying to force a fake chuckle to lighten the mood.

He gave a little smile and slowly sipped the water. When he was finished, he handed her the glass back and she placed it on the end table.

"Can you try to talk to me?" she asked again.

He nodded. "Not sure what happened. Just started to feel sick."

"When?"

"Last week. It came on slowly."

"Can you walk?"

He shook his head "no."

"Can you breathe okay?"

He shook his head back and forth in a response that said, "Sorta."

"Are you in pain?"

He nodded.

"Where?"

He rolled his head in a semi-circle.

"Huh?" she questioned.

Again, he rolled his head in a semi-circle.

"Does that mean, 'Everywhere?'"

He nodded.

She reached to lovingly touch his foot, but he winced the second her fingers met the edge of the quilt. She recoiled, eyes widening in disbelief.

"What on earth is going on with you?" she mumbled in a hushed whisper, half hoping he wouldn't hear her.

He slowly shrugged and closed his eyes for a moment.

"Not Coppleysites. Not a cold. You're freezing, not burning," she rattled off the list of possibilities that swarmed in her brain. "I'm not a resource on elf diseases or anything like that, ya know," she tried to joke. "What did the Medic Elf say about this?"

He touched his four fingers to his thumb, brought his hand to his mouth, and opened and closed his lips as if he were eating an invisible piece of bread. She scrunched her nose for a second and then finally realized what he was trying to say.

She waved her hands frantically in the air. "Oh! Oh! Something you ate! The Medic said it was something you ate!"

He closed his eyes and gently nodded.

"But what? What did he say it was?" she asked. "Like, do you think you were *poisoned* or something?"

He didn't nod or shake his head; he closed his eyes and breathed deeply. A frightening rattle in his chest startled her when he inhaled.

She put her face in her hands and rubbed her temples with her forefingers. "Do you think someone purposefully did this to you?" She was determined to get to the bottom of this.

He wearily shook his head. "Too many of us," he grumbled. He was right about that. Other elves were sick: Jolley, Blithe, Barkuss....

"I'm not sick, though," she said, not really addressing him, but more of working the angles out loud. "And Sturd's not sick."

Suddenly, a putrid smell overpowered the air, and she nervously looked up. "Just speaking his name makes my stomach turn!" she said. Banter's eyes were closed, but that rattle-like chuckle escaped his mouth again.

"Nessie," he managed to groan.

"What? Are you hungry? Do you want me to get you some Nessie Fruit?"

Using most of his energy, he shook his head side to side frantically. "Ness-eeeee," he moaned a little louder, putting emphasis on the last syllable.

She was still puzzled. What in the world was he talking about? "Banter, I can go get you some Nessie Fruit if you want it, but I...."

"No!"

She stood up, scared. Banter's body tensed from beneath the blanket. And then it hit her like a pickaxe to the front of the skull. Nanny Carole's tales came jostling into her memory... the Nessie Fruit. "Banter, tell me right now, does the Medic think the fruit is what's making elves sick?"

He closed his eyes and nodded, his weak head barely bobbing up and down. His body relaxed.

"And he didn't give you anything to help you? Isn't there some kind of medicine, or grulish, or *something* to help you?" she pleaded, her voice rising in anger and fear.

He shook his head again.

"But, I don't understand. I'm not sick! And why hasn't the Medic told all of us? We need to warn everyone!" she yelled frantically as she violently stroked the top pieces of her hair into a tight-knotted bun.

"Can't," he muttered.

"No. Of course you can't. I can! I need to go Aboveground, Banter. Things have been bad down here for far too long and there ain't nobody down here who's gonna help us. If that stupid doctor of ours isn't going to show us the decency and respect we deserve and refuses to warn us...."

"Panic," Banter said.

"So? There are ways of doing things and ways of saying things. There's gonna be a helluva lot more panic down here if elves start dropping like flies with no good reason. You're in bad shape! And if that idiot isn't going to help you, then I have to go and find a way to get to the Boss's Headquarters and get you the help you need."

"Can't," he muttered again.

"No. Of course you can't. But I can. And I will!"

"No Pass!" he exclaimed followed by a series of coughs.

"Pass? I don't care about that," she declared. "I'm not gonna need a Pass, Banter. I have the List! The one that Sturd destroyed last year. I picked it up and put it back together. Barkuss helped me. It's about time that Sturd paid for his actions. I knew that the no-coal thing was a bad idea, and the Council needs to know just how out of control that monster is!"

His eyes widened. "But you know...."

"Sturd will say I'm Defector. Yes. Let them all come for me. Let them try to come for me."

"You don't know the way," he said, managing to muster up some strength to sit up.

She thought about this for a few seconds and smiled, "Yeah. But you do. And you're gonna tell me!" He shook his head in protest, but she stared at him and nodded her own. "Yes. You're going to help me. You know the way to the Mouth. Tell me how to get to the Guards."

"No Pass!"

"I told you already! That 'No Pass' stuff is nonsense, Banter! I know you know a way! Magic or no magic, I don't care. You have to tell me. Banter, Barkuss went to his den sick today, too," she started to raise her voice, "and I'm not going to sit back and watch my friends die. You clearly need help, like yesterday! Now are you going to tell me how to get out of here, or am I going to have to ransack your den to find something that will? You know you can't stop me, Banter."

"But Sturd...."

She threw her hands in the air and rolled her eyes, "Sturd Shmurd. I don't care anymore, Banter. I don't care. Do you understand that I *don't care*? Let him *try* to do to me what he did to Pepper Brightly. If it means getting you help, so be it. It's worth it. *You're* worth it!"

Banter knew he had to let her go. Her determined and pleading eyes told the story of a girl locked in a cage, and if this was to be her savior's mission, he could not deny her that.

His hand appeared from underneath the quilt again, and he pointed his twisted and weak finger to the dresser on the opposite side of the room. "Third one. Folder."

She opened the third drawer down from the top, and just as he said, there was a folder inside. Inside the folder were construction specs, data charts, before and after renderings, and a map with Elvish writing on it.

"The map, I'm guessing?" she asked with her back still to him.

He grunted a yes.

She closed the folder and angrily turned to him, "But I don't speak Elvish. And neither do you. So this is no good to me."

"Floorboards," he groaned, the rattling in his chest getting louder.

She dropped to her knees in front of the dresser and ran her fingers across the wooden planks. She hadn't noticed before that the bedroom had wood flooring. All den floors were rock, so what was this all about? She soon found out when her fingers felt a dip in the wood, like a carved opening. She gripped the notch tightly and lifted up. The floorboard gave way in her hand and revealed a small opening in the rock floor beneath. There was a piece of frosted plastic within and nothing else.

She removed it and held it in the air. "What the hell is this?"

"Elvish," he whispered.

And like a light bulb firing off in her brain, she anxiously opened the folder, took out the map written in Elvish, and placed the frosted plastic over it. The other documents scattered onto the floor like a pile of disturbed leaves. The ancient letters of the map transformed underneath the plastic into words that she could read and understand. From what she could decipher, it would take her at least two hours to make her way to the Aboveground, and if she left now, she would get a good head start before anyone even knew she was gone.

"I'm going now," she said with finality. "Thank you for this. I'm going to get you help. I'm going to get us all help." And with that she walked over to Banter's weakened body and lightly kissed his cold forehead.

"Good luck," he whispered, and she walked out of the den.

Chapter Twenty-One

H E WATCHED FROM A DARKENED CORNER, INHALING HER STRAWBERRY scent as it wafted in the air long after she had raced past him. Her ashy black hair danced right underneath his nose as he crouched low behind the crags. She glided like the most beautiful Graespur, her feet seemingly not touching the ground as her urgency (for whatever it was that was so urgent) propelled her forward in the night. Her hair draped the wind like soft gray wings set atop her arched, delicate back. She was a vision of loveliness, and his mouth watered at the thought of what she tasted like. Was she salty? Was she sweet? Would her gentle flesh melt in his mouth like butter on the finest of meats?

A low hunger-rumble worked its way throughout Sturd's belly.

When Ember was gone from his sight, he emerged from his hiding position and made his way into Banter's den. He knew there was something going on, and he was determined to get to the bottom of it. He entered Banter's bedroom like a snake creeping up on its prey.

Banter was now fast asleep, dreaming of Ember getting help and getting him better. It was a pleasant dream that relaxed all his muscles for the first time in a week, but reality forced his eyes awake the second Sturd opened his mouth to speak.

"Banter! Poor Banter!" Sturd exclaimed, clicking his tongue against the roof of his mouth in mock pity with a "tsk, tsk, tsk" sound.

Banter's bloodshot eyes flashed wide for a second when he saw Sturd standing in his room.

"Somebody sick?" Sturd's derision continued. "What a shame. Ya know you don't look so hot. In fact, you look quite frozen!" He laughed.

Banter shuffled his body under the quilt. He was trying to sit up, but it was no use.

"Relax, brother, relax," Sturd coaxed. "I just want to talk, and of course, to see how big brother is doing. I believe someone else was here earlier to see you, isn't that right?"

Banter stared him down and made no effort to speak.

Sturd slithered closer to the bed. "I'll take that as a yes. Now, I know you and Skye are good buds and all that, and she was probably over here just checking up on you, right?"

Banter didn't move a muscle.

"*Right?*" Sturd screamed in frustration.

Shaken, Banter finally nodded.

"Hmmm," Sturd continued, "and that's fine and dandy and all, but what really concerns me, what I find to be truly suspect, is why our little Skye girl jetted out of here like a reindeer on the Big Night."

Banter shrugged and shook his head.

"Come on, Banter, tell baby brother what had Emmy-poo all worked up?"

Banter closed his eyes and cocked his head back onto his pillow. He felt cornered, like a trapped animal, and he knew there was no escaping Sturd's cage. Sturd continued to eyeball the room when he noticed the papers scattered on the ground beside the dresser and the secret compartment in the floor opened. He raised his eyebrows in curiosity as he bent down and fingered through the papers.

"Hmmm," he said again as he leafed through the pile, "lots of construction stuff, whatever. But there had to be something else here. Why in Claus's name would you reveal to her your floorbox? Ya know, I have one too. And I only keep the most sacred of documents tucked away there. I know you did, too, cause that's kinda the reason why they're there. You must have had something so precious there, something so important. Now the questions are: what was it, why did you give it to her, and what is she doing with it? I *will* find out. You know this, right? You have to know this. You can't *not* know this."

Sturd moved over to the edge of the bed, papers still in hand. Banter opened his eyes to look at him. He was so very weak, and so very cold. Sturd could feel his body shivering with sickness through the mattress. He smiled and touched Banter's leg.

"Poor thing," he whispered as he puckered his lips out. "Hey! I have a marvelous idea! Let's play a game! I'll tell you what's going on and you tell me where Skye girl's off to. Sound good? Good. Here we go. You're dying, dear brother. I think you know that, though. You're sick.

Lots of elves are sick. Something's wrong with the fruit. But, I kinda think you already know that one, too. You're so smart, aren't you, Banter? So, let's see, wanna know why I'm not sick?"

Banter shut his eyes tightly in disgust. If it really was the Nessie Fruit that was making the elves sick, it was obvious why Sturd wouldn't be. Sturd didn't eat Nessie Fruit. Everyone knew what Sturd ate....

"So, I played my part of the game, now it's your turn," he sang in a maniacal tone as he looked down and rummaged through the papers again. "Oh, wait. You probably can't talk. I'll tell ya what, I'll rattle off some ideas and you can nod or shake your head whenever you feel like. That sounds splendid to me!" He clapped his hands overdramatically.

Banter deeply inhaled with that horrid rattling sound quickly following. Sturd puckered his lips again in mock sympathy. "Wow," he derided, "that sounds awful! All right, enough of that. Let's have it. These papers are in some sort of cluster, like they all go together somehow. Do they?"

Banter made no movement or reply.

"Do they?" Sturd repeated. When it was apparent that Banter was not going to play his little game, or give any type of hint or clue, he became agitated and shifted on the bed. "The only reason why you shouldn't be answering me is if you're dead! DO THEY GO TOGETHER OR NOT?"

Banter winced at Sturd's screams, and finally, regretfully, nodded.

"See, isn't that better? Cooperation, brother, cooperation," Sturd said smiling and calming down. "Now, from what I can make out here, these construction prints are for some kind of gate, or walkway, or something that would go *around* something else. Am I close?"

Banter closed his eyes.

"Good, good, I thought so. So, these coordinates and other charts here have some sort of magical property. Some of this here is written in Elvish. Can't really make it out, but this here symbol is a protection rune. So, you were planning to build some sort of gate around something to protect it?" Sturd ran his fingers through his hair with frustration, nearly pulling out a large clump. "But there's a piece missing. And that's the piece you gave Skye. Am I right?"

Tears were starting to stream down Banter's cheeks. It was only a matter of time before Sturd had it all figured out and captured Ember. He wept at the thought of what he would do to her.

"Oh, grow up!" Sturd chided as he began to lay the papers across Banter's legs on the bed. He stood up and puzzled over them, looking from one page to the next, trying to figure out a pattern and make sense of a connection.

"This would be a lot easier if you just *told* me what was missing...." he said as his voice began to trail. Just then he noticed there were numbers hand-written on different areas of each page, as if to throw someone off track. But not Sturd! "101, 101-A, 107, 103, 102, 109, 110-A, 109-A, 109-B," he read as he turned each page over and over. There was the key. There was the common denominator. He finally pieced the pages in order and fanned them out with his thumb.

"110 is missing," he declared. "That's what you gave her, isn't it?"

Sturd descended upon him, his face within inches from Banter's. Banter could feel Sturd's hot breath by his mouth, and although it carried a rancid odor, like that of rotted flesh, the warmth felt good against his own icy lips.

"Isn't it?" Sturd growled a low animal growl through his gritted teeth.

Banter quickly nodded and closed his eyes once again. There was no stopping the tears as they streamed down his face in uncontrollable waves.

"Time's up, brother. Game over. Ember has page 110, and from what I can see, it's some sort of map, right?" he cooed.

Silence and tears. Banter knew there was nothing he could do to stall any longer.

"I said, TO WHERE?" Sturd screamed, his voice penetrating Banter's small eardrums, his hot breath like fireballs on Banter's face.

Realizing he wasn't going to get an answer from tight-lipped Banter, Sturd pulled back and breathed deeply. He started talking to himself, piecing together all the possibilities—the who's, the where's, the why's, the how's. "The Medic," he began. "No. Doesn't add up. He can't help her even if he tried. What about West Valley? No. Those crazy girl elves are useless and pathetic. She wouldn't dare try to make it to the Mouth...."

Banter's body had reflexively twitched when Sturd said the word *mouth*, and Sturd—with his heightened senses and keen perception—had noticed the slight shift of movement and seized the opportunity to pounce.

Sturd once again took a step closer to Banter's bed and propped himself on his hands. His red eyes widened as he stared at Banter in disbelief. Banter must have given Ember a map. That meant Ember was going Aboveground. That meant Ember was now a Defector! That meant Ember was now officially *his*! His stomach moaned at him at the very thought of Ember, an open fire, flesh roasting on the spit....

Sturd looked at Banter and cocked his head to the side. "You're dying," he said again in a flat voice. "Here, brother, let me help you!"

And with that, Sturd's twisted fingers were tightly wrapped around Banter's throat. With every last ounce in his body, Banter thrashed against the wicked embrace, but he was too weak with sickness to fight back. His eyes bulged in fear and pain as Sturd's firm grip squeezed the last of the air out of Banter's fragile lungs like deflating the air from a week old party balloon. Sturd knew Banter would soon succumb to the force of his hands, so he loosened his grip and pressed his mouth onto Banter's.

As Banter's final exhale escaped his lips with an eerie rattle, Sturd breathed deep his brother's last breath. Kneeling up on the bed, Sturd let Banter's death breath wash over him in a near ecstatic moment. Death filled him with new life. He sucked it in, held it deep within his own lungs for as long as he could, and when he felt the swoon of unconsciousness start to creep upon him, he exhaled slowly and steadily. Then he stood up and placed the folder back into the dresser drawer.

"I have an alarm to sound," he said, chuckling as he left the den.

Chapter Twenty-Two

EMBER WASTED NO TIME AS SHE RACED THROUGH THE CAVES. SHE HAD NO idea how long it would be before Sturd, or Corzakk, found out she had gone, and she wasn't going to take any chances. She knew exactly what they did to Defectors - *You poor girl, Pepper Brightly* - and that was a fate she was so desperate to avoid. Banter was sick; Barkuss was getting sick. Would she get sick, too? That didn't matter now. Banter was on his death bed, and that was enough to drive her into action. Apparently, their good-for-nothing Medic was just that – good-for-nothing! Now, getting Banter help was her one goal, and the only option she had was to make her way to the Mouth to get Aboveground.

The map was very detailed and it looked like it was part of some larger plan. From what she could decipher, the Mouth was going to be protected by a lighted gate that connected to a path. The magic gate was going to make the opening of the cave invisible. Who knew? Did that mean they were going to get rid of those Guards? She wasn't too concerned with all the working details. It meant nothing to her. What she did care about was making it safely to her destination.

Construction of the cloaking gate had not yet begun. In fact, poor Pepper Brightly's escape attempt had probably prompted these construction plans, no doubt. Thank Claus these plans were weeks away from coming to fruition.

The map instructed her to get to Barrier Holt, a section of the Mines that had long since been abandoned. Every elf who either grew up, or was transplanted Underground, was told of the story of the goblins—filthy and demonic creatures that made their Home in Barrier Holt. There was supposedly a truce made between the elves and goblins, so the story went. No elf was to enter their domain, and in return, they would leave all elves alone. Coal Elves were told of the horror stories if this truce was ever breached. Goblins would rip elves from limb to limb and cook their bodies over open flames. No elf she knew of dared cross over into Barrier Holt. No elf even dared to speak the name of the long-forgotten territory.

But, now, as she studied the map in Elvish and pored over the blueprints for the supersonic cloaking gate, she understood why those tales were told in the first place. Goblins didn't exist—at least not in the Mines of the North Pole. It was all fear. All mind control. All a way to prevent the Coal Elves from ever reaching the Mouth! Barrier Holt *was* the Mouth, and the only way to get to Barrier Holt was to cross the Ignis River to Sandstone Shelf and proceed through the abandoned catacombs and hallways.

Cross the Ignis? Great. How am I going to do that without getting noticed?

It was late, and hopefully there wouldn't be anyone around to question what she was doing.

The rafting station was dark, and best of all, elfless. A few twinkling helmet and lantern lights in the distance meant some elves were traveling, but she noticed that most of the lights she saw were headed *away* from Sandstone Shelf. The elves who worked there were probably making their way back Home to their dens. This was a good thing for her. She needed to go *toward* Sandstone Shelf, and the fewer elves around, the better.

She found a raft on the bank of the river and began to untie the ropes when she heard footsteps behind her. "Hey stranger!" a voice cheered.

Startled, she wildly jerked her head around to see who was there.

"Easy, easy," the voice coaxed. "What's got you all crazed!"

It was Tannen. His green eyes glittered in the darkness of the cave.

She sighed and let her tense muscles relax a bit when she realized it was him. She rolled up the map and placed it in her back pocket. "N-nothing," she stammered as she fidgeted with the paper and plastic translator.

"Nothing? You're just as jumpy as a chinchi, out here late at night getting a raft to go Claus-knows-where. That's nothing?" he inquired, flashing a bright smile.

She blew strands of hair from her eyes. "Yeah, nothing," she repeated as she bent over to continue to untie the raft.

"Here, let me help you."

"No!" she snapped. "I got this, I'm fine."

He stepped back a bit and lowered his head. Realizing her tone of voice, she paused for a second and inhaled deeply. She peered up at him through the ashy strands of hair that fell back onto her forehead. He looked like a jagged puzzle piece, his eyes cast down, biting his lower lip in nervousness. Through the pieces of her black hair, his image was cut up and monstrous. She had to create this image of him in her mind in order to shut him out, make him less desirable, and make him less elf and more repulsive monster. She exhaled, and with her forced breath, the hair blew up again, and she was able to see him clearly. Defeated Tannen. Clueless Tannen.

I-wish-I-could-have-fallen-in-love-with-you, Tannen.

His gaze shifted to his boots and he began to apologize, "I'm sorry if I offended you. I really don't know what I did to….."

She breathed deeply again. "Nothing," she huffed. "You didn't do anything to offend me."

He raised his eyebrows in confusion, and she knew that now was the time to tell him the truth.

"It's my fault," she confessed. "I shut you out. I just couldn't… didn't want to get too close to you. You're a really good friend, and there's just some stuff that I… I just don't want to involve you in my craziness."

"I don't mind," he said with a smirk. "A little crazy never hurt anyone, did it?"

Great. There he goes again with those big green eyes and that charming smile….

She couldn't help but smile back. She hoped he couldn't see her blushing in the darkness. "I'm serious," she pleaded. "There's stuff that could get you hurt… or worse… and I…" She tried so very hard to sound foreboding, but it was so very hard to be serious with a smile on her face.

"So, now you're all tough-girl renegade?" he joked.

"Something like that," she mumbled in a soft whisper as the smile melted from her face.

He stopped and his smile vanished, as well. He took in the severity of her tone, and realized this wasn't a joke.

"So, what are you doing out here?" she asked as she turned back to fiddle with the raft.

"Fishing," he answered matter-of-factly as he lifted his box. "Ya know, since the stream at Onyx Alley is closed off, I thought I'd try my luck in the Ignis."

She climbed on to the raft "Well, good luck to you." And she started to drift into the river. *This may be the last time I see you.*

"Wait!" he yelled, dropping to his knees and pulling the raft back to the dock.

She sighed again. "Tannen, I really don't have time for this. I'm kinda in a hurry!"

He forcefully pulled the raft back to the dock. "Tell me where you're going! Tell me what's going on!"

"I can't!" she screamed back at him, trying to tug away from his grip.

"Then I'll come with you! Whatever is going on, let me help you! I don't care what it is! Just let me help you!"

"You can't," she growled.

"Yeah, whatever," he said as he jumped onto the raft.

"Tannen!"

"Look," he calmly began as he pushed the raft far out onto the water, "I just miss my friend. And you can't lie and tell me nothing's going on. Let me help you. Even if you won't tell me what's up, let me help you anyway."

She rolled her eyes. It was a losing battle with him. "I'm sorry," she finally apologized. "I'm sorry for everything. For abandoning our friendship. For ignoring you. For not letting you in. I really liked spending time with you. But there's just... I don't know... stuff, I guess. Stuff that I have to do, and stuff that I have to deal with."

The List. The spreading sickness. Where did Tannen fit in this world of hers? She wished there could have been a way to make the pieces match up, but right now, there was no squeezing him in. No

matter how attracted she was to him. No matter how much she genuinely enjoyed his company.

He put his hand on her knee. "I know. You have secrets."

"Lots!" she exclaimed as he smiled at her. "And it's like, I'm kinda
bound by those secrets. And I'm not truly 'free'. Does that make
sense?"

"I think I get it," he responded.

"I don't want to keep secrets from you. Does that make sense, too?"

He brushed the hair from her eyes. "Perfect sense. But why are you
running from them? Your secrets. Why are you trying to get away
from them all?"

She clasped his hand at her cheek and brushed the back of it with
her forefinger. "No, no. Just the opposite."

"Well," he said, looking deeply into her eyes, "you let me know
when you've got everything sussed out. No questions asked. I'll be
waiting for you, you know."

And with that, he placed his hand on the back of her head and
drew her closer to him. Her body shivered as she felt her mouth
instinctually open to accept his kiss, and her mind suddenly went
blank.

Where was she?
Where was she going?
What was she doing?
Why was she doing this?
What map?
What mission?

This moment was intoxicating, almost like the dance she danced
with Barkuss's super- sweet super-secret grulish. Heavenly. A sweet,
otherworldly swoon. The bobbing of their heads, and the rocking of
the raft on the river lulled her to a safe and comfortable place. She
delighted in the gentleness, yet firmness, of his touch as he ran his
fingers through her ashen hair. She marveled at the softness of his lips
opening and closing on her own. His lips were warm and the insides
of his mouth tasted so sweet, like almond sugar cookies with a light
Nessie Fruit glaze….

She suddenly pulled away in horror, breaking from her romantic trance, and quickly snapping back into her painful reality. The sweet taste of Nessie Fruit danced on her tongue like a disturbing reminder. *Banter. Sick.*

"I... I'm sorry," she stammered as she broke from his embrace.

"I know. I know," he smirked as he watched her curl her knees to her chest. "You got... stuff." And they both giggled.

"You do have to tell me one thing, though," he said.

"What's that?"

"You have to tell me where you're going. If not, we're just gonna wander aimlessly on this river!"

"I suppose so." She sighed heavily. "Sandstone Shelf."

He raised a suspicious eyebrow. "What's in Sandstone Shelf?"

"No, what's *through* Sandstone Shelf," she corrected.

A wave of terror briefly washed over his face. His sparkling green eyes flashed dim with grave concern. There was only one place through Sandstone Shelf, and that place was forbidden to all. "Okay, I'll play," he began as his voice transformed to a tone of seriousness. "Em, tell me, what's through Sandstone Shelf?"

She looked at him as if to say, "You know the answer to that!" but she knew he needed to hear the actual words from her in order to process what was going on. "Barrier Holt," she said bluntly, lowering her voice.

He paused, digesting the enormity of her words. Barrier Holt could only mean one thing. "Okay," he said breathing deeply and still trying to process. "What business do you have in Barrier Holt?"

Just then, a blaring siren echoed through the cavern walls. They both took their hands and covered their tall ears to mask the sound. It was the Defector alarm, one that he had heard all too recently. His face dropped in horror when he saw her guilt-ridden eyes pleading with him.

"Ember!" he shouted over the deafening wail. "What did you do?"

"The Mouth!" she screamed back over the rising, groaning din. "I'm going to the Mouth." She moved her mouth wide to exaggerate the words as if she were speaking to a deaf elf. "I'm going Aboveground!"

Chapter Twenty-Three

L EAVING TANNEN WAS EASY. THE ALARM WAS SO DEAFENING THEY
couldn't hear what the other was saying, and Ember wasn't very
good at reading lips. He got the raft to the bank of Sandstone Shelf, as
he yelled at her, narrowed his eyes, and waved his arms wildly in the
air in protest. It was no use. She was going through Barrier Holt, and
there was nothing he could say, yell, or gesture, to change her mind.
When he realized all his efforts were futile, he yelled something that
sounded something like, "Good luck," and, "Almonds tall struthers!"
He was obviously mad. Disappointed. Confused. All of the above.

When she had gotten off the raft safely, he turned it around onto
the river and headed back the way they came. And that was it. As she
made her way stealthily through Sandstone Shelf, she realized that
analyzing what had just transpired between them was not her top
priority; the repartee between them, the dreamy kiss… that would
have to be saved for a later time, and figuring out what "almonds tall
struthers" meant? No, she needed to focus on the task at hand.

Finding the gates was easy, too. Not a problem like she had anticipated. She remembered the way the rocks had felt, and looked, and
even smelled. Even though the path was ever changing, she knew
exactly which way to go by the changing of temperature and the
changing of the rock texture. It was as if she was working on instinct,
and she only glanced at the map once or twice to double check that
she was in fact headed in the right direction. Her only concern was
how she was going to pass through the gates. She didn't have a Pass
this time and she had no idea what she was going to do or say when
face to face with the Guards. She paused when she came upon a
familiar glistening giant gray boulder. She was close.

She ran her hand over the surface of the boulder. The façade was
rough, crunchy. It *was* some sort of fairy dust that was glittering on it.
She brought her hands to her face to examine, and sure enough, they
were covered with the colorful sand-like substance, like a thousand
grainy rainbows coating her palms. She continued to run her hands
up and down and back and forth across the stone to guide her along

the path as her hands collected more and more of the mysterious particles. Her steps grew quicker, more frantic, and her will and desire became so great she thought her heart would burst. *How in the hell am I going to do this?*

And then without warning, the frost melted in the center of the rock wall, creating a opening to the Aboveground. Sunlight filled the cavern with a soft glow, the way it had looked the day that she went Home. This time, there were no gates, and no Guards. *Look at that! Didn't even need a Pass! Just some more razzle dazzle.*

She took a deep breath and passed through the opening, expecting to hear an alarm sound automatically, or even be speared through the back. But nothing happened. No sounds, no menacing Guards to haul her back Underground.

Just ice. Lots of it.

She took one step onto snowy ground, and was suddenly lurched forward on a patch of slick ice. She landed hard on her back, her knees tucking awkwardly to her chest. She felt something lash at her back, followed by a warm, wet sensation underneath her jumpsuit. *Great. I'm cut open.*

Her eyes were still closed tight, and she had expected to at least see bright shadows behind her eyelids, or the shadows and shapes of a brilliant day like the hundreds of butterflies flitting about the garden in her courtyard, their iridescent wings catching the thin rays of light from the sun. It looked dark behind closed eyes. It *felt* dark, and there was a burning mold smell that permeated the air. Slowly, she began to open her eyes, and when they were at full vision, her jaw dropped at the sight she saw.

Burnt wood—piles of it littering the snowy ground. That was what had ravished her back and caused her to bleed. Her small hand moved to feel the wetness on her jumpsuit, and she assessed it wasn't too bad, just a little cut, just a little blood. Looking beyond the field of burnt wood was a different story. It was much colder than she had remembered; the sky was shrouded in clouds of thick black smoke, preventing the sun from penetrating the land. There were no signs of birds or other woodland creatures, and the smell of death and disease hung heavily in the air. She stood up, glanced around one last time, and made her way to her old town of East Bank.

East Bank was almost unrecognizable. There were no smells of the roasted chestnut street vendors, or the faint whiff of black toy lacquer from the numerous toy making shoppes. Her nose scrunched as she inhaled the new putrid odors of the burnt wood and filth. The streets were near empty. What was usually a busy city teeming with smiling and singing elffolk was now reduced to a mere ghost town. She heard a loud *POP-POP-POP* sound in the distance, and soon a snowfall began to descend upon the streets. It was a gray snow that reminded her of coal dust. When it landed on her sleeve and didn't melt, she realized it wasn't snow at all. It *was* dust. Ash. Probably from whatever was now in flames on the horizon.

"Just like Home," she sang, and paused for a moment when she realized that she had actually referred to the Mines as Home… out loud.

She was in shock at the state of affairs Aboveground. *What the hell is going on around here?*

And then she paused and chuckled at the irony of it all. The ones who lived the best and had all the advantages were in a state of emergency, their once blue and white and sunny world reduced to the dreary gray ash like the Underground. *What's that word they call something like this in the human world? Karma?*

Not really having a sense of where to begin, she decided to seek help from the one elf who had lent her a kind hand before. She walked through the deserted streets to East Bank's town square. She would talk to Slarrett, the Inn Keeper, who had been so kind to her those months ago.

But, the Inn had transformed greatly since she was there last. The beautiful tapestries in the entranceway were riddled with a layer of ashy dust; the once lush décor was now home to a series of intricate cobwebs. It appeared as if the Inn had been abandoned, but Slarrett was there behind his desk, sitting in the eerie silence with his head engulfed in his hands.

The bells on the door sang out behind her when she entered the lobby. Slarrett, startled, looked up from his desk and narrowed his brow. As she approached him, she noticed his cheeks had sunken in and his skin had turned an awful shade of gray, like a layer of death washing itself slowly across his face.

"Slarrett?" she questioned when she reached the desk.

He stared at her a few moments longer. The dark circles under his eyes were like two black patches stamped on his face. When he finally recognized her, his eyes lit up in surprise and he straightened out his back.

"I remember you!" he said in his high pitched voice that was softer, quieter.

She meekly smiled a fake smile in hopes not to scare him. "How are you, Slarrett? You don't look so good."

"Don't feel good either. Haven't really eaten in a few days. Trying to avoid that sickness, but it's not looking so good. What brings you back here?"

"I need to get to the Boss's Headquarters. A friend of mine is very ill, and the Medic isn't of any help down there. I need to see if there's anything I can do or give him, or... or... I was wondering if you could help me...."

"Ahhh," he sighed, "guess they sent you back 'cause you're the most familiar with this place. But Headquarters? I'm not sure how to go about getting there."

Slarrett's body was overcome with a deep coughing spell. His body doubled over in uncontrollable heaves, the rattle sound reminded her of the one she heard from Banter—worse than Miner's cough; worse than a Coppleysite cough. She made a move to help him, but he raised his hand for her to back away. When the coughing subsided, he stood; a trickle of blood running down his nose. He took the back of his hand and wiped it away, leaving a red trail along the side of his boney cheek.

"Oh, my!" she exclaimed. "Let me help you!" and she made a move toward him, but he jerked away.

"It's okay," he answered tiredly. "I'm getting used to it now. When you're the only one left, you have to adjust to the ways things are."

"Only one left?" she inquired with a hard gulp.

"Yes," he answered in a somber tone. "Everyone here was ill and went Home. Poor Joona didn't make it."

Joona. She remembered Joona. He was the one who served her the night she had stayed here.

Didn't make it?

"What's going on here, Slarrett? What's happening up here? What's with the fire and smoke and all that?" she asked frantically, trying to piece everything together.

Slarrett hung his head low and shook it side to side slowly. "That Coal-less Night messed everything up. We all blamed you Coal Elves for not doing your jobs, and the Council was indifferent about where the blame actually fell. Now everyone is sick."

The reality started to creep its way into her mind. Everyone was sick—not just Banter, who was on his deathbed; not just Barkuss, who was showing early signs of being sick; not just Carson Blithe or Jaffert Jolley, who had been MIA. It was widespread. All over. Under *and* Aboveground. The problem was larger than she had thought.

"Well, what is the Council doing about all this?" she replied anxiously.

"Oh, yeah," he sighed. "They say they're working on a plan; that we all need to be patient. They're aware of the situation, they're getting right on it, and we need to hang in there."

Her voice rose in anger. "That's it? That's all they said?"

"No. They think the burning of the infected trees is going to help out, but that will take some time. They said something about the Big Night and a new List and something about...."

He stopped in mid-sentence as another coughing fit hit him. This time it lasted longer than the first.

"Think, Slarrett, think!" she implored when he was steady on his feet. "It's important that I get in contact with someone. I need to get to Headquarters and talk to someone in the Council. I need to help. I need to do something. Please, tell me everything you know!"

Slarrett was in a daze. He was weak with hunger and sickness, and his high-pitched voice was shaky. *If I touch him, will he be as cold as ice, like Banter?* She didn't know if Slarrett was even aware of his surroundings. What he needed was to be in a bed somewhere with a glass of warm water at his disposal. He smiled at her, but the corners of his mouth barely made a dent in his cheeks. She tried to smile back, to give him some sense of comfort, but it was no use.

"The Council is going to hold another meeting tomorrow night," he began.

"A meeting? Where? When? What are they going to talk about?" she asked in a calm tone, hoping to coax the information out of him.

He laughed a delirious laugh, and his eyelids were barely opened, "C'mon, they sent you back up here. You should know all this, Coal Girl."

But she didn't know all of this, because she hadn't been sent. She was on her own, a fact that she had purposefully not mentioned. He stiffened up at her lack of response, his ears pointing straight in the air, as if sensing something was amiss. He mustered up as much energy as he could to keep his composure.

"Yeah," he began, the word slithering out of his mouth, "how about you show me that Pass of yours?"

She gulped and stared at him, hard. The only paper she could show him was her reconstructed List, but now, with his suspicious, half-dead eyes glaring at her, she wasn't about to let him know she had it.

He stared back, every ounce of energy within him to keep his eyelids open. The silence lingered in the space between them.

He cleared his throat and feebly held out his hand in a motion for her to place the Pass within his weakened fingers. But there was no Pass to show—she knew it; he knew it; *she* knew *he* knew it. And the silence that grew began to heighten, electrify. He coiled his fingers one by one until his hand was a balled up fist.

"Slarrett, you and I both know that...."

"Get out," he snarled.

She closed her eyes and sharply shook her head. "I'm just here to help," she pleaded, "and you were the only one who I thought to come to. Please, Slarrett, just tell me what you know. Tell me about the meeting. I have to do something, anything!"

"Just get out," he repeated. "They'll kill me if they know I'm talking to a Defector."

"But, you're dying anyway! Let me try to help you," she desperately screamed at him.

"Get out!" he repeated. "This sickness is a better fate than what they would bestow upon me. Give you information? I'd rather die! Just...." and before he could continue his tirade, another coughing episode overtook him.

Defeated, she turned around and walked back onto the streets of East Bank, knowing Slarrett probably wouldn't make it through the night.

Chapter Twenty-Four

EMBER LOOKED AT THE GRAY CLOUD SKY; THE SUN WAS TRYING SO HARD to poke its rays through the thickness of the smoke, but it was a futile attempt. The lack of sunshine dropped the temperature many degrees; her lips were cracked and dry from the cold, and the tips of her pointed ears were raw and red. It didn't take long for the blood on her back to dry. The bitter cold air must have sped up the process, because she could now feel the crusted over scab brush against the material of her jumpsuit. She arched her shoulder inward and tilted her head to try to see her back. A stain had seeped its way through the fabric, but was barely visible against the black color of the suit. She shoved her hands in her pockets, fingering Banter's map with one hand and caressing the sacred List with the other.

What was she doing here? What was she thinking? What was she trying to accomplish? It was obvious the Council knew what was going on, and it was obvious there was no rush to rectify the situation. How did she think she could possibly get Banter help if Aboveground was in such a state of disarray? Help was *not* on the way. There was no cavalry coming with rescue, and she was certainly no stranger to this feeling of hopelessness.... *The Boss is* not *coming. Help is* not *on the way.*

The meeting the Council was going to hold was probably going to tell the elves things they already knew mixed in with lies and false hope. And just who did she think she was? Ember Skye, Coal Elf. *Girl* Coal Elf, no less. That fire in the pit of her stomach had driven her to defect, and try something... anything; that was the same fire that had forced her to pick up the scattered pieces of Sturd's List and spend months diligently piecing it back together. It was a want, a desire, a need, to do and be something, someone *larger* than herself. It was a want, a desire, a need, to give meaning to her seemingly meaningless life, to have a purpose. And now what? Just where was that desire leading her? Back to the Mines to be executed and cannibalized by Sturd? Or to a life of hiding Aboveground?

Great. I'm screwed either way.

It was only a matter of time before the search parties made their way Aboveground to look for her. Sturd would force Banter, and Barkuss, and Tannen to explain every little detail of their last encounter with her, for sure. Poor Banter would probably be too weak to say much, Barkuss would no doubt spill his guts out in fear, and Tannen would....

"Almonds tall struthers?"

She walked the streets aimlessly, taking note of the desolation and near destruction of everything that previously existed here. She wondered if she should go to her mother's mansion in Tir-La Treals, but she let that thought escape her mind as quickly as it had rushed in. The sun was starting to set—at least that's what she thought was happening—because the gray smoky sky started to darken some more. It would soon be even colder; she would need to find a warm place to stay, and fast. The Fish Market had a shed where they kept tools and supplies. It had looked abandoned when she passed by there before, and maybe she could sneak in and stay there for the night. It was the only option she could think of.

On her trek to the Fish Market, she came upon the Reindeer Stable. The wrought iron fence that surrounded the property was rusting over, and the trees and shrubs that once decorated the landscape were now overgrown and choked with weeds and moss. A layer of ash decorated the tops of the snowcapped shrubs like gray icing on a vanilla birthday cake. The Reindeer Trainer, Kyla, knelt next to three snow mounds in front of the porch of the house. Yellow and white flowers adorned each mound, but they, too, were sprinkled with fallen ash. Kyla was huddled over them whispering to each one. Her hair was tied in a knot at the top of her head, and her purple coat was torn at the shoulders. Ember leaned her arms against the fence, and it creaked loudly in the still of the late afternoon. She shuddered at the sound.

Kyla looked up from the mounds, her eyes wide in surprise. She motioned for Ember to enter when she recognized who it was. Ember entered the gate and walked up the pathway to the house.

"Coal Girl!" Kyla exclaimed when she approached. "Now what brings you back up to these parts? Certainly not on holiday, I would presume," and with that, Kyla threw her arms around her neck in a warm and friendly embrace.

"True," Ember replied as she tried to smile back. After breaking hold of Kyla's embrace, she stepped back and surveyed the scene of devastation. It was appalling—the smoke, the ash, the smell. Her mouth dropped open at the sight.

"Yea," Kyla agreed in a faraway voice. "It is nice to see you again, considering, ya know. So, what brings you back?"

She deeply inhaled. "It's a long story."

Kyla looked thoughtfully at the mounds at her side. "Well, time is all I seem to have these days. The sickness took my whole family. Momma, Poppa, my sister, Tyla."

Ember shook her head in sympathy and wondered about her own family. Was her mother still alive? What about Ginger and her baby? Nanny Carole? Were they okay? "I'm sorry to hear that," she replied, trying to offer some sort of comfort.

"Thank you, but there's nothing you could have done," Kyla said with a sad voice.

The wind began to pick up and the sun struggled to sink lower on the horizon. She knew she had to get going to one of the sheds at the Fish Market before nightfall. "I hope things work out for you. I probably should be going. Besides, I don't have a Pass, and you'll probably not want to continue this conversation much longer."

Kyla's eyes were distant and there was very little expression in her face and gestures. "Why would I care about that?"

"Seems like most elves would. I'm trying to get to Headquarters and I thought someone up here might be able to help me. I went to the Inn Keeper thinking he would be able to steer me in the right direction, but that was obviously a dead end. So, I'm kinda stuck. I just needed to do *something*. Does that make sense?"

"Perfect. Come inside. It's getting dark. Since the burning of the Groves, it's much colder at night than it used to be. I have some cocoa and cookies on the stove. You can spend the night here, too, if you like. It's been a few weeks since I've had any elf to elf interaction."

"Sure," Ember responded with a nod, and Kyla led the way into the house.

The kitchen was warm and the soft glow of the candles made their shadows dance on the walls like ghosts at a ball. Ember sat at the table and thanked Kyla as she served her. The cocoa was bitter, old. Even the peppermint swizzle stick couldn't mask the underlying taste of expired chocolate. The cookies were okay. Chocolate coconut chip. The edges were slightly burnt, the obvious work of an amateur baker. Nanny Carole would have never let the edges burn like that, but then again, Kyla wasn't a baker. She was an orphan Reindeer Trainer trying to survive on her own.

Regardless, Ember wasn't about to complain for it was the only thing she had eaten in almost a day.

Kyla sat down and took a bite of one of the cookies, her jaw working her teeth through the hard parts. She closed her eyes as she swallowed down, then frowned and said, "Sorry."

Ember waved her hand in the air as to say "forget about it!"

"How come you haven't gotten sick?" Ember finally asked after some time of silence.

"I'm not sure. I guess I only eat the bare minimum of the fruit. I never liked it straight off the branch, if you know what I mean, and I would only use it sparingly on my other food. My sister, Tyla, worked in the Groves. Her exposure to it was constant, and I assume that's why she got so sick so fast. Momma and Poppa loved Nessie. They would eat a whole fruit for morning snack and one for dessert after dinner. Like I said, I never cared for them like that. I've managed to get by this long with doing what I'm doing, but in all honesty, it's only a matter of time. What about in the Mines? What's it like down there?"

Kyla's frail hands wrapped around the mug, and she brought the beverage to her lips and took a sip. The bones were practically jutting out of her fingers, and her veins were raised against the flesh like dark blue chinchi tunnels raised under the dirt of the Mines. It was obvious

Kyla wasn't eating as much as she should be, but Ember understood she was only trying to avoid the sickness as best as possible.

"I hate to say it," Ember said, "but our situation down there isn't nearly as bad as up here. The sickness hasn't hit us so hard, and it's probably because none of us ever eat Nessie Fruit 'off the branch' as you say. There's no way for us to get them fresh like that, so I guess the sickness is slow working. A few of my friends are sick, though. One is actually pretty bad right now, but no one has died. At least not that I know of, yet."

Yet.

The distant look clouded Kyla's face once more. Was she thinking about her family? "So, you said you came here to help?" she asked, breaking the silent stare of her mug.

"Y... yeah," Ember stammered, "but, I have to be honest, I have no idea what I'm doing, or what I *can* do. Like I said, my friend, Banter, is really sick, like really bad, and the Medic was not helping at all. So, I took it upon myself to get help. I don't know, I thought maybe the Council could help? Maybe point me in the right direction, refer me to an Aboveground Medic, something like that. All I know is, I've gotten myself into a lot of trouble, and if I don't do something quickly, it ain't the sickness that's gonna get me."

"Headquarters," Kyla blurted. "That's where you need to go. That's where the Council is."

"Yeah, but how do I get there? And would the Council even see me? And what would I say to them if they did entertain my presence? That old Inn Keeper told me they were holding a meeting tomorrow night."

Kyla quickly shook her head. "That won't help. It's not really a meeting. They're basically getting a representative to come over a loudspeaker with some information. They've done it before. It's a waste of time. You won't be able to speak to an actual person."

"So, they've had these so-called meetings before?"

"A few times. But they basically say the same things."

"What do you mean?"

"The Coal-Less Night. It's all because of that. The Council seemed like they were trying to put the blame on you guys. They said you Coal Elves destroyed the List to see what would happen, ya know? Like some weirdo experiment."

Ember's face flushed in anger as her hand reached for her pocket. The List was tucked away safely. *Lyn Vincent, Lee Martin, Luke Williams*, all nestled together on a piece of paper under her bottom. "No," she corrected, "just one Coal Elf... Sturd. He's bent on being in control. He took it upon himself to destroy the List. But it goes beyond that. He's seriously out of his mind, and that's another reason why I need to see the Council. Something seriously needs to be done about him."

"Well, whatever he did, and for whatever reason he did it, it created a disaster. That night sealed our fates. There was so much happiness in the world because even the naughty kids were rewarded. That energy, that 'over-happiness' upset the balance of things. Made the Nessie Fruit grow uncontrollably and rot. The Grove Elves didn't know what to do; there was so much of it growing wild at such a fast pace. My sister worked in the Groves, and one afternoon I filled in for her. It was brutal. Chaos. Nessie Fruits were falling to the ground...."

Ember gasped. "The ground?" The reprimanding hand of Nanny Carole came crashing down on her mind's eye.

Kyla just stared. "There wasn't anything that could be done. There was nowhere to keep it all. If they hit the ground for just a second, everyone thought it would be okay. 'Cause really? What would a split second matter? Apparently, that contributed to the problem—added to the sickness. From there, things just spiraled out of control. The key would be to get to Headquarters yourself, but that's a tricky thing, and I don't think you'd be able to...." Kyla's voice trailed as she sat back into silence.

Ember raised an eyebrow in interest. There was something in Kyla's slight shift of mannerism that alerted her attention.

"It wouldn't work," Kyla was whispering to the floor. "You don't know the words. You wouldn't know how to steer."

"Wait! What are you talking about?"

"No. No. No. It really wouldn't work, and you'd probably get yourself killed. I'd go myself, but what do I know? I don't know what to do." Kyla mumbles streamed together in frantic whispers.

"Wait. Just slow down. Explain to me what you're talking about, please."

Kyla stopped and shook her head out of her trance. Her eyes met Ember's and she took a deep breath. "I know how to get to Headquarters. But you couldn't do it. Not unless you speak Elvish."

Ember reached across the table and grasped Kyla's boney hands. "I don't understand," she pleaded.

Kyla backed away from Ember's grip. "No. There's nothing you can do. Besides, the Council hasn't listened to any of us up here. There isn't any kind of cure or antidote. What makes you think you'll have any luck?"

Ember's outstretched arms slouched on the table. Her head crashed to the wood with a slight *thud*. It was hopeless, and obvious, that any amount of begging and pleading would be useless on Kyla.

As her body hunched over the table, her head huddled within the crevice of her arms, she felt the map in her front pocket digging into the ridge of her folded stomach. The plastic cover that helped her read the map was pinching at her belly flesh, and she suddenly realized something: she couldn't *speak* Elvish, but she could *read* it.

Ember stood up calmly. "Kyla, I have this," and she pulled out the map and translator from her jumpsuit. "This was given to me by my friend, Banter, the one I told you about; the one who's very sick. He thought if I could bring back some kind of help, any kind of help, it would be worth it for me to defect and try. This is a map. It shows the path to the Mouth of the Mines—it's the passageway that bridges the Aboveground to us. Anyway, it's supposedly a highly guarded secret. Look, it's written in Elvish, but if I put this piece of plastic on top of it, the plastic acts as a translator. When I place it over the map, it allows me to read the words. That's how I was able to get here on my own without a Pass." She spread the map on the table so Kyla could get a better look at it. "Kyla, I have to try," she continued. "I have to try to see the Council, state my case, and get some direction. If it's useless, then so be it. But I can't *not* try. I can't let Banter die without giving it my best shot!"

A string in Kyla's heart twinged. Momma, Poppa, Tyla… gone. Soon she would be gone, too. What kind of elf would she be if she at least didn't help Ember in her plight, regardless of how fruitless she thought it would end up?

Kyla stood up and walked around the table to where Ember had laid out the documents. "Hmm." She examined the plastic translator. "I think this actually could work."

A glimmer of excitement coursed through Ember's fingers. "Talk to me, Ky! I know you are thinking of something."

"A little while ago the Council representatives came to judge my reindeer. They took most of my team, but the one most notably left behind is a Shadow-Deer. The Council never takes Shadow-Deer, regardless of their lineage or abilities."

Kyla paused.

"Okay, continue," Ember urged, her voice rising in anticipation.

"I'm not sure. I was always told it was so, but never really knew for a fact."

"Knew what? What are you talking about?"

"Asche. My Shadow-Deer. The one they left behind. He under-stands Elvish."

"And…?"

"Well, it's just that, reindeer who know Elvish are supposedly wired to Headquarters."

Ember's face twisted in confusion. "What do you mean 'wired?'"

"Wired. Like instinct or something. Like it's in their blood to know."

"Wait. Are you saying that your reindeer, Asche, could take us to HQ?"

Kyla ran her fingers through her hair. "Not sure. And it wouldn't be 'us.' I don't have a proper carriage to hitch. He would have to be saddle-ridden."

"Do *you* speak Elvish?"

Kyla nodded.

"So, *you're* gonna go to Headquarters! *You* need to go before the Council!" Ember shrieked with excitement.

"No, I'm not," Kyla responded in a monotone voice. "I have a sick baby deer. Viella. I won't leave her."

Ember huffed in frustration. *Great. Let the entire elf race rest on the shoulders of a sick reindeer. Your reindeer's going to die, and so will you, Kyla.*

Kyla looked over the map a few more minutes, "But...."

Ember's ears perked up.

Kyla opened one of the kitchen cabinet drawers and pulled out a piece of paper and a pen. "But... hmmm, let me see." She began to write something down. "This translator can make Elvish readable, but could it do the opposite?" She wrote "Happy Birthday, Kyla and Tyla" on the paper and held the plastic translator over it. Just as she had suspected, the words transformed before her eyes. It was the ancient language... Elvish.

"Can you read this?" Kyla asked.

Ember strained to make out the words, and struggled with the pronunciation, "*Uhlantang Daagen*, Kyla *oft* Tyla?"

A smile swept over Kyla's worn out face, and her opal eyes lit up with hope.

Ember scrunched up her nose. "What does it say? Did I say it right?"

"Happy Birthday, Kyla and Tyla. And yes, you said it well. Diction is off a little, but we can work on that!"

Ember beamed. For the first time since she arrived Aboveground she actually felt like she was getting somewhere. "Well, Happy Birthday!" she exclaimed.

Kyla gave a solemn nod. "Thank you, Coal Girl. Now let's go get Asche! Ever ride a reindeer before?"

Ember gulped hard. "Um, yeah," she stammered nervously. "About that...."

Kyla frowned at Ember's apprehension. "You can't be serious. You're the fearless Coal Girl! You risked your life to leave the Mines, and you're going to tell me you're afraid of a little reindeer ride? No way. Not letting that happen. Come with me out to the stable. Let's get Asche from his stall, away from the others."

Wait? What was that? Stall? Almonds tall stuthers?

I'll stall the others?

I'll stall the others! A giant grin plastered itself on Ember' face. *Thanks, Tannen.*

Asche stood proudly in his corral. His coat was a magnificent shade of shadow gray, and his antlers were thick and sturdy like a crown made of strong, velvety bones. His piercing blue eyes stood out like two twinkling stars against a black-fur sky. Ember approached with great caution, respecting the authority of this stunning beast. When she reached the barricade of his corral, he lifted his head high above the railing and scooped his head forward to meet hers.

"You can pet his nose," Kyla said when she reached the stable door-way. "He likes that!"

Ember gingerly reached her hand forward to feel his velour muzzle, and as if on instinct, Asche moved his nose directly into her palm.

She caressed him with long, gentle strokes. "I remember you," she whispered. "I watched you train that day. You are the most beautiful animal I've ever seen."

There was a weird sort of electric feeling as she ran her hands across his nose and moved them gently to brush his face. His eyes were all-knowing, like he had a secret that only Ember could learn, and for some strange reason, she felt an immediate connection with him.

"He loves the attention!" Kyla noted. "You keep buttering him up like that, and he'll be faithful to you forever!"

Ember smiled, but never once looked away from Asche. She was enthralled with his presence, his dominating aura.

"C'mon," Kyla said, breaking Ember's awestricken trance. "Let's get him saddled up and the basic ground rules down."

Chapter Twenty-Five

TIME—THEY HAD VERY LITTLE LEFT. KYLA KNEW TRAINING EMBER TO FLY in such a limited amount of time would not be an easy task; nonetheless, they worked a basic course throughout the frigid night. Asche took directions in both languages and worked hard despite Ember's awkwardness and uncertainty. The first break of morning light against the horizon was their indicator to stop, that the task was now at hand. Ember had succeeded in the basic steering, flying, and overall maneuvering. The Elvish and sudden change in atmosphere as they climbed above the land was something else to be dealt with, but Kyla knew Ember would tough it out no matter what happened.

Working with Asche was a tremendous experience for Ember, and she marveled at how well he responded to her every slight movement. His hearing was keen, as he was able to pick up even her quietest whispers against the whooshing night air.

Kyla shrugged wearily, "I guess this is it." The last swarm of Graespurs fluttered overhead against the rising dawn.

"You think so? I don't know. I'm still a little shaky about the landing part. My left arm tends to pull up a little too hard and...."

"Relax. Asche knows. No matter what, he'll see you through it."

Ember looked at Asche. His crystal blue eyes sparkled in the quickly fading darkness. His majestic head nodded at her, as if he were giving her reassurance that she could actually pull this off.

Ember smiled. "All right," she said with renewed confidence, "let's do this!"

Kyla reached into her coat pocket and handed her the paper with the instructions on it. "This is what you need to say to him. This is the only way he'll lead you there. Say these words exactly as they appear in the translator, and Asche will take care of the rest. When you feel the pressure changing, that's your cue to recite this. And remember not to panic when the pressure change happens. You'll be pretty high up, and it might feel hard to catch your breath. Breathe deep and slow. If you start to panic, you'll make yourself pass out, and honestly, I don't know how Asche will react."

If I pass out, Asche will bring me right back here.

Even though she had the translator at her disposal, she committed the Elvish words to memory; she wasn't about to take any chances with fumbling over the plastic and paper, and trying to steer correctly.

Kyla walked over to Asche and kissed his muzzle. "Be a good boy," she cooed to him. "Take care of Ember. You're *hers* now. Do you understand me?"

Asche responded with a gentle nudge to Kyla's shoulder.

Kyla felt the tears welling up inside her. She knew by letting Asche go on this mission with Ember, she was essentially letting him go. This is what he was meant to do, Kyla knew that now. He belonged to Ember, regardless of how their journey turned out. "Do as she says, and keep her safe," she continued as she rubbed his muzzle lovingly. "Work with her if she's a little unsteady. Take her to the mountain, big guy. I'm counting on you. I'm so proud of you." Then, she whispered something to him in Elvish. He bleated like a calf and nuzzled against Kyla's cheek.

Kyla handed the reins over to Ember. "Here," she said with a small sob. "Take care of my boy, okay?"

She solemnly nodded as she tightened the leather straps around her palms. "Thank you. You have no idea how much this means." She mounted the deer and righted herself on the saddle.

Kyla raised her hand and silenced her. Then pointing to the three mounds on the ground, Kyla whispered, "I do know."

Ember gave a small smile and leaned forward to stroke the back of Asche's dark head. "Ready, boy?" she asked, and he responded with a nod. Without further hesitation she called out, "*Oontza ahnga, Aschen!*"

Asche, startled by the authoritative command, took to the sky in a flash. Ember's body jolted forward from the force of the movement. She tightened her grip on the brown leather reins and tightly closed her eyes. Her stomach dropped violently as Asche ascended higher into the sky, but it felt as though it rushed back up to her throat when he stabilized his altitude. Slowly, she opened her eyes. The sky was like a dark blue blanket with a million tiny white holes punched through it. There were no clouds up where they were, and there was also no visible land below.

Asche was fast! Remembering she actually had to guide him, she tugged a bit on the reins. Her hands were numb and sweaty from holding on so fiercely. Ashe moved up a bit more, and she could feel the pressure change that Kyla had warned her about. The cold of the height licked at the tips of her ears. *Breathe. Slow and deep. Slow and deep. Don't panic now.*

"We're really high up, aren't we, Asche? Past the other side of the horizon."

Asche kept steady under her shaky control. He was a working reindeer now, and he knew there was no time for affection or play. When he had his reins and saddle on, there was only one thing in his mind.

Slow and deep. Slow and deep.

The air was getting thinner, and she was beginning to get a little light-headed. There was a sweet candy smell in the air, and if she just closed her eyes for a second, she knew she would be in the most fabulous bakery surrounded by the most scrumptious desserts. The heavenly smells of chocolate chip cookies and white macadamia nut fudge wafting throughout the storefront. Every bit of delectable confection right at her fingertips....

Fingertips!

She had started to drift into a dream and had almost dropped the reins, but Asche jolted in the sky, his front hooves rising up to a violent stop. She jolted forward as well, and re-tightened her hands around the leather straps. He had felt her weakening grip, and stopped to wake her up.

"Good boy!" she said when she realized what had happened. "C'mon, I think it's time we get to HQ."

She was ready. It was time. The words she had memorized danced in her mind like a child's song from Old Nanny Carole's repertoire, and she even sang it over and over to the tune of "The Mists of the North."

Take me to that sacred place, beyond the land of the Elves. Take me to that sacred place that belongs to the holy Claus.

Over and over to herself in the words and language of her mother and father and sister and nanny and friends and grandelves and great-grandelves and great-great-great-great-great grandelves, until no longer was she mumbling the coded mantra in the language she knew. The words flowed from her lips in peculiar form, like second nature, like rhythm and poetry and water and something that felt and sounded so wrong, but so right and clear and natural....

"*Frelda gnaffa zynne cormeg utz drefflig,*" she called to him in a strong voice, one that knew the words, had said them from birth; in a voice that was firm and confident.

Asche, hearing the ancient song, made a sharp right turn and dipped downward. She gasped as her stomach once again did flip-flops.

"*Frelda gnaffa zynne, au Clausen!*" she called out the last command, and he dipped a little lower before shooting up into the sky like a rocket shooting into space. She closed her eyes again (tighter this time), and without even realizing she was doing so, held her breath. *Great. I'm gonna die, like right now!*

It was hard to tell how high up they were, or even exactly where they were, but suddenly she felt sun shadows against her closed eyelids. When she opened them, she was confronted with a place she had never even dreamed of before. For one thing, there was land with a purple mountain range against the sunny horizon, and a permanent rainbow arching across. She could make out a small village below with a train racing along a track, its puffs of white smoke coughing out of the stack in heart-shaped clouds. The pressure in the air was normal now, and it wasn't nearly as cold. It looked like the North Pole—the Aboveground—but it wasn't; this place was magical, otherworldly. This place was something different. *Somewhere different. Somewhere over the....*

"I'm dead, aren't I?" she whispered to herself.

Asche shook his massive head, his heavy antlers rocking her back and forth.

"We need to get to the Council. Maybe even to the Boss, but that would be pushing my luck, wouldn't it be? He's got to live around here somewhere. Maybe up in that mountain over...."

At that instant, a team of reindeer descended upon her and Asche, surrounding them in the air. It was a crew of four butter-colored deer pulling a dark navy blue sled with bright yellow stripes down the side. There was a circular emblem on the sled door bearing the swirled "C" wrapped in holly leaves—the emblem of the Council.

The driver elf in the sled came over a megaphone. "Stop right there!" his voice said blaring in her ears.

She froze and jerked the reins down hard so Ashe would come to a halt. He stopped and hovered in the air as the blue sled circled around them a few times.

"Ember Skye!" the elf shouted. "Hold your reindeer steady! Do not move another inch! I am coming to hitch you to my sled!"

She sighed a sigh of relief as the sled slowed down beside them, but Asche was not as relaxed; his movements were jerky and he was uncomfortable with the glowing tether the elf attached to his collar.

"It's okay," she said, patting his back. "It's okay." But his grunting and snarling was unsettling.

"Okay, now," the elf commanded, "get on in!"

Without hesitation, she shimmied her body from the saddle and into the official sled. She sat next to the elf, who was wearing a blue stocking cap and a blue and yellow vest, like some sort of uniform. "Thank Claus you got me when you did. I didn't know how long it was going to take me to get to the Council."

The elf didn't respond. He instead reached into a brown sack and took out another glowing tether, like the one he used to harness Asche to the sled. *What is that for?*

And then, something didn't feel right. She couldn't quite put her finger on it, but she paused for a second. "How did you know my name?"

The elf unraveled the rope. "Hold still!" he yelled. Quickly, he gripped her arms and wrapped her up.

She thrashed and screamed against his hold, but it was no use, the rope was thick and powerful, and held her in place. Every time she moved against it, she could feel it tightening around her small body. There was no use. She was caught.

"Wait!" she shouted in a frenzied voice. "What are you doing? You don't understand! I'm here to speak to the Council! I need help! We all need help!"

He ignored her pleas and sat back in his driver's seat. "You are unauthorized to be here!" he said in a robotic tone. "You're a Defector from the Mines, and are now trespassing in a highly restricted area. I have jurisdiction to take you into custody where you will be sentenced for your actions."

Custody? Judged? Sentenced? Her head swam with surreal thoughts in this surreal land. The sled began to move. Asche struggled against the movement. He moaned and thrashed, but he, too, was feeling the swell of the clasp from the magic tether.

How could she have been so stupid?

No. Not stupid. A little blind, maybe, but not stupid. She knew they would be searching for her, and they were already here, waiting, prepared. And now she was going to be judged, and no help would come to her friends.

Judged? By whom? The Council?

"So, what are you, like an Enforcer Elf, or something?"

"Yes," he huffed.

"And like, you're taking me where? Jail? Court?"

"I have specific instructions to take you to the Council, immediately!"

So, maybe all hope isn't lost just yet.

He looked back at her and narrowed his eyes when he saw her smiling. "What are you so happy about?" he hissed in disgust.

"Oh, nothing."

The elf grumbled at her response. "I can't stand looking at your face!" He reached back into his brown sack and pulled out a smaller bag. "Smile under this!" he snarled as he threw the bag over her head.

And she did. The whole sled ride over she smiled, for she knew she was going to be *exactly* where she wanted to be; she was getting a first class escorted ride to her intended destination: Headquarters!

Chapter Twenty-Six

EVEN WITH THE BAG BLINDING HER, SHE KNEW THEY WERE CLOSE WHEN the Enforcer's reindeer slowed down and began a steady descent. Asche had long stopped thrashing against the tether, and relented to settle down. When they finally landed, she could sense they were parked somewhere high because she hadn't felt a sudden drop in her belly and the reindeer's descent was a quick one. The wind rushed through her ash-caked hair with deep, howling noises that blew puffs of dust into the air. Even through the sackcloth over her face, she could feel the wind's frigid chill against her cheeks.

The Enforcer got out of the sled and grabbed her by her tied hands. He led her down from the seat and began walking.

"If I untie you," he said above the howl of the wind, "you have to promise not to run."

"Sure," she replied from within her head chamber.

He unraveled the ropes that confined her body. "If you run, you'll just fall over the side of the building. We're on a roof right now, so stay close to me."

"Oh, really?" she answered sarcastically. "I couldn't tell."

"Well, if you're going to be like that, you can keep that bag on your head!" he yelled indignantly.

"Whatever you say, chief!" she countered nonchalantly.

The elf pulled her forward like he was dragging cattle across an open field. Her feet weren't ready for the sudden movement, and she stumbled over herself, her knees buckling onto the cement roof. The Enforcer chuckled loudly when she slipped.

"Hey!" she sang out from underneath the sack. "It's not nice to laugh at other's misfortune!"

The Enforcer snorted one last time as she rose to her feet. "Keep moving!" he barked as he shoved her shoulder.

Finally, he opened up a door and dragged her through a tunnel-like structure, and from what she could sense, the cylindrical pathway was like some sort of bridge. The flooring they walked upon was some sort of hard surface, tile perhaps. She imagined what the view would be like from up there, a beautiful picture of the sprawling landscape below. She could hear the wind pounding against the tunnel-structure, whooshing across the valley like waves crashing onto an open shore. Soon, another door opened and they stepped into a large room. It smelled new, like fresh paint and recently laid carpet, but there was also another familiar scent that permeated the room. She figured it was her own burning-dirt-smell wafting in the air.

The escort dragged her to a couch and commanded her to sit. Her small body sank into the soft cushions, nearly swallowing her whole. *Expensive and luxurious. Only the best, right?*

She heard whispered chatter between her escort and someone else, and could sense the presence of a few other elves in the room, elves she knew who were staring at her, for sure. *Probably never even seen someone like me.*

"No, no, no!" she overheard a woman elf say in a frantic voice after some more whispering.

"Well, I was just doing what they said to do! Where do you want me to leave that deer?" the Enforcer cried in his creepy baby-elf voice.

Asche. They're talking about Asche.

"Is it tied up? Okay, good. Leave it on the launching pad with your sled. You need to stay here in case we need you!"

"Fine, fine," the Enforcer grumbled in defeat.

"And get that bag off her head, please! They'll be very upset with you if they think you treated her with any hostility!"

"But she was the hostile one!" he cried out again.

"Just do it, Kipper!"

In seconds the sackcloth was ripped from her head, and Ember struggled to adjust her eyes to the bright lights of the room. It was an office. A waiting room with cream-colored walls and artwork depicting scenes from different Big Nights, and just as she had suspected, a beige shag rug adorned the floor. There was a desk in the corner where the secretary Kipper had been arguing with sat. To her left and right, large brown couches lined the walls, and in front of her stood Kipper.

"You're all theirs," he said as his upper lip curled in a sneer.

She stared at him, and as he moved away from her to sit at one of the other couches, a vision came into sight from across the room. She blinked her eyes a few times to try to shake the confusion and unfamiliarity of her surroundings from her brain, but the figure was still there. He was still there. And the smell was still there.

Sturd!

Sturd sat on the opposite side of the room, his face twisted in a half-smile, his red eyes burrowing holes within her very soul. She blinked again, trying to force her imagination to dream up someone else, anyone else, to be sitting there staring at her, but it was no use. There was only Kipper to her left, and Sturd straight ahead.

"I knew I smelled you," she calmly said to him.

Kipper turned to her. "That's enough, girl. You're not to talk to him."

She ignored him. "This whole situation reeks of you," she continued, her voice raising a level in volume and anger.

Sturd stared at her with no response; he just continued to grin, his small, shifty eyes opening a bit to show the complete fullness of their blood red color. Kipper shifted to the edge of his seat out of concern for the events unfolding in front of his eyes.

She stood up from the couch and began walking over to Sturd. "What are you doing here anyway? You here to take me back? To punish me? To kill me? Why don't you tell the Council what you do to Defectors in the Mines? I think they'd be real interested to know!"

Kipper stood up and got in front of her before she could reach Sturd. "That's enough!" he yelled at her. "Sit back down!"

But she continued to ignore Kipper and moved to the side so she could see Sturd in full view. At this point, he was laughing wildly, a rollicking belly laugh that infuriated her even more. The secretary behind the desk looked nervous. Her eyes widened in fear and she picked up a telephone and dialed frantically.

Ember stood with her arms outstretched and took another step forward. "C'mon, Sturd!" she egged him. "Punish me! Do it Pepper Brightly style! Right here, right now! Show everyone how…."

Kipper slid up behind her, grabbed both her arms behind her back, and dragged her back to the couch. "I said, that's enough!" he screamed.

She bucked wildly against his hold. "What's with you and tying me up?" she spat at him.

Kipper twisted her arm and she yowled from the pressure.

The secretary behind the desk slammed the phone down onto its handle. "They want them! Now!"

Kipper pushed Ember toward the beige-colored door. "Let's go!" he snarled. "You too, come on," he called over his shoulder at Sturd.

She continued to fight against Kipper's grasp. "Yeah, yeah, let's go!" she yelled. "Drag me around some more, chief! Watch me fall and laugh, chief!"

She was wild, like an enraged animal locked in a cage. Her hair was tousled about her head and there were tear streaks down the sides of her cheeks; her jumpsuit had holes at the knees from when she had previously fallen down. Not exactly how she had planned to confront the Council, but then again, she hadn't planned on running into Sturd here, either.

The Council's Chambers was not what she had expected to see. In her imagination, she had envisioned a grand throne room where each of the Council members sat regally on golden chairs. There would be lavish tapestries and curtains made of silk, and the members would wear the finest clothes in the entire Pole. But that's not what was in front of her. The Council's meeting room was rather boxy and plain, with a long, rectangular table in the center. There were piles of papers scattered along the table top, and in the center was some sort of radio device with three antennas protruding from the top and a flashing red light which was currently blinking.

Five elves sat behind the table: three men and two women. The women's hair was tied back tightly in buns, the men wore glasses down low on their noses, and all five of them wore black robes with purple cords around their necks. There wasn't much distinction among the five of them as they all looked similar in size and stature. Perhaps they were a family as well? They spoke quickly and quietly to one another, their voices garbled amidst the acoustics in the room.

There was something in their mannerisms that caught her attention immediately—one of them was in charge, the head honcho. By her position at the table, and the way the others intently waited for her approval and direction, it was apparent that Councilwoman #1 held all the cards. She sat in the middle of the panel, practically separating herself from the others. When they mumbled, not once did Councilwoman #1 turn her face to the others, rather they leaned in toward her to catch her ear or listen to her own mumblings. The rest nodded in unison as she spoke; it was clear she was their unofficial leader. The Council was supposed to be an equal entity, yet there was definitely a sense of a power play among them.

Nevertheless, this was Ember's time. She was finally standing before the stone-faced judges, with Sturd at her side, fearful and frozen, but ready to plead her case.

"Ember Skye," Councilwoman #1 began, "it has been brought to our attention by Sturd Ruprecht that you have defected from your duties in the Mines. Is this true?"

"I... I had no other...." Ember stammered, stunned and unable to think clearly. She had planned over and over in her mind just how this scene would play out, but now that she was there, really there, before them, her mouth and mind locked up and she was left a bumbling fool.

Sturd's eyes locked with Councilwoman #1's for a brief and unsettling second, something Ember was keen to take note of.

Kipper pulled up on Ember's arm, making her wince.

"Thank you, Mr. Gulch, that'll be all," Councilman #5 interrupted. "You may go back to the waiting room until we call for you."

Kipper reluctantly let go of Ember's arms, bowed his head at the Council, and walked out.

"Miss Skye, a simple 'yes' or 'no' would suffice," Councilwoman #2 continued.

"No," she replied.

The Council collectively raised an eyebrow.

"No, you did not defect from the Mines? Is that what you're saying?" Councilman #4 asked.

"No," she continued, "I meant it's not a simple answer."

The Councilmen sighed. The two women picked up their pens and wrote something on the paper before them.

Councilman #3 exhaled, "Miss Skye, we certainly don't have time for semantics, as you know we are dealing with a dire situation. Did you or did you not defect from the Mines. Answer the question. Yes or no?"

Dire? Interesting choice of words....

She shuffled her feet and stared at the floor. Putting this situation into words that somehow made sense was not an easy thing to do. She knew what she felt; she knew what her intentions felt like; she knew the desperation inside her when she looked at Banter sprawled out helplessly on his bed; she knew the dread she felt to think the same fate would befall Barkuss, or Tannen, or even herself. But to vocalize those deep inner feelings? Certainly not her forte!

"Yes. I did defect," she said, eyes still transfixed on the ground. "But it was with good...."

Councilman #3 looked up and down the table at the other members, and after each gave a nod of their head, he reached toward the radio device and pushed a switch upward. The red flashing light stopped blinking and turned green. A static hiss echoed from the speaker.

"Well, then," Councilwoman #1 continued, "under the Twelfth Provision of Regulation 6, we, the Council of the Pole, in full representation of the Claus, hereby release you to Sturd Ruprecht, and render you to the jurisdiction of the Mines. Thank you, Mr. Ruprecht, for your quick response in this matter. The punishment of this elf is in your hands and...."

Sturd took a step toward Ember, his wicked smile still plastered on his face.

"Don't you touch me," she hissed at him. "Wait!" she yelled, addressing the Council. "This isn't fair! Let me explain. I defected because I needed to get *here*. I needed to speak to *you*. I needed to tell you what was going on down *there*! I've been through so much just to get here. Please, just give me a moment of your—"

Councilman #4 spoke up. "Did you not think we already knew what was happening? How could we not? Are you that foolish?"

The other Council members let out a forced sounding chuckle.

She took a step forward toward their table, and their collective eyes widened as if to say *how dare you approach us*. "But, you don't understand. You're *not* there. You're *not* in the middle of it. And the Mines aren't half as bad as the Land-dwelling elves. So many are dying, and even more are suffering."

"And we are working on a resolution," Councilwoman #1 said sternly.

"It's not fast enough," she whispered, assuming no one would hear.

Councilwoman #1 banged her fists on the table. "Don't you dare question our authority!" she shouted.

"Do you not think we suffer too?" Councilwoman #2 chimed in, taking her cue from her leader. "We've been dealing with this on a higher level as well! We have been..." and her voice trailed as the emotion overtook her, heaving her chest with suppressed sobs.

Councilman #5 took the frantic woman's hand into his own, "Easy," he coaxed. Councilwoman #2 dipped her head into his shoulder and shut her eyes. Ember could see tears pooling at the base of her eyelids.

Councilman #5 was more at ease, more relaxed. His eyes were calming, and he wasn't as hard as the others. He spoke in a soft, gentle voice, "We know how the problem started," and he quickly glanced at Sturd and back to Ember, "and how the fruits have been destroyed. We have been working diligently to rectify the problem and restore order. And while we, the Council, recognize that your intentions were noble; while we understand you were just seeking help for your people, you broke protocol, and are therefore responsible to answer to Mr. Ruprecht."

Sturd snickered as she gave him a sideways glance.

"Protocol? I... I don't understand. There's still protocol during a time like this?" she begged, bewilderedly.

"That's quite enough, Miss Skye," Councilwoman #1 asserted. "Mr. Ruprecht, I think it's time you took her and left."

"As you wish," Sturd replied. He shoved her by the shoulders toward the door. At once, the Council members shifted in their chairs and began to get up to leave. Just before Councilman #3 could pull the switch on the transmitter so it blinked red again, Ember jerked her shoulder loose from Sturd's bony hand and raced toward the table.

"Wait!" she shouted at them again.

"What now, Miss Skye?" Councilwoman #1 huffed in aggravation.

She thumbed her finger at Sturd. "The List. The one he destroyed," she began.

Councilwoman #1 and Councilman #3 jerked their heads toward each other instinctively and both narrowed their brows. Councilwoman #1 then quickly glanced at the table, at the transmitter device in the center, then back up at Ember with a suspect look.

"What about it?" Councilman #3 asked with an alarmed tone to his voice, then he, too, looked over at the transmitter, back at Councilwoman #1, and back to Ember.

Sturd narrowed his eyes. "Yeah, what about it, Skye?" he whispered demonically into her ear.

"I have it," she declared. "It's preserved. I mean, I fixed it. I fixed it, and I have it with me right now. "

The Council began to buzz:

"What is she talking—"

"How could that be—"

"What does she mean by—"

Councilwoman #1 stood straight up and wiped her forehead with the back of her hand. "This is certainly not the time for games, child," she said with a crackling voice.

She reached into her back pocket and procured the tattered document, unraveling it to the floor with its jagged edges. "Look, I'm not playing games, I swear, Your Honor."

There was a collective gasp from the Council, and the familiar buzz again:

"How did she—"

"Is it possible that—"

"Could it be the actual—"

Sturd stood frozen with his mouth opened wide, exposing his pointy teeth.

"Bring it here!" Councilman #4 called, and Ember walked in front of the List, dragging it behind her. The Councilman cautiously cradled the paper in his hands as the others (except for Councilwoman #1 and Councilman #3) crowded behind him in awe. They were buzzing yet again, but this time, she couldn't make out any of the words.

"Explain the meaning of this!" Councilwoman #1 cried out with fury, silencing the droning buzz.

She swallowed hard, digging deep to find her voice, to find the confident words. "The day Sturd announced to us in the Mines that we wouldn't be needed to collect any more coal that year, that the List was being ignored, I had a terrible feeling it wasn't right. Sturd tore up the List, and after everyone left the rally, I stayed behind and picked up the pieces. My friend, Barkuss Dwin'nae, and I spent the last year putting it back together, and I've tried to keep it safe since."

"Did you say Dwin'nae?" Councilman #3 asked suspiciously, and she nodded her head.

Sturd let out a small gasp as he nervously ran his fingers through his hair. "I knew you and your little crony were up to no good!"

A buzzing noise came through on the transmitter and the Council stood still, looking at each other in shock. She couldn't decide whether the expressions on their faces were that of anger, fear, or happiness.

"Leave! Both of you!" Councilwoman #1 demanded. "Somebody get Pennybaker in here immediately! We will call for you both when we need you!"

Ember's stomach dropped. She hadn't been separated from the List since the day she collected its torn segments, and she didn't feel comfortable leaving her List with the Council at all! Her mind raced with what they were going to do with it. As she reluctantly opened the door and stepped back into the waiting room, she saw Councilman #3 press a button on the radio receiver as he huddled over it, whispering.

Kipper, who had been waiting for further instructions, raised an eyebrow when Sturd and Ember came back into the room.

"So," Sturd said as they sat back down on opposite couches, "that's what you've been hiding this whole time!"

"Shut up. You're just mad cause you're not gonna get to eat me."

"Don't be so sure of that, Defector! Your fate is still up to the Council, and they may just—"

Suddenly, Harold Pennybaker, the liaison between the Above and Undergrounds, came dashing through the office door; Harold Pennybaker—head of List Communications—with his full, healthy-looking cheeks and cotton-candy colored suit. He glanced quickly at them, flashed his badge to the secretary at the desk, and hurriedly flew into the Council's Chambers. Harold Pennybaker, the phony elf with the big slick smile who gave all the Quarterly Meeting speeches. "Good job, so-and-so, for collecting the most coal! Excellent work, whatever-your-name-is, for officially shutting down this section of the Mines." Names he read off his list and forgot the second he said them out loud.

Why would the Council need to see him about this?

Pennybaker disappeared behind the beige door of the Council's Chambers. Her mind began to fill with so many theories and suppositions that her body felt weak and numb. She could only imagine what was being said to him.

The secretary's phone rang, and after she hung up she announced, "Mr. Gulch, come here please." Kipper approached her desk. She whispered something to him, and he left in a hurry.

"Sturd Ruprecht," she continued in an official tone. "And Ember Skye, the Council wants to see you both again."

Sturd pushed his way in front of her. She barely made it through the door, as Kipper was closing it behind them. Harold Pennybaker was standing in the middle of the room before the Council. The List was still visible on the table; it appeared to be all right, unscathed. The transmitter light was still green as well.

Councilman #3 lifted up the List. "Mr. Pennybaker, do you know what this document is?"

Pennybaker cleared his dry throat, "Yes, Your Honor. It's the Naughty List."

"And how do you know that, sir?" Councilman #4 questioned.

"The red and green names, and the black lettered title."

"Mr. Pennybaker," Councilman #3 continued, "is this the List you were assigned by us to render into Mr. Ruprecht's possession?"

"Yes, sir, it is."

"Did you at any time tell Mr. Ruprecht that the List was to be declared null and void?" Councilwoman #2 piped in.

Harold shook his head. "No, ma'am. At the last Quarterly Meeting, I announced that the Light List provision was to be invoked, as per Council orders, but I never once told Mr. Ruprecht that the List was to be destroyed, or abandoned." Harold looked nervously around the room.

Sturd was stone-faced, not showing any emotion at all.

"Mr. Pennybaker," Councilwoman #1 spoke up, "do you know this young Coal Elf next to Mr. Ruprecht?" She pointed to Ember.

"No, ma'am, I… I mean, I know her from the meetings in the Mines, Ember, but I don't *know* her. We've never spoken."

The Council members looked at each other and nodded their heads in freakish unison.

Councilman #3 waved his hand signaling him out the door, "Thank you, Mr. Pennybaker, that will be all. You are dismissed." Pennybaker turned on his heels, said not another word, and quickly made his exit.

"Miss Skye, would you please step outside for one more moment while we address Mr. Ruprecht?" Councilman #4 said gently.

Ember nodded and left the room. *That was really weird.*

After ten minutes, the door opened again, and Sturd came bustling out. He no longer had his usual maniacal grin, and the lids of his blood red eyes were puffy and worn. He kept his gaze on the floor as he approached her.

"They want to see you now," he mumbled.

Chapter Twenty-Seven

THE ROOM WAS SILENT. THE JUDGES WERE LIKE STATUES IN THEIR SEATS. Cold faces and hard eyes stared at her; even the one gentle Councilman's face was riddled with seriousness. The transmitter's light was still green. Ember surmised it was either recording pieces of the conversations, or someone was listening in on the other line. *The Boss, perhaps?* Her List was unraveled on the floor in front of the Council's table, but laid out next to it was another document that was curiously similar—the paper crisp and bright white, in stark contrast to her tattered and yellowed one.

As she stepped closer to the table, she could see names scribbled in reds and greens on the fresh paper: *Logan Alessio, Madison Star, Alaina Morgan…* it was a List! A new List with so many names! Some were familiar, ones she had committed to memory for the last year, but oh, there were many new ones! She took a step closer to examine the new List, but one of the Councilmen cleared his throat, stopping her in her tracks.

"We know you know what this is," Councilwoman #1 said in a monotone.

She nodded, a quick nod.

"We have been compiling the new List," Councilwoman #2 interjected, "because we have realized it's the only way to help clear up this situation."

She thought about that for a moment. What good was a new List going to do *after* the fact?

"We will be returning to the usual way of doing things. Mr. Ruprecht has been given sentence for the acts he committed and will serve his punishment accordingly," Councilman #5 confirmed as the Council nodded in agreement.

"Miss Skye, why did you collect the List Mr. Ruprecht destroyed?" Councilman #4 asked.

She paused. How could she possibly put into words the feeling of dread she had as she watched the remnants of the List fluttering to the cave's stony ground? How could she possibly explain the sense of urgency and ownership that overcame her as she laid all the pieces on her kitchen table, and diligently worked night and day to restore the sacred scroll? How could she possibly translate the feelings of ecstasy that rocked her body every time she recited the memorized names on the List? How could she construe to this panel before her how her whole life had been good, charmed, until the moment she stepped foot in the dusty Mines; that taking control of the List gave her life a weird kind of meaning and purpose?

Scrambling in her brain for all the right words all she could mumble was, "I don't know."

The Council gave a collective sigh. Councilwoman #2 huddled into the ear of Councilwoman #1, cupped her mouth, and whispered something. Councilwoman #1 narrowed her eyes and slowly nodded at what was being said to her.

"Well, then, I suppose there's nothing left to say," Councilwoman #1 announced to all present.

"I just knew, all right," Ember blurted in a low voice.

"Excuse me, Miss Skye?" Councilman #4 questioned.

"I just knew," she repeated, louder, "about the List."

"What about the List?" Councilwoman #1 sternly asked, her voice bleeding with venomous agitation.

"I knew it was wrong to destroy it. I can't explain it. I don't think I can put it into words. It just *felt* wrong to me, and fixing it up just *felt* right."

Councilwoman #1's face twisted into a semi-snarl. The other Council members started to grumble again, and almost immediately, another buzzing sound came through over the transmitter. Councilman #3 pressed a button on the device and a mechanical voice on the other end called out, "P70, 24."

The Council's eyes widened in shock.

"What?" Councilwoman #1 screamed in confusion. "We've never invoked *any* Provision of Regulation 24!"

"P70, 24," the mechanical voice repeated.

The other members shifted nervously in their seats. Fear crept up on Ember, freezing her in position. Councilwoman #1 became enraged and pounded her fists on the table again.

"No! No! No! No! No!" she screamed. "This is *not* what we planned on do..."

"P70, 24," the voice repeated, but this time there was anger behind the distortion. "Una!" the voice bellowed, "this is your mess and I'm cleaning it up my way! Pick up the receiver! Pick it up, now!"

Councilwoman #1's face dropped and was drained of color. Council members' first names were forbidden to be spoken aloud. In fact, no one even knew they even *had* names. Ember tried to muffle an instinctual gulp, but Councilman #5 apparently heard it and widened his eyes.

This is your mess? And then it came to her. This whole tribunal had felt weird to her because it *was* weird.

It was bogus. A set-up. A fake. More lies. That was a common trend these days.

The Council knew about this all along; this wasn't Sturd's plan, it was *theirs*. It was *their* weirdo experiment. The "Harold Pennybaker Show" was to somehow cover their own butts, and Sturd was their fall guy!

Could the Council possibly have wanted to destroy the entire Elf Race? And if the Council was behind it all, did that mean the Boss had known about it? Was that mechanical voice on the other end of that radio *the* Boss?

She looked at Councilwoman #1. Her stone-wall face was like a porcelain statue, and her eyes were ice blue. Suddenly, Ember felt an overwhelming sense of fear when she stared too long into those cold and calculating eyes.

Quickly, Councilwoman #1, Una, picked up the handset of the transmitter. She listened intently to the set of instructions being given to her from the other end. The other Council members were obviously upset and fidgeted in their seats.

"Yes, yes," she answered through the phone. Then she covered her mouth with her hand so that her voice sounded muffled, and so Ember couldn't read her lips.

"Okay, okay," Una said in conclusion as she passed the phone to Councilman #3. He, too, listened with a defeated expression on his face. It became obvious to Ember at that very moment that Councilman #3 was Una's second in command. After Councilman #3's instructions were completed, he passed the phone to Councilman #4.

It went on that way for at least a half hour until all Council members were informed of what they were to do. Councilwoman #2, who was last to receive the message, placed the handset down on the receiver when she was done listening and clasped her hands gently over her heart. The green light was still on, and Ember detected the same low static sound she had before.

"There have been new developments in the plan," Councilwoman #2 said, looking at Ember and back at the rest of her colleagues.

The Council members straightened up in their seats. Una inhaled deeply. "The only solution," Councilman #4 began, "is to manage both the old List and new List. The idea is to meld them together. And yes, this is something that we've spoken about at great length."

More Council heads slowly nodding. "The plan is to cross-reference the two," he continued. "If a name appears twice, then that child would receive extra coal for the two years-worth of naughtiness. If a name only appears once, on either List, that child would also be punished, regardless of which year their name showed up."

Una ran her hand across the top of her head and slicked her hair back tightly. She exhaled with a loud "huff" and slammed a fist to the table. "Quisto!" she yelled. "Would you just get on with it?"

"But what do I have to do with all this?" Ember wailed in confusion.

Quisto cleared his throat.

Una picked up a pen and began tapping it against the wood of the table. "Proceed," she commanded.

"Miss Skye, under the Seventieth Provision of Regulation 24, we, the Council of the Pole, in full representation of the Claus, hereby re-assign your Life Job. No longer will you report to the Mines under the supervision of Sturd Ruprecht."

A collective silence from the Council rose up.

"What?" she asked in shock.

"Miss Skye, you are now in full charge of the List. We know this is a bit sudden, but we are confident you are capable of this responsibility. The task at hand will take time and diligence, but it seems to be the only way to bring back balance and restore order at the Pole."

Her head swam: Re-assigned? No more work in the Mines? Did she hear him correctly?

"Your Shadow-Deer will be taken care of at the Main Stable. We know that he understands Elvish. You will need to study the ancient language, as well, in order to complete your duties."

"Wait! Wait! Wait!" Ember shrieked as she waved her arms in the air. "Slow down there! I'm still digesting the whole 're-assignment' thing. What do you mean that I'm in charge of the List? Isn't that Sturd's job?"

"He's no longer needed in that department," said a stone-faced Councilman #3.

"No more mining for me? But, do I still have to *live* in the Mines?"

"That's entirely up to you," Quisto said gently.

"And I have to learn Elvish?"

"It's the only way to bypass the Boss on the Big Night," Councilwoman #2 added.

"Okay, now I'm confused," she said, shaking her head back and forth.

Una rolled her eyes in aggravation. "Dear, sweet child," she began with a poisonous sarcastic tone, "it has been brought to our attention that the Boss no longer wishes to deliver coal. This is a responsibility he no longer wants to carry out. It has been brought to our attention that because *you*..." she said the word "you" as if she were spitting nails from her bowels "...have demonstrated appropriate foresight and concern for *all* elfkind, you would be best suited for, um, possession of the new Lists and all Lists from here on in. Your duties will consist of cross-referencing the Lists for the upcoming Big Night, managing the proper coal load, and delivering the coal to the appropriate recipients."

"The Boss wants you to do this. The job is yours. He chose you," Quisto said flatly.

"Me?" she asked, and the word sounded idiotic to her as soon as it reached her ears.

"Yes. You," he confirmed.

"I have to deliver the coal. To the kids. On the Big Night," she stammered, trying to process the news out loud in hopes of comprehending the gravity of it all.

"Yes," Quisto responded. "You will have your own sleigh and deer. You will be trained as quickly as possible to reach our fast approaching deadline. Again, I repeat, you will be the sole deliverer of the coal."

"But you must never intercept the Boss," Councilwoman #2 chimed in. "There are strict rules about that. There are Elvish chants that will help shroud you and your Shadow-Deer during the night in case contact is ever made. All will be revealed during your training. The Sled Elves will begin work on a temporary sleigh for you and your cargo. Sleighs usually take at least a year to build, but they will produce something suitable for the upcoming Big Night."

"And of course, you will be trained in Big Night delivery procedures," Councilman #5 inserted.

More instructions and information were spewed at her in rapid fire fashion. She was fuzzy and confused a little by the abruptness of everything. Her mind was having a hard time wrapping around the idea of never having to work in the Mines again, something she had dreamed about for so many years! She moved towards the Lists; they were lying side by side on the table and had spilled out onto the floor. She took one in each hand and began scanning the names. The feeling of excitement and purpose swelled within her as her eyes danced up and down and back and forth in a hypnotic rhythm.

"My own sleigh? My own Shadow-Deer? Elvish lessons? Delivery procedures?" her thoughts manifested into audible words.

Una sighed heavily. "I knew this was a bad idea," she groaned as she leaned over to Councilman #3's ear. "She's not going to be able to handle...."

"But the Big Night is still six months away!" she exclaimed, snapping out of her dazed state. The promises and possibilities of what the Council presented her with were simply mesmerizing, but the reality of the situation crept its way back to the forefront, enraging her soul. "This is all well and good," she continued indignantly, "but explain to me how this is going to help us elves now?"

The Council fell silent once again. Each member looked up and down the table with cold, knowing glances.

She persisted, "Don't you understand that we need help *now?*"

"Miss Skye," began Quisto, "we've already been through this. The plan we've laid out for you is the only one we've got."

"It will be a long six months," Councilman #3 said, quite insincerely Ember noted, "and many elves will suffer and possibly die, but their sacrifice will not go unnoticed. The best we can do is advise on watching your Nessie Fruit intake."

That's the best you can come up with? Sacrifice? Is this the type of garbage you tell them at your so-called meetings?

The eyes of the Council stared her down, waiting for some sort of response. Una struggled to withhold a wicked sneer, convinced Ember would decline their proposal.

Ember looked down at the Lists again. It was hard not to. Their power drew her in and seduced her attention. She knew she could do this. She felt it in the deepest part of her being that this was what she was *meant* to do. From the very first moment she ever laid eyes on the List—to the prospect of having *two* of them in her possession—she was certain this was her ultimate calling. And then, for the first time in a long while, the voice of her father echoed out in her ears, *"This is what the Boss wants for you... apparently the Boss has got it all figured out."*

Her face lit up with confidence and she couldn't help but smile. Although spoken so long ago in a much different context, she knew her father would want her to do this. He had said it himself. He never thought she'd end up down in the Mines, and maybe this was a sign from him that she had bigger things to accomplish.

"Fine," she finally replied, her eyes not once looking at the Council.

"Fine?" Una angrily questioned.

"I'll do it," she calmly declared, her grin widening at the thought of all the endless possibilities her new Life Job would bring. "I'll take the job."

EPILOGUE

İT'S PRETTY DAMN COLD UP HERE," EMBER CALLED TO ASCHE AS HE RACED
across the moonlit night. "Maybe next year I should wear a hat." She
reached up to flake tiny ice crystals away from her ear tips. It seemed
to be twenty to thirty degrees colder here in the air, and Asche's
lightning-like speed only magnified the painful chill.

She looked down at the paper in her hand. "Only a few more stops
in this quadrant."

Asche snorted, his white cloudy breath huffing into circles above
his antlers. He was almost totally camouflaged against the night sky;
if not for the light of the beaming moon, he would have been invisible to her.

She coughed. Actually, she had been coughing here and there for
a few days now, but this was different; this cough was followed by a
slight tightening in her chest and a rising liquid in her esophagus. She
spit into her hands the second it reached her mouth, and she looked
down at her exposed palms. It looked like black ink covering her fingers, but she knew in proper lighting it would be a dark red.

Although she had had the opportunity to leave, she had decided
her Home was in the Mines. Ebony Crag. Her humble den. There was
truly nothing left for her Aboveground, and she felt she would be able
to carry out her duties more efficiently if she stayed below. She would
be able to better regulate coal production, keep a closer watch on
the intake and output, and what did the Council call it? Productivity
inventory calculations? *Whatever that meant.* She was still trying to
make heads or tails of the "newness" of her role. She knew she could
do it well by staying where she was.

She had full access to go Aboveground, which she rarely used.
Kyla was her contact on Land. She had survived the sickness and
Ember trusted her to be her eyes and ears. And the thought of leaving
Barkuss was enough to make her stay in the Mines. After the death of
Banter, how could she leave him? And of course, there was Tannen.
She did enjoy revisiting her friendship with him, even if she did insist
on keeping him at arm's length, Catta-car rides only. Oh, Tannen!

Tannen Trayth. Descendant of the Tree Elves, Tannen. *I-would-fall-completely-head-over-boots-for-you-Tannen-if-I-didn't-have....*

Another episode of coughing shook her to the core. She could feel the blood rise in her throat, but she swallowed hard, forcing it back down again.

Asche slowed down, preparing for their next stop. The sleigh hovered a few moments and she marveled at the glorious scene below her. The human world glittered with snow and lights, and she knew somewhere in those houses, tucked away in their beds, were little Jimmys and Janeys dreaming of toys, and dollies, and candies, and games. She smirked as she patted the Lists in her coat pocket. There were no dollies or toy cars in *this* sleigh! She then reached into one of the bundles of coal and filled a satchel with enough for Robert Berringer, who had made the List two years in a row.

"Please, Claus, let this work," she mumbled as she closed her eyes and hoisted her body down a red brick chimney.

The unnatural movements and contact with large amounts of coal made her nauseous and weak, but if these deliveries were going to save elf lives, she was willing to endure it. So much had happened in the last six months; so much pain and suffering and grief; so much loss. She knew pain. She knew suffering and loss. No elf, Land or Below, went unscathed.

Her list of casualties was almost as long as the List itself. Banter, bold and brave, gentle and stern, gone forever. Mother, too weak and mentally deficient, was one of the first elves to be struck down. Ginger, her sister, survived long enough to give birth to her son, Devlin. Vonran, Ginger's husband, survived long enough to render custody of his son, Devlin, to Nanny Carole. So many elves. So many good lives taken away so abruptly.

And suddenly, as she popped up the chimney and back onto the sleigh, Sturd's face flashed in her mind.

Sturd.

He was to make his return to the Mines in a few weeks after having to spend some time Aboveground. The Council thought it best if he "relaxed" and "sorted things out." Six months. That was the time limit for Sturd to "find himself." Again, whatever that meant. The reality of it, though, was he was coming back, and the Council, in exchange for his "forced holiday," had promised him an elfwife, one that would "undoubtedly work out this time."

Curious. After all that he had done, after all the chaos he created, this didn't seem a fair enough punishment.

She felt no sense of justice, or satisfaction, with Sturd's apparent "slap on the wrist." It left her feeling angry all over again, and she nearly gagged at the thought of Sturd returning to the Mines with an elfwife. Or was that more blood filling up in her throat and closing her windpipe over?

Light was starting to creep on the edges of the horizon. Knowing she risked crossing paths with the Boss, she shouted to Asche in Elvish to pick up the pace. "*Oontza ahnga*, Asche!" she yelled, and he reared up on his hind legs and shot forward like a bullet.

She held the reins tightly as the force of his acceleration knocked the wind out of her. She tried hard to catch her breath, but was overcome by more coughing. She tried to breathe deeper, but the familiar scent of dirt and dust blew out from an opened coal bundle and directly into her nostrils.

More body-rocking coughs, and then the rising of more blood into her mouth. When it finally came up, she wiped her hand on her coat, and just before it was clean, she saw a tiny white worm slither onto the floor of her sleigh and up the side of one of the bundles of coal. Her blue eyes narrowed in defeat.

Great. Just what I damn need. Coppleysites.

Such is the life of a Coal Elf.

About the author

Maria DeVivo is a native New Yorker who has had a lifelong love affair with 'the pen.' A graduate of St. John's University with a BA in English Literature, she has a passion for all things mystical and mythological. She has taught seventh grade Language Arts since 2000, and in 2010, designed the curriculum for an academic elective class entitled Folklore where she has been able to share her passion and knowledge on concentrated topics such as folktales and mythology with her students.

Having grown up in a large Italian/Irish family of five children (where Maria falls as the oldest, and of course, wisest) the mystery and wonder surrounding holiday traditions were a main staple of her upbringing. At the age of seven, when her mother finally admitted the "truth" about Santa Claus, Maria became somewhat of a "Santaphile," an obsession that has rooted its way deeply into every fiber of her being. She's one of those people who cry when Santa makes His grand appearance at the Macy's Thanksgiving Day Parade. Couple that obsession with a spark of creativity for all things dark and twisted, and her debut novel *The Coal Elf* was born.

Maria resides in Florida, with her husband, Joe, and daughter, Morgan.

www.mariadevivo.com
www.facebook.com/mariadevivoauthor

Don't miss any of these
other exciting SF/F books

Angelos
(1-933353-60-0, $16.95 US)

Dragon's Moon
(1-933353-53-8, $14.95 US)

Gaea
(1-60619-183-7, $18.95 US)

Griffin's Fire
(1-60619-210-8, $16.95 US)

Griffin Rising
(1-60619-212-4, $15.95 US)

Jerome and the Seraph
(1-931201-54-4, $15.50 US)

Nine Lives and Three Wishes
(1-933353-55-4, $13.50 US)

The Nameless Prince
(1-60619-243-4, $16.95 US)

Valley of the Raven
(1-933353-75-9, $16.95 US)

You, Me, Naideen and a Bee
(1-60619-208-6, $19.95 US)

Twilight Times Books
Kingsport, Tennessee

Order Form

If not available from your local bookstore or favorite online bookstore, send this coupon and a check or money order for the retail price plus $3.50 s&h to Twilight Times Books, Dept. LS1112 POB 3340 Kingsport TN 37664. Delivery may take up to two weeks.

Name: _____

Address: _____

_____

Email: _____

I have enclosed a check or money order in the amount of

$_____

for _____ .

If you enjoyed this book, please post a review
at your favorite online bookstore.

Twilight Times Books
P O Box 3340
Kingsport, TN 37664
Phone/Fax: 423-323-0183
www.twilighttimesbooks.com/